MELOV'S LEGACY

also by Sam Ross
HE RAN ALL THE WAY
SOMEDAY, BOY

MELOV'S LEGACY
BY SAM ROSS

SECOND CHANCE PRESS
RD2, Noyac Road
Sag Harbor, New York 11963

Originally published by Farrar, Stauss and Company
under the title *THE SIDEWALKS ARE FREE*

First republication in 1984 by
SECOND CHANCE PRESS
RD2, Noyac Road, Sag Harbor, New York

Copyright© 1950, 1977 by Sam Ross. All rights reserved.
Printed in the United States of America.
This book or parts thereof may not be reproduced
in any form without written permission of the publishers.

Library of Congress Catalogue Number: 84-050877
ISBN: 0-933256-56-6 (cloth)
      0-933256-57-4 (paper)

MELOV'S LEGACY

# BOOK ONE

HOMECOMING

CHAPTER ONE

1.

Hershy was the first to know that his father was coming home from the war. The letter, dated November 15, 1918, had come in the afternoon mail. His mother, who had never learned to read, hunched tensely over the round kitchen table as he studied the sprawling script and read aloud. When he finished, he looked up and saw tears in her eyes.

"What's to cry about, Ma?" Tears always bewildered Hershy. They came to him only when he was hurt or raging mad. But grownups—you could never tell about them; they cried when they were happy, too.

She answered him by spattering his face with kisses and tears.

"Holy Cry, Ma."

But she didn't give herself over to weeping for long. She had to get ready for Papa. Suddenly Time, which had seemed endless, became a raging flood, a fierce hurricane, a runaway train, charging down upon the Melov household. Time, suddenly, gave her a most peculiar feeling in the belly. It wouldn't let her eat, and it broke up her sleep, and it made her eyes look like two bright lamps. Time became an overwhelming demon as the floors were scrubbed, the furniture washed and polished, the bedding aired, the clothes put in order. She even bought Hershy a new suit; but in this instance, where money and foresight were involved, time was plentiful, you couldn't be too careful.

"But, Ma," he said, when she seemed to be considering carefully the last of two dozen suits he had tried on, "ain't it too big?"

"What's big about it?"

"Look."

The jacket hung loose from his slender shoulders, with the sleeves reaching his dirt-caked knuckles; the baggy pants billowed over his knees and were slipping off his waist. He groaned as she slashed tightly the belt of his pants and then of his jacket. Appraising him, as he stood strapped by the belts, she said: 'It's all right, Hershel, you'll grow into it."

"But, Ma, it hurts my belly. I can hardly breathe."

"Never mind, it hurts. Remember, you're a growing boy. I can't buy you a new suit every Monday and Thursday."

"But like a clown I'll look. Pa'll laugh on me."

"Clown, *shmown*. By next Pesach, for the spring holiday, it will fit you like a glove. You'll grow into it."

That's the way it always was: you'll grow into it. He never got anything to fit him right away, not even shoes. How long was it going to take her to admit he was grown up, to buy him clothes that would fit him now, not three years from now?

His mother also found time to make him polish his scuffed shoes every day, so that they might look like they hadn't just been dragged out of a garbage can, but getting a shine on them was impossible.

"Well, the feet are not so important," she decided. "Nobody should look on the ground anyhow. But at least we can make your head shine."

So she bought a jar of Vaseline and began to train his hair. But when his pillowslip became greasy and his fingermarks began to show on everything he touched, she decided against continuing the practice.

On the day, finally, of his father's homecoming, Hershy didn't want to go to school, but his mother wouldn't hear of it. "*Gottenyu*," she said, "my little God." Time, the beast, was already on her back, preventing her from doing the million things she had to do; she was not going to be burdened with him around the house, too; he was going to go to school, that's all, and that was final; and he was going to get all dressed up, in case Papa should come home while he was still in school, because today he had to look like a gem, like the great big diamond of his father's heart. And she warned him solemnly that she would break every bone in his body if he was not a good boy on this day.

He protested, though, when she tried to make him wear a pair of white stockings, left over from his cousin Rachel's childhood. What did she want, all the guys to call him sissy? Did she want he should come home with black eyes?

No, she only wanted him to look like a prince. She only knew that white was the color for the rich, the great, the respected.

In the old country, yah, but how many times did he have to tell her this wasn't the old country? How many times did he have to tell her that he didn't live in a palace or a *schule*, but in the United States, on a street in the Northwest Side of Chicago called Thomas Street, where the only kind of stars you saw came from fists, how many times?

All right, she'd let him wear black stockings.

She then almost strangled him with an old necktie of his father's, which was so long that he felt it below his groin after tucking it into his pants. But what was she going to do with his hair, his wild Indian hair? Beads of sweat burst out on her forehead as she struggled with it. At last, with the help of the Vaseline and after breaking half the teeth of the fine-toothed comb, she managed to get what resembled a part.

Finally, his neck craning from the wrinkled collar and

tightly knotted tie, his belly cramped by the belts of his baggy pants and loose jacket, his mother beamed at his shiny face, his sticky blond hair, his blue eyes, his small bony nose, his fair skin, his protruding ears, his bulging lips, and proclaimed him a beauty, a picture of a boy.

"My beauty, my gem, my handsome Cossack," she said, as though chewing him up through the expressions. "Papa will never recognize you. You've grown so big since he went away. Papa will eat himself alive at the sight of you. Now go to school before *I* eat you up."

But before he left, her face changed, became stern. "Remember," she warned him, "I'll break every bone in your body if you're not a good boy today, if you come home dirty."

Then he left, watching over himself and his new clothes as though he were carrying eggs, the terrible responsibility of keeping himself clean and good for a whole day being almost unbearable, making him wish, almost, that his father was not coming home. Outside, he remembered, luckily, to kiss the mezuzah on the front door entrance: that might help him out; anyway, it was supposed to keep all evil away. On the way, the spirit of his father suddenly appeared to aid him further, for in him stirred a powerful incantation his father had taught him long ago.

One evening, he remembered, while alone on the street, a shadow had begun to flutter about him. The thing paralyzed him, but just as it reached to swallow him up he screamed and ran into the house. His father lifted him to his chest and held him close until his wild heart was calmed, and when he found out what had happened his father wrinkled his brow and then decided to let him share the knowledge of a great magic secret, which had been handed down by the old sages of Israel.

"From now on," his father said, "when you're alone and frightened, all you have to do is say: 'Shabriri . . .'"

"Shabriri," Hershy repeated.
"Briri."
"Briri."
"Riri."
"Riri."
"Iri."
"Iri."
"Ri."
"Ri."
"Repeat it."

Heshy repeated the chant and then said: "So what happens when I say that?"

"If you say that, and while you're saying it, anything that frightens you will begin to shrink, until, as it hears its name grow smaller and smaller, it becomes nothing, vanishes, pouf, like smoke. See?"

It was a powerful piece of magic, for since then, whenever he was alone and frightened, nothing had ever happened to him after he spoke these strange words.

Now, to fortify himself further, he said aloud: "Shabriri . . . briri . . . riri . . . iri . . . RI."

Now, he said it.

Now nothing could happen to him.

And, strangely enough, nothing did. He was teased and taunted, certainly, but not enough to get fighting mad; he was too well protected. He didn't even mind it when the guys went to the park to play football after school. And, when he got home, even his mother was surprised.

He had come quietly up the back stairs and stood for a moment looking through the kitchen windows. His mother sat stiffly at the kitchen table in her best black dress with the white lace collar, staring at the nickel-plated alarm clock that stood on top of the stove. Her hair, dipped along her forehead and braided in a thick biscuit in back, was still wet from a recent bath and had a patent-leather luster; and her face, with its strong nose, gleaming cheekbones, full lips, and deeply set eyes, seemed set in a frame of lace. The room was immaculate, with the bleached oak floor still damp from scrubbing; there was a wet sheen on the sink, the polished coal stove, and the oilcloth on the table.

"Man," he said, startling her as he walked in. "Man alive, is it clean."

She studied him carefully, and then said: "You're a good boy, Hershel. An angel."

"Because I didn't get dirty?"

"Yes."

"Papa helped me."

She became excited. How? Had he seen Papa? Where was he?

"It was Papa's magic helped me. I gave everybody the *Shabriri*. See?"

She relaxed, sighing from the depths of her swollen corseted bosom, and smiled. He liked the way her eyes gleamed and the way her face grew round and soft when she smiled.

"You look pretty, Ma."

She kissed his hair and stroked it with her hand. "I wish Papa was here already," she said.

"Me too. He'll see me in my brand-new clothes and then I'll be able to get in my old clothes and go out and play."

"Play here."

He looked around, wondering what to do. He couldn't go into the front room and ride the rocking chair; his mother wouldn't let him. He couldn't play with her; she was too old. Maybe he could practice up on his catching. He took a sponge ball out of a drawer in the pantry, where he kept his belongings, and began to bounce it off the wall.

"Hershel."

"What?"
"I just cleaned the house."
"So?"
"So stop it."
"So what'll I do?"
"Something else."
He put the ball away and saw his marbles in the drawer. He took a few out, placed them on the floor, then got on his hands and knees and, with his bull's-eye knick, tried to hit them.
"Hershel."
"Huh?"
"Look what you're doing with your new suit.
"But the floor's clean, Ma."
"You'll wear the pants out."
"Crying out loud, Ma, what'll I do?"
He picked up the marbles and reluctantly shot them into his drawer. He studied the pop-bottle corks and some of his father's old union buttons, then drew out a stack of limp cards with pictures of baseball players. He propped them up one by one on the windowsill and tried to imitate the batting, pitching, and catching forms of the great ballplayers.
"Hershel, can't you sit still for a minute?"
"Aw, Ma, I got to do something."
"Then read me a story."
"Ah, all right."
"What will you read?" she asked eagerly.
"I don't know. What? History, Geography, Good Health?"
"Good Health."
He brought out the Good Health book, opened it on the table, and began riffling the pages. Hey, there was a lulu, one he hadn't read aloud yet. All about the Black Hole of Calcutta. He began reading laboriously, but his mother followed

closely, nodding her head, gasping, folding and unfolding her hands, stirring in her chair. When he finished, she said: "Is that true, Hershel?"

"Sure, Ma. It's in the book. It got to be true."

"Imagine that."

"So from now on, Ma, we got to have the windows open at night, even in the winter."

"We'll see."

"What do you mean, we'll see? What do you want us to do, die some night from the bad air? You want us to keep on breathing poison all the time?"

"It'll cost too much to heat the house."

"It'll cost more if we get flu or something."

"Robbers could get in through an open window."

"Robbers! What could they steal?"

"Shut up."

He knew that she hated to be reminded that there was nothing of great value in the house. But he insisted: "How about it, Ma?"

"I'll think about it."

He knew that from now on there'd be open windows in the house. She believed in the Good Health book. So did he, but he wouldn't always admit it, especially when the book prescribed things that hurt, like iodine.

"Now what, Ma?"

She didn't answer. Her eyes were misty and there was a distant look in them. "All I've missed," she said, shaking her head. "Like a pig I was brought up. I have to come to a child to learn, to a child that *I* should be teaching."

"That's all right, Ma." But he liked the sense of power he got from teaching her; he liked her dependence on him for certain information which only his father could give before he went away. Maybe his mother was right; there was something holy about the written word. "You want me to read something else?"

"No, sweetheart."

"So what'll we do?"

She shrugged her shoulders.

"Can I go in the front room and ride on the rocker?"

"No, you'll get it dirty. I didn't clean all day for nothing."

"Then how about letting me play shooters or with the rubber ball?"

"No."

"Then let me go out." He saw her hesitate. "Aw, Ma, I got to do something. I won't do nothing outside, I promise. I'll just wait for Pa. Maybe he won't be able to find the house. So I'll see him and show him where it is. Yah, Ma, that's a good idea."

"But you won't get dirty?"

"I promise."

"Remember, Hershel, if you do."

"I'll just wait for Pa."

Released, at last, he banged the kitchen door shut and jumped down the rutted back stairs three at a time.

Outside, a few girls were playing jacks on a porch, and below them a girl was skipping rope, but he couldn't play with them. Some little kids were shooting marbles on the earth between the sidewalk and the curb. When he tried to butt into their game to show them how to really play, they began to yell and swear at him. A few big guys, standing outside their basement social and athletic club, chased him away when he tried to listen in on their conversation. He wished his own pals were on the street instead of in the park playing football. They were a fine bunch of guys, he told himself, leaving him alone. He'd get even with them someday.

"What do you say, Pa?" he said aloud. "Come on home already."

He picked up a chicken-coop stick and ran it over the separated slats of a wooden fence. Suddenly, in hearing the clunking sound, a kind of music seemed to thrum out of the fence, and he became a part of the street's rhythm. He kicked a can and caught a cymbal tone from the asphalt pavement as the can clanked along. He jumped high in the air: a brittle twig snapped as he flicked it, he crunched over some dried leaves that fell, and he felt that he himself had set the rustling tree above in motion. A horse and wagon clattered by, and then Tony the bananaman filled the street with his lusty voice. Windows screeched along their rusty lines, and women poked their heads out to call Tony or to listen. Their calls were like a shrieking chorus behind Tony's big, buoyant voice. Hershy thought: someday he'd get a big belly like Tony, tie a red-and-black handkerchief around his neck, and become a singer: *O solo mio, O solo you-O.* Even his own mother leaned out of the window and shook her head while listening.

"No bananas today?" Tony sang to his mother.

"No bananas today," his mother sang back, followed by pleased laughter.

"Oh, that Tony," Mrs. White shrilled. "He should of been in the opera."

The voices died down, seemed to flutter through the passageways, from where the wash could be seen on the clothesline, and in their stead came a whipping breeze that filled up a sleeve, a shirt, a bedsheet, a towel, a stocking, a pair of bloomers.

Hershy then gazed longingly at the fences framed about the lawns. He wanted to jump on them and walk on them, but resisted the temptation; he might fall off and get dirty. Anyhow, he was the world's champion fence-walker, so he didn't need too much practice any more. But someday he was going to get a wire or a strong rope and string it across his back yard and practice for the circus. Hershy the Great. There'd be a big spotlight on him, like the way he had seen it as a little kid the time his father had taken him to the circus; he'd be a million miles above the people, touching the sky, and they'd look to him like pebbles with open mouths. Hershy the Great. Then he'd get off the street and live in a palace like a king with his mother and father and Rachel. King Saul. King David. King Solomon. And King Hershy. Hershy the King. But the crown of the king became heavy on his head. It meant leaving the street and the guys. He didn't want to do that. Not after all the fights he had had. Not after getting to know it so well.

He knew the street when it had ice on it and when the asphalt got sticky from the heat; he had jumped, walked, hopscotched, slid, coasted, fallen, and played over every inch of it. He knew the curbs from sitting on them and leaping from them, from using them as bases on the corner when playing kick-the-can baseball, and from the angry, cracking, popping sounds they made when he and his gang roasted potatoes in a bonfire. He knew the sewers, especially how to stuff the drains with leaves on a rainy day so that he could go wading and sail paper boats; he knew the sewers, too, from being lowered into them, with a big guy holding his ankles, to fish for the grimy balls that fell in. He knew every back yard, passageway, basement, and back porch from playing hide, redlight, and run-sheep-run. He knew the garbage-heaped alleys from rat-hunting expeditions. And he knew the magic of the night, under the yellow arcs of the lampposts. Gee, how he knew this street—better than any he had ever lived on. Simply because he had lived on it longer.

2.

Before his father had gone away, they had never lived in a flat more than a year. He didn't know why they always had to keep moving, but once his mother said: "We move because it's the only way to get a clean, freshly painted, aired-out, brand-new flat. Sometimes we get a month's free rent, too." Each year, it seemed, she forgot the heartache and turmoil of moving, the many new fights Hershy had to get into on the new and strange streets, and the tearful partings when the fights were over.

Long ago, they had lived around Maxwell Street, the pushcart neighborhood to which all Jewish immigrants first came, but he was too young to remember it, except for one incident, which brought him his first present. He had tripped on a broken stair and fallen to the bottom of the stairway so hard that his father had to carry him back into the house. He couldn't remember the pain he had felt, but he did recall that his father, not knowing what to do, left the house and came back with a bright-red cardboard fireman's hat, and he got well and strong in an instant. After that, the only time he ever got a present was when he was sick; sometimes he got a nickel on Hanukkah, the Jewish Christmas, but that never seemed like a real present.

Once, when his father wasn't working, they moved three times in one year. One place was above a stable off an alley, with a toilet in the yard that had a hole in it; he got sick then because it was too cold to go down there in the winter and because he was afraid of the hole and the dark. Besides, they were the only Jews on the street. All about them were Italians; his mother didn't know how to talk to anybody; he didn't, either. He had a fight every day, and once his father came home with a bloody face. The next day they moved again, to a street where everyone was Jewish.

When his father got to work again and the job began to look steady, they decided to move to a cleaner, bigger flat in a better neighborhood. They moved to the Northwest Side, near Western and Division streets: a neighborhood, his mother said, which wasn't all played out, and where there was a park nearby to enjoy. Plenty of goyim lived there, but also plenty of Jews; one, then, couldn't be a total stranger. Besides, they were getting up in the world, his mother claimed: the streets seemed bigger, and there were trees one could look at, and she could hang out her wash without fear of getting it full of smoke from railroads and factories, and she could breathe air that wasn't always filled with the stink of slaughtered animals from the stockyards. People, she insisted, had to better themselves.

Year after year, they moved farther west, closer to Humboldt Park; now they were only a couple of blocks away from it. On the other side of the park lived his rich uncle, who owned a laundry, an automobile, and a brick house. His mother always looked toward the other side of the park, and said someday, with God's help, they'd live there; meanwhile, they were close to making the jump across. But before his father left, he said to his mother: "Please, do me a favor. Keep your eyes off the park. Keep calm. Make the landlord clean the flat. And don't move. I want to come back to something I'm used to." Perhaps they'd have moved again, because the autumn his father was away she did look for new rooms, but flats were hard to find, and they remained where his father had left them.

He wondered if his father would remember the street and the house they lived in. After all, his father hadn't lived there very long. Besides, his father had been to so many places, a million miles away, it might be hard to remember. His father had known the street only in the early hours of the morning when he went to work and at night when he came home, so how could he be expected to recognize the street and the house? Maybe his father was lost; that's why it was taking him so long to come home. Maybe he should wait for him on the corner, or by the streetcar, so that he could show him the way home.

I'll show you, Pa, he said silently, imagining himself leading his father home. I know the whole neighborhood by heart. Sure, Pa, I explored it. When I grow up big, I'm going to be an explorer. I been practicing and I'm learning good. I'll take you in the park, too. I'll show you where I fish, by the bridge, under a tree. I'll show you Bunker Hill. We play cowboys and Indians there. I'll show you where you get the boats to go rowing on the lagoon. Yah, Pa, I'll show you.

He remembered suddenly the statue at the entrance to the park. It was of a miner with granite muscles, bent on one knee, and embracing a little girl. Every time he saw it, or remembered it, something big began to thump in him. Maybe that's the way his father'd come home. He'd see him on the street and he'd run to him and his father'd get down on one knee and wrap him up in his strong arms. Jesus, Pa.

But maybe, if he went to the carline, he'd miss him. He'd better stay in front of the house.

He wondered what his father looked like now. He remembered that he was a very big man when he left, like a tower; he had to bend his head way back to look up at him. Since his father had gone away, his mother had grown shorter and shorter, and now he didn't have to bend his head back to look up at her face. But his father, maybe he was like a giant now, with muscles busting out of his clothes, like the miner in the park.

Oh, hurry on home, Pa. Hurry. Hurry.

CHAPTER TWO

1.

Waiting on the wooden stairs of his front porch, wishing that he could slide down the black iron rails on the sides, Hershy scanned the street, ready to rush up to his father at the first glimpse of him. Suddenly a fear came over him that he might not recognize his father. The picture he held of him in his mind was vague, the edges blurring as he tried to make it sharper. A shadowy figure of his father rose in its stead and began to accuse him of not being a good son. He felt himself shrinking backward, yelling inwardly: I know you good, Pa. I know you real good.

2.

He knew, for instance, that his father's name had not always been David Melov. In the old country it had been David Melovitz. But when he began living in Chicago the mailman would never call his name when he brought the mail.

"It's a hard name to pronounce," the mailman complained. "All you itzes and ovitches and skis. When I come home, not only do I have to put my feet in a hot liniment bath but I also have to spend all my money on candy drops to take out the cramps in my tongue. Do me a favor, then, and change your name."

His father wouldn't listen.

"Don't do me a favor, then," the mailman said. "Instead, let me give you a piece of advice. You're a greenhorn, aren't you?"

"Yes," his father said.

"You want to get along in this country, don't you?"

"Certainly."

"You don't want any trouble, do you?"

"God forbid."

"Then cut out the itz and be an American."

His father wouldn't budge.

"Look," the mailman said. "If you didn't mind having a piece of your rosebud cut off, why should you mind knocking off a little itz?"

His father didn't know what the mailman was talking about; he knew only that he was fighting hard to keep his name. But how hard can a man fight? He was so worried about his wife, pregnant with Hershy in Russia, that to get mail from her promptly he had to change his name to Melov. After that, he felt like a real American. The mailman gave him immediate service, yelled his name all over the building, made him known, and became a friend. It was his first introduction, his father explained, to a great American phenomenon: the tendency of people in America to equalize themselves and to lose their identity.

3.

That happened before Hershy was born.

But as he grew up, always gathering information and learning secrets, trying to solve the mystery of himself and the world about him, he found out that older people lived in and talked about mostly two things: the past and tomorrow. Talking about the past made them feel stronger in the present and gave them the hope for tomorrow. The hope, in their relating the sharp contrasts of two worlds, seemed to rest finally in him, for they always said: "It's your America, Hershy."

His father, he learned, had never known a childhood as it is experienced in America. He was the eldest son of a *sofer*, a pious man who writes out the Scrolls of the Torah and who also copies mezuzahs and other Hebrew religious writings. He was expected, then, to follow his father's footsteps, and, in preparation, had spent his whole childhood in a *schule*, stooped over the long tables, reading by the flickering lights of candles, rocking with prayer and study: play was a thing which only the rich and the idiots and the *mujiks* could enjoy. But David did not want to be a *sofer*. It had bent and gnarled his father and had made a stranger of him. For his father, gone sometimes for months in his travels through the province of Kiev to do his work, was seldom home. Even David, his own son, hardly recognized him when he did come home. And his mother, left dumb and slightly deaf from an attack of scarlet fever, suffered her loneliness in silence. In her muted way, she made her son understand that she, too, did not want him to become a *sofer*, but that, being a woman, she could do nothing against the dominating will of a father.

David wanted to be a carpenter, instead, like his mother's father. As a small child, before his grandfather died, he was fascinated by the patterns in the grains of wood, the shavings curling out of a plane, the sawdust spraying from the bite of a saw, and the power of the hammer. The rhythmical sounds and movements pleased him, too. But the touch of smooth surfaces against his fingers and the magic of seeing things put together made him jump with joy. Later, he liked the smell of the forests outside his village and was overwhelmed by the thought of felling a tree and shaping it to any form he desired.

The decision of what he was to do with the rest of his life rested finally in himself. For, just before his *barmitzvah*, the day a Jewish boy becomes a man, his father left in the snowdrift dead of winter on a trip through the province, promising that he'd be back for his son's *barmitzvah*, but he never returned. His father, who always insisted upon being thoroughly clean before he would begin work on the Scrolls of the Torah, had come to a village where the whole water supply had frozen. He had no alternative but to go to a nearby river, chop a hole in the ice, and bathe himself. Soon afterward, he fell ill with pneumonia and died dreadfully, away from home, with his pus-filled lungs choking him to death.

Alone, then, David became a man on his thirteenth birthday, a man who suddenly was able to shape his own destiny, with his childhood left behind in the old yellow pages of a prayer book. Immediately afterward he went to Kiev to become apprenticed to a master carpenter, armed with the proper papers of permission to live in the big city; for in those days a Jew was not considered a citizen, and God help you if you were caught without a yellow pass.

At the time, he was a slender, bony, hollow-faced boy weighing eighty pounds. He thought of himself as a man, for officially he was one, but the terror he felt when he first saw Kiev could only have gripped a child. Houses seemed to lie on top of one another. Houses, drawn by horses over shiny rails, with jabbering people tangled in them, clanged through the streets. Countless spires, with ugly jagged fingers, pointed accusingly at the charred heavens. Bulbous domes, like the diseased noses of drunkards, sniffed the sky. He could hardly breathe from the smoke that pocked the city and from the suffocated-looking people that wormed about him. He shrank against the buildings as he walked, trembling within an utterly strange and hostile world.

Finally he found refuge in the master carpenter's house and vowed that he'd never wander from it. Even after the older apprentices laughed at his fears, he seldom wandered from the immediate neighborhood. The one time he did, aside from visits home, he was attacked by a gang of older boys who, when they found out that he was a Jew, beat him so violently that he could barely crawl home. Besides, there was no time or energy to wander far. He had to get up at dawn to mourn for his father, then work until the sun went down. At night he slept in an attic with nine other apprentices, which wasn't much different than at home where everyone slept and lived in the same room. All in all, he had traded one room for a more crowded room, a dark smelly *schule* for a darker smellier hole.

Gradually, after the year of mourning for his father was over, it became harder and harder to go through the morning and evening ritual of prayer. Hard work and piety somehow did not go together. Time was too precious and the body was overwhelming in its demands. In this frame of mind he began to heed a new kind of philosophy that was being expounded by Jewish trade union leaders and socialists. They said: "Destroy the delusion of the Messiah." That was like saying: "Destroy Judaism." They said further: "What is the Messiah? It is nothing more than man's dream of a better life. But why hope for a better life after death? Is it wrong to hope now? Why not hope today for tomorrow? Let man himself become his own Messiah. In man alone rests the fulfillment of tomorrow's dreams." Slowly, he began to drift away from the rigid training of his earlier life.

But before his apprenticeship was over, he became fervent again in his religious observances. During a pogrom that occurred in his home village, his mother, his older sister, and her husband were killed. His younger brother Yussel was away at the time, learning to become a tailor. And Rachel, his sister's little child, was left unharmed; she had been in the outhouse during the massacre, paralyzed by the terrifying screams.

Soon afterward, Yussel, on his way back to Kiev from the village, met a drunken Russian officer on the road. The Russian officer, who had been left behind with a peasant girl after a night of drinking and gambling, was lost, and he commanded Yussel to take him home. But on the way the officer passed out, and Yussel robbed him of his winnings and ran off to America.

This left David completely alone, cut off from the world, except for his niece Rachel, who was taken in by a cousin in a nearby village until he could support her. He mourned a year for his dead ones, rocking with prayer and beating his breast. Slowly, the guilt he had felt in having turned away from God began to dissolve. And presently, purged of neglect and sin through prayer and the sweat of his daily labor, he was able to sleep through a whole night without waking up in a cold fright from a horrible dream.

Then he met Sonya. He was visiting his niece Rachel at his cousin's house in the village of Narodich when he saw her. Afterward, in remembering, it seemed to him that at one moment he had been living a deep, internal life, and at the next moment he had been suddenly sprung from a dark prison to face a warm, glittering world.

Back in Kiev one night, in the attic with his friend Hyman Bronstein, who had begun his apprenticeship with him, he said: "Hyman, are you awake?"

"No, but I can hear you."

"I met a girl, Hyman."

"Where?"

"In Narodich."

"So?"

"I'm going to marry her."
"Are her parents rich?"
"No."
"Don't be a fool, David. Remember, we promised each other we'd go to America."
"She'll go with me."
"How do you know she'll have you?"
"She has to have me. For once, something good has to happen to me."
"But who is she? Who are her parents?"
"Her father is a poor baker."
"Then you won't get a dowry."
"That's not important."
"Oh, you fool. Remember, you are the son of Hershel Melovitz. It's almost like being the son of a rabbi. You can have anybody you desire. You can get a large dowry, enough to make you a master carpenter, enough to get you to America, enough to let you live like a king for the rest of your life. Don't be a fool, David. Don't throw yourself away on a piece of flesh."
"That's the way it is, Hyman."
"And to tell me this you woke me up?"
"She's a picture of a woman."
"Let her be a picture, but a gold frame around it wouldn't hurt, either. Go to sleep, you idiot, and dream of another picture."

But he couldn't go to sleep at once. He was too full of the beauty of Sonya's face, of her strong arms and back as she carried water from the river, of the shape of her bare feet and solid ankles as she stepped over the earth, of the sound of a comb choking through her thick black hair, of her young bubbling laughter, of the smell of fresh bread, deep and warm and earthy, about her. The image of her grew fuller and fuller, and one day he wrote to his cousin asking her to make a match. He also wrote to his younger brother Yussel in America, taking it for granted that he was rich, asking him to send the fare to Chicago for him and his future wife.

At the time (Hershy heard this from his mother in conversations with her sisters or Rachel, which always left him bleak and frightened), Sonya had plenty of suitors, one in particular who later came to Chicago to make a fortune. And he (David), though he was nineteen and thought of himself as a full-grown man, had no conception of his appearance to others. Actually, he looked like a slightly overgrown, deprived child, with protruding ears and hollow cheeks and cavelike eyes; he had no teeth, either, since he had had them pulled out in order to evade being drafted into the army.

But Sonya had no choice. She was a poor girl, one of four sisters, two of whom had already married plain, common men, one a harness-maker and the other a tailor, and she had a younger sister who couldn't get married until Sonya did. For a girl to have a choice she needed wealth, her family had to make rich offers, as though the man were a God. Whatever she dreamed she would have to forget; her other suitors were nothing, nobodies, no matter how good they looked. She was fortunate that a man like David was eager for her. He was a good man. He came from a fine family. He was highly educated. Why, he was even able to interpret the Talmud. He was a man, coming from the family of a *sofer*, who could ask for blood if he insisted. And apparently he loved her, for no man in his right mind, who could marry into a fortune, would marry a girl whose parents had no dowry to offer. Besides, she would do what her parents told her. She would marry David. She would be happy with him and would give him children. Love was for the idle and rich. Love was a dream. A woman was life. And a poor woman had to face life, that's all.

Still, she tried to postpone the marriage. When he came back to Narodich a few months later, she thought she had been given a weapon for delaying it, for he was all set, immediately after marrying her, to go to America. He was disappointed, he explained, that there wasn't another steamship ticket for her; but his brother Yussel had written that he could only afford one ticket; however, in a short time, both of them would have enough money to send not only for her but also for little Rachel.

She wouldn't hear of it. He had no right to marry her before he left, she argued. What if something should happen to him on the way? What if, after he got to America, he forgot her? No, he had no right to laugh. That had happened before to countless girls. She had to think of herself. What was he thinking of, to marry her and then leave her, perhaps with child? Wouldn't it be better if he went to America and then, if he sent for her, get married there? (Her plan was to get him to bring her to America; but once there, free of her parents, she would go to work and marry a man of her own choosing.) That seemed just and right to her. So wouldn't he please tell her parents of the new plan, since only he could postpone the wedding? But he wouldn't listen. He only knew that without her he could go nowhere, he could do nothing, and that knowing she was his he could go and then place the world at her feet. And, not being able to dissuade him, with her parents insisting, she gave in finally. Then, in the month she became pregnant, he left for America, to face with great hope a fearsome new world and to lay at her feet the world he had promised her.

And she was left alone to face the maddening sights and sounds of young people in love, the anxious men who still wanted her, and the bleakness of an empty bed. There she was left, growing bigger every day with the child that was in her, with a nameless fear flooding her whole being. When a dog howled at night or when an owl hooted in the trees, she almost died of fright over their omens of death. When her loins ached, she was happy, for she was told that she was carrying a boy. When her belly pained, she cried; it was the sign of a girl. But finally, through joy and fears, signs and omens, a boy one day and a girl the next, the child wouldn't stand for any nonsense; he came out yelling as if the whole world belonged to him. And his yells, it seemed, brought passage for them and Rachel to America.

The crossing was a nightmare. But when she arrived and saw the spacious three-room flat, with windows, and three soft chairs, and a carpet, and two separate beds with soft mattresses, and the magic of gaslight, she forgave him (David) all the suffering he had caused her. He was a rich man, she thought, at least a baron. She wept with joy, and through her tears she fell in love with him.

But, as her values changed, she found that she was really married to an ordinary workingman, a nobody in a world of struggle to become a somebody. Still, life was better, even when jobs were scarce or poorly paid. And in their common problems, her first burst of love settling into a sense of loyalty and duty, they grew closer and closer together.

4.

Then came the war. Hershy was seven years old. His father, upon learning of Russia's conflict with Germany, clasped his hands tightly and said: "Thank God." His mother gasped and wrung her hands; she had two brothers in the Russian army. And Hershy said: "What's the matter?"

"Nothing, nothing," his father answered. But he lifted him to his chest and held him close. Hershy knew that something was wrong, but he also felt that nothing could harm him. "Thank God we're safe in America," his father said.

War, for his father, was nothing more than a battle for dirt. The soldiers will fight, he said, and the czars, the kaisers, the kings, and the generals will be called heroes. The poor people will gain nothing but suffering and sorrow; the only earth they could possibly win was the plot of earth all people are destined for after they die. The rich had worlds to win. And the Jews, for certain, had nothing to gain. Thank God, he said, America was a country that was free of the iron fist. Thank God, the children could play at war without meaning it.

But gradually the war came closer and closer, and then, in 1917, three things happened which Hershy could never forget.

5.

His father came home early one day, dressed in his best clothes and carrying a brick of ice cream.

"Look at me," he said. "Just look at me."

"All right, I'm looking at you," said Hershy's mother. "What is there to see?"

"Do I look the same?"

"Why should you look different?"

"Because I feel big. So big, I can't express it. You're now looking at a new man, a real American, a genuine Yankee. You're not looking at just plain David Melov now. You're looking at *Citizen* David Melov."

His mother, in trying to hide her deep emotion, said: "So what am I to see, stars on your hat, red-white-and-blue stripes on your suit, a goat's beard on your chin?"

"Ay, Sonya, you should have seen me sign my name. Others sprawled their names all over the paper. Me, I fitted my name right on the line, so delicate, so refined; it was a pleasure to look at it; even the judge was delighted. And you should have seen how I got on with the judge. You'd have been proud of me. The judge said: Who was the first president of the United States? I said: George Washington. The judge said: Who is the president of the United States today? I said: Woodrow Wilson. The judge said: What does the United States mean to you? I said: The United States is a free country. The judge said: Would you fight for the United States to keep it free, even lay down your life for it? I couldn't answer for a minute. But the judge helped me out when he said: If you lived in Russia now would you fight for her? And I said: No. Then he asked: Why? So I said: Because it is not my country, I couldn't fight for a pogrom-maker. Then, when the judge asked me again if I'd fight for the United States, I said: Yes. And he said: All right, you'll make a good citizen. And he said further: Sign here."

"So, to be a citizen, you have to fight then?"

"No, it's just talk. We're not even at war yet. But here, at least, I'll have something to fight for, if I have to, even if it's for a piece of paper that makes me a citizen. In Russia, though, a Jew is not even a citizen and he is forced to fight."

"Who would take you to fight anyhow?"

"Don't belittle me. I'm an important man now."

"Maybe you are. Maybe now you'll be a somebody."

"Why, am I not a somebody already?"

"No, I mean a real somebody."

His father swore in Russian. "Are you never satisfied?" he said.

"Yes, I'm very satisfied now. I'm proud of you. I only want to be prouder." She kissed him.

But Hershy was truly satisfied. "Then you're a real American, huh, Pa?" he said.

"Yes, Hershel. You have a father now that you should never be ashamed of. You have a father now that you can be proud of."

That evening, Hershy swelled with greater pride; his mother had planned for this day, knowing that her David would not fail her when it came to something that required learning, and had invited their relatives over to celebrate.

Uncle Yussel was away in California, and Rachel was out dancing. But Uncle Hymie, the rich one, without whom no gathering was official, drove over in his new Studebaker touring car. Uncle Hymie was his father's best friend from Kiev. He was also married to Sonya's younger sister: he had fallen in love with her when he went to Narodich to attend David's wedding; and later, after being presented a ticket to America by David as a dowry, married her.

As usual, he honked his horn a good minute before coming up. And, as usual, Hershy ran down the stairs to greet him and Aunt Reva, and had to go through a boring ritual before he could get into the car.

First, he had to ask where his cousins, Manny and Shirley, were. They were at home with the maid. Then he had to say, *Aleichem Sholom,* peace be with you, after Uncle Hymie said, *Sholom Aleichem.* Then his Aunt Reva would stop fixing her furs, which his mother always touched with trembling, envious hands, and would place her diamond-fingered hand on his head as though crowning him for having done something admirable. And his uncle, wreathed in smiles, would look down at him from his height of black, wiry hair and crunched, blinking eyes.

"Noo, Hershel, where are you running?"

"To the car, to the car."

"And where are you going?"

"Around the world, all around the world."

"And what will you be around the world?"

"An explorer, a discoverer."

"No more moving-and-express man?"

"Sure."

"No more Samson?"

"I'll be Samson, too."

"And a racer, too?"

"Sure. Can I go drive now, can I, can I?"

"But where did you get this new craze, an explorer?"

"Columbus was an explorer."

"Oh, then that's a good thing. So go ahead, Hershel, and be a Columbus, but find gold, too. When you get older you'll learn that gold can never hurt you."

Then Hershy ran off and leaped into the leather front seat of the touring car, without opening the door, just like Douglas Fairbanks, and began going *rrrrrrrrrr* all over the world a million miles an hour. His trip was interrupted twice. Uncle Ben, the fruit peddler, who was married to his mother's oldest sister, came by with his wife, but Hershy was too busy killing off a pack of whooping Indians to pay them much attention. Then Uncle Irving, the card player, woman-chaser, and former tailor, who now worked for Uncle Hymie as a laundry driver and who was married to his mother's next oldest sister, caught his eye; but Hershy was too busy machine-gunning an army of Huns from his roaring airplane to say hello. Then, just as he was about to win by a mile the daredevil speed championship, his mother called and made him come into the house. And there, around the kitchen table, watching them hold lumps of sugar between their teeth as they sipped tea out of glasses, and as they smacked their lips with praise while they ate the strudel and taigloch his mother had prepared, he flowed into the hero his father had become.

Now, his father could become a man of property.

Maybe, Hershy thought, his father could get a car, now that he was a citizen.

Now, his father could be anything he wanted, could do everything he desired; he was a man with rights.

Maybe, Hershy thought, his father would buy him everything he wanted. Maybe he would buy his mother a fur coat and diamonds, then she'd never be jealous of her younger sister, and she'd never scare him with the stories of all the wealthy suitors she could have married. Maybe everybody'd be satisfied.

His mother, glowing with pride, visioning a new world, laid a tombstone on the past. And the others began to erect a monument to the future.

Now, with citizen's papers, David Melov had the right to become an American *goniff*, a thief with honor. Now, initiated in the uses of the toilet, the faucet, the brick house with more than one room, he could delve into the greater magic of America. With the courage he had shown in leaving behind pogroms and a piece of dried-up black bread, in being able to tear up his roots to replant himself in richer earth, he could now go on to bigger and better things. Nobody could rightfully call him a greenhorn any longer. He could be like the children and shout: It's a free country. Yes, now, as with the children, it was his America.

His father admitted it was a wonderful life.

Uncle Hymie wanted everybody to observe who was talking. The citizen. The silent one, the man of few words, from whom you could seldom get a peep. Suddenly, because he is now a citizen, he thinks he has a right to talk. All right, Uncle Hymie shushed everybody, it is free-speech time. Talk.

But his father didn't talk. Instead, everyone laughed. And Hershy, bursting with pride, jumped on his father's lap, and yelled: "Hot dog, Pa!"

6.

Hershy felt even more secure as an American when, soon after the United States entered the war, his Uncle Yussel became a soldier. Hershy hadn't seen him in a long time, not since he had gone to California, where they made moving pictures. In fact, Hershy hardly knew him, for he was always traveling. It seemed to him that Uncle Yussel traveled purposely so that he could bring back to him a million stories of the splendor and excitement of new worlds, then just as he was about finished telling his stories he would be off again. But actually, Uncle Yussel was never able to get used to the freedom of movement he had in America. Here, he said, a man could move constantly, there was always a job for him, he could go anywhere, and he had to keep testing the truth of this. Besides, he was a restless man; it was easier to move than to try to calm himself.

"You ought to get married and settle down," Hershy's mother once said.

"How can I?" he answered. "The only woman I could be happy with is already married."

"And who is that?"

"You."

His mother poked him with her elbow. A pleased smile lighted up her face. And she said playfully: "Go flirt with someone else, Yussel. Why, there are so many beautiful women in America."

"But none as beautiful as you."

"Liar. But you're a sweet liar, Yussel."

"Besides, American women are too greedy."

"Get a greenhorn, then, right off the ship."

"They spoil too quickly."

"Then what will you do? A man can't stay single all his life. He needs children to bear his name."

"Someday I'll go back to Russia and find a nice, respectful, obedient, beautiful Jewish girl, and bring her back as my wife."

"You've been saying that for years."

"Or I'll wait for Rachel to get older and marry her."

"Don't ever say that, Yussel, not even in jest."

For that was the secret of his restlessness; he was in love with Rachel. It was first discovered when Uncle Yussel came back from one of his trips and found Rachel suddenly grown into a woman. He flung her away when she rushed up to him and wanted to be fondled, he refused to be too close to her, but he could hardly stop staring at her.

"What's the matter?" Rachel asked one day.

"Nothing," Uncle Yussel said, his face agitated. "Nothing."

"Don't you love me any more?"

"Sure. Sure."

"Then why don't you hold me and kiss me and tell me some stories?"

"No. I'm too busy, too busy."

Hershy heard him say to his mother: "She was just a baby when I left. Now look at her. *Look at her.*"

And Hershy once caught his mother discussing it with his father.

"It's horrible," his mother said, "a man should feel like that about his niece, his own flesh and blood."

"Don't talk nonsense," his father said. "Yussel has a natural love for Rachel, the love of an uncle who has worried about her since infancy."

"You're blind, David."

"You're the one who's blind. In every tender look you see a love affair. Can't people love without desire?"

"Oh, are you blind, David! And oh, how Yussel must suffer."

It was hard for Hershy to relate Uncle Yussel's suffering to anything specific, especially to this vague thing called love, for Uncle Yussel seemed to be a happy, joyous, exciting man, always ready with a tender pinch of one's cheek, always ready with a smile or joke that brought laughter, always going away and coming back with strange, fantastic stories of faraway places that kept everybody awake night after night long after bedtime. He liked the stronger attachment Uncle Yussel had for him since Rachel grew up, but the notion that it was horrible for people of the same family to be in love confused him.

"So," he said to his mother one day, "what if Uncle Yussel is in love with Rachel?"

"Who told you?"

"I know."

She stared at him in amazement. "How could you know?" she asked.

"I know. So what if he is?"

"It's a sin, it's against the law."

"Why?"

"Their children can be born crazy, deformed, God knows what."

"What if there are no children?"

"Without children, there is no love."

She couldn't explain it further. She walked away from him, leaving him more confused, and she muttered: "Go talk to a child. But how could he know? There must be a devil in him." Then he heard her sigh: "Oh, how Yussel's soul must ache."

For what? Hershy wondered. He knew what his soul ached for: a football, a baseball uniform, a cowboy suit, an electric train, to be a great pitcher or halfback. What could older men ache for? They seemed to have everything: strength, big muscles, fearlessness, money, freedom of movement, powers of speech. Even Rachel had big aches. It seemed that one day she was a part of his world, and the next day she had moved into another. Everybody began to look differently at her. It seemed as if one day she had been playing with dolls, and the next day she had filled out and thrown them away; and, as her flesh began to hide her bones, as she became curvier and bigger, she suddenly got a big ache and drifted far away from his world. Why, he wondered, did all older people groan with aches? When did you suddenly start hurting, without falling down or being hit or getting sick?

When Uncle Yussel left for California, Hershy's mother said: "Come back with an actress, Yussel."

"Maybe I will," said Uncle Yussel.

"And bring me back a horse, like Tom Mix's Tony," said Hershy.

"All right," said Uncle Yussel.

"Do me a favor," said Hershy's mother. "Look around and find an actress and bring her home."

But Uncle Yussel brought back only himself. The day he came back, Hershy was playing on the street with some kids when they saw a man in uniform walking toward them. He was the first soldier they had seen and they stopped playing to admire him. Then one of the kids yelled: "Hey, that's your uncle, Hershy."

He tripped as he rushed to him, but he felt no pain from the fall, only his throat hurt. His uncle smiled, caught him in his arms, lifted him up, and sat him on his shoulder.

"Yo, man, look at that soldier."

"Look at that Hershy. That lucky Hershy."

"That your uncle, Hershy? Your uncle, for real?"

But Hershy couldn't answer. There was a big, hard pain in his throat.

In the house, however, everybody acted differently. Rachel flung her arms about Uncle Yussel and kissed him, then she backed away to admire him.

"You're so handsome, Uncle, so, so handsome." She threw her arms around him again and began to cry.

Hershy's mother and father looked stunned at first. Then tears began to seep out of his mother's eyes, and his father felt the sleeve of the uniform as though he were appraising the material.

"Now I'm a regular Yankee," Uncle Yussel exploded.

· 35

"You're the most beautiful Yank in the world," Rachel said.

"The hat, Uncle Yussel, let me wear the hat," Hershy shouted.

Uncle Yussel whirled the boy-scout-looking field hat to Hershy. At the sight of the hat covering Hershy's whole face, everybody smiled, timidly at first, and then laughed; the tension was gone.

"How?" Hershy's father managed to say. "Why?"

"I was on my way home," Uncle Yussel said. "Suddenly, that ugly Yankee with the goat's beard pointed his finger at me and said: I want you. So go carry on a fight with that rawboned Yankee."

"Yussel, Yussel," Hershy's mother sighed. "What's going to happen to you?"

"Nothing," Uncle Yussel said. "Ever since I've been in this land I've wanted to go to Europe. Now I can go free, at the government's expense. Maybe I'll find a wife there."

Hershy's father shook his head sadly. Uncle Yussel slapped his back.

"It's a lively world, David," he said. "Things happening all the time. Things always changing. Yesterday a tailor; today a soldier; tomorrow, maybe, a general. Who can predict the future?"

His eyes began to wander. When he looked at Rachel he shook his head and suddenly seemed to remember something. "Fool," he called himself. "How could I have forgotten to bring something? Come, Hershel, take a walk with me."

Hershy walked down the street with him, swollen with pride. He gripped his hand hard as the people stared at them. His voice was tight when he spoke.

"When you going away to fight, Uncle Yussel?"

"Tomorrow."

"Tomorrow? Wow!"

"Early in the morning."

"Wow! Pa going with you?"
"No. One soldier in the family is enough."
"Will you bring me back a German helmet?"
"Certainly."
"And a gun?"
"A great big one."
"A gas mask, too?"
"Of course."
"How about a medal, a pile of medals?"
"If I become a hero."
"Gee, Uncle Yussel. Gee."
"What's to cry about?"
He couldn't help it.
"Take me with, Uncle Yussel. I'll be your mascot. I'll load your rifle and bring you water when you're thirsty and I'll never get in your way and I'll go to sleep early and I'll eat a lot and everything."
"Don't cry, baby. Don't."
They stopped in front of a sporting goods store.
"What would you like, Hershel?"
He swallowed hard and said: "A bat."
"That's all?"
"A glove, too."
Then, with bat and glove in hand, choked with gratitude and pride, he went into a jewelry shop with his uncle and watched him buy a lavalier for Rachel, a cameo ring for his mother, and an Elgin watch for his father.

That night, when everyone was asleep, Hershy woke up and stared at his uncle a long time as he slept on the front-room couch. He tried on his coat, which hung to the floor; he put on his hat and practiced saluting. Then he kissed him softly and went back to sleep. When he woke up, Uncle Yussel was gone.

7.

Soon afterward, Hershy's father left also, to help build barracks at southern army camps. The war, then, seemed to have caught up his whole family, except himself and his mother. Uncle Yussel was overseas. His father was working for the army. Even Rachel was helping out: going to dances at canteens to help make the lonely boys from faraway places a little happier, she said, with his mother warning her: "But don't make them too happy, Rachel. Remember, a woman has only one precious thing to give a man. Taking care of a house, cooking, bringing up children, all that comes later. But a man will die if he gets a piece of damaged goods. So remember, Rachel, don't make them too happy."

But Hershy felt that he was out of everything. It seemed to him that he was among a gang of guys who were choosing up sides, and he was praying and begging to be picked, but nobody even looked at him, and finally everybody moved away and began to play, and he was left alone. He felt even worse when the airplane became firmly established as an instrument of war. Oh, if he was only old enough. Oh, would he fly, like an eagle. Oh, would he be a pilot. Why did it take so long to be old enough? Why did it take so long to grow up and be big enough? Why couldn't a guy jump into the world, bang, and be a big fighting man who could do anything?

"Thank God you aren't grown up," his mother said. "You have plenty of time to do the things you have to. There will be many things for you to do, don't worry, when you do grow up, and I hope it won't be fighting. Before you know it, you'll be grown up, you'll be a man, and then you'll be wishing you're a child again. You will see."

But Hershy couldn't see. How could anybody wish he was a little kid?

His mother, for whom worrying was not only an occupation but also a luxury, seemed to exhaust herself with all her worries. She fretted about his father and Uncle Yussel, about her two brothers in the Russian army and her parents in Russia, from whom she hadn't heard since the war began. She even worried about Rachel.

"Rachel, why don't you stay home sometime?" she nagged.

"What will I do home?"

"Keep me company a little."

"Aw, Ma." (She always called her aunt and uncle ma and pa.)

"But what do you do night after night?"

"I told you. A million times I told you."

"You're selfish."

"Why am I selfish? All day long I work, I'm a dog. At night I want to breathe. I go to my dancing class and I feel like a fairy tale. Or I go to a dance and meet a boy. I feel important. Everybody wants to dance with me. Everybody is nice. They make me feel like I got a big place in the world. I learn all men aren't bosses, pushing you around. I learn men got hearts, too. They want to do things for you, turn worlds upside down. You feel like a queen. All I want is a little fun, a little pleasure. Is that selfish?"

"Yes."

"Aw, Ma."

"Do I have fun? What pleasure do I have?"

"But you've got everything."

"Yes, I have everything, including a cold bed and a crazy pain in my belly. Go, go dance, but be careful."

Her worries, it seemed, shifted to him. It got so that he could hardly do anything. If he was a minute late to a meal or bedtime or anything, thunder from her face crashed down on him. She kissed him more often, stared at him longer, held him tighter when she hugged him, wanted him with her even when he was in the way; sometimes he didn't know what was coming over her and what she wanted from him. It made him wish with all his might that his father was home; then she wouldn't make him stay in the house so much, it would be easier to get out at night, and he could stay up later. He also wished his father was home because he would get into fewer fights, or he would feel stronger when he did get into them; and he wouldn't always be hearing: "Remember, Papa said you should be a good boy." It felt funny to be aware of his father about the streets and in the house, even though he was nowhere to be seen. Sometimes it seemed to him that his father was never coming back, and it frightened him.

The only time he felt good about his father not being home was at night, especially if he was afraid, when his mother would let him sleep with her. That was better than sleeping alone on the daybed in the dining room, where it was cold and ghosty. In bed with her it was always warm, he was always protected, he was afraid of nothing, he never got bad dreams, and he didn't even mind it when she sometimes put her arms around him in her sleep. That was the only time he didn't mind being a little boy, and he didn't care what the old people from the old country said about it being a sin to sleep with his mother. He was always sure to go to sleep on his father's side of the bed when a *landsman* was visiting at night, especially the one who had been a suitor of his mother's in the old country and who was now a successful customer peddler and who was still, according to his mother, in love with her. Hershy hated him, the way he looked with his tobacco-stained mustache, hairy nose, and fierce eyes, so unlike the clean face of his father; he hated the way the *landsman* would sit heavily and sigh and transport his mother back to Russia, to mysterious days he knew nothing about; he hated the way they sometimes spoke in Russian so that he wouldn't know what they were saying; and he hated the way his mother looked, so warm, glowing, and excited at times. And always, when he was told to go to sleep, he backed away, glaring, to her bed. Once she asked him why he did that.

"I don't know," he said. "I'm afraid."

"Why, suddenly, are you afraid?"

"I don't know."

Then he heard the man say: "I thought he was a big boy."

"On the streets he's a giant, a hero," his mother explained. "But at night, in the house, he shrivels into a baby."

"Shame on him. When I was his age I wandered over the countryside; I was getting ready to start working for a living."

"In America they're different. Men are babies, and babies are frightened mice."

"You spoil him, Sonya."

But he wasn't spoiled, he told himself. He'd grow up someday. He'd show them who was spoiled. He never fell asleep until the man left, his body tight, his heart hammering, especially when they spoke in whispers or when they were silent.

But his father made himself felt often enough to prevent anything from happening. He seemed to come home in person, announced by a shrill, marble-like whistle, which the mailman blew before delivering his letters.

At first, the letters came with a laborious, sprawling handwriting on the envelope, but inside was a strange, tiny, compact handwriting in Yiddish, which neither he nor his mother could read. Then they'd walk across the park to visit Uncle Hymie and Aunt Reva to get the letter read. Afterwards, he'd play outside with his cousin Manny, or they'd go for a ride in his uncle's car, or he'd watch his aunt make his mother gasp with envy in showing off a new dress, a new jewel, a new piece of furniture.

· *41*

"Live, sister, live," his mother would say.

And on the way home, she'd say: "Papa slaves for a piece of bread. And my sister lives like a baroness. Oh, how people with a dollar can live."

"But we ain't poor, are we, Ma?"

"No, we're not poor. We eat well, we have a flat and a stove to heat it, and we sleep well. But other people *live*."

"How come Pa ain't rich like Uncle Hymie?"

"How come?"

"But maybe Pa'll come home with a lot of money. Then you'll have things like Aunt Reva, and Pa'll have a car, and I'll have a million things like that punk Manny."

"Maybe, maybe. But maybe is such a long time. Anyhow, Papa doesn't have ulcers, nobody hates him, he has no sins on his head."

"Is that what's the matter with Uncle Hymie? Is that why he wants to bring a rabbi from Russia over here after the war?"

"Shah, it has nothing to do with you."

"Okay, I was just talking."

But usually, after a reading, they talked about his father. And afterward, until the next letter came, his mother would take the blue-lined paper with the peculiar script on it from the cut-glass bowl in the china closet and stare at it, then mutter the phrases she remembered from Uncle Hymie's reading.

In one letter, his father wrote part of it in Russian, which he couldn't understand but which embarrassed his mother. She smiled awkwardly through Uncle Hymie's reading and the loud laughter, sly talk, and knowing elbow-pokes that followed. And when they got home, she said: "Hershel, from now on *you* write the letters to Papa, and you tell him to write us in English. Everybody doesn't have to know everything."

"Why, what'd Pa write, you know, where it was in Russian?" Her cheeks turned red and she said: "You're too young to know."

What could his father have written? he wondered. But he never found out, for his father, apparently, never repeated the secret after he began to write in English. The letters were brief and simple, sprawled over three and four pages, which was done purposely, his father explained, so that Hershy would find them easier to read. And he wrote back what his mother told him, but he always added his own postscript: "I am a good boy, Pa. Ma told me to tell you." Once he added: "Ma told me to tell you she wants you should say to her again what you once said to her in Russian on a letter." But his father ignored the postscript.

Sometimes he protested and wanted Rachel to answer his father's letters, but she was too busy.

"That's all I got to do, write letters," she said.

Actually, Rachel couldn't write much better than himself. She was nine years old before his parents learned that she had to go to school and how to go about getting her into one. In classes with children three and four years younger than herself, she suffered horribly through five years of school, flunking twice, before she quit. Hershy's father had to lie about her age, saying she was sixteen, when the truant officer came to the house. But since there was no record of her birth and since she did look mature, she was allowed to leave school and go to work. Hershy's father hoped his dead sister would forgive him. God knew he had tried his best. Besides, she seemed better equipped to become a dancer. Her soul yearned so hard to become one, especially after the first excitement of going to work in a dress factory wore off. Besides, women didn't need too much education to fulfill their role in life. Also, he argued, a woman didn't necessarily have to know the sum of two and two, or who discovered what, in order to be a good wife and mother, which, despite her dancing, he knew she was going to be.

So Hershy, during his father's absence, was the official letter-writer and reader of the family, the bridge between his father and mother. Once, however, a letter wasn't received in over two weeks. His mother sat up late worrying. When it was time for the postman to arrive, she trembled for the sound of his whistle. And every day she made him read the last letter over and over, trying to interpret some sign from it to relieve her fears, until they both knew it by heart. Then a letter finally came, and some of the writing was blurred:

"Yussel is dead. He was killed in France. The Germans killed him. All week I sat *shiva* (in mourning). Bitter tears are in my heart. They run down my face. Now all I have is you, dear Sonya. My dearest son, Hershel. My precious Rachel. You are my life now. Do not let anything happen to you. Be a good boy, Hershel. Be a good girl, Rachel. Take care of them, Sonya. Take care of yourself. My whole heart loves you."

His mother burst into tears. She drew the shades and told him to run out and buy a glassful of tallow with a wick in it. She lit it when he came back. And then she took off her shoes and stockings and sat down on the floor and began to rock back and forth. His legs began to tremble; then he, too, began to cry, and he sat down beside his mother.

"Me, too, Ma? Should I do it, too?"

"No, dearest, you don't have to."

"Why don't I have to, if you have to?"

"I don't have to, either. I don't know what else to do. I just don't know what else to do."

She flung her arms around him and drew him onto her lap and rocked him back and forth, and he felt her hot tears drop on his face.

8.

Soon afterward, all the whistles and horns in the world began to blow. People went crazy. The war was over. And then his father wrote that he was coming home.

CHAPTER THREE
1.

It was almost as Herhsy had imagined, only his father didn't have on a miner's cap, nor was he in short sleeves and overalls, nor was he made of granite, nor was he carrying a lunch pail. Instead, he was wearing a gray hat and a black coat; and his thin, hollow-cheeked, bony face seemed lost under the hat and crunched within the high stiff collar.

Hershy wouldn't have recognized him as he turned the corner onto his street but for the chest of tools he was carrying on his shoulder and the old cardboard suitcase he was holding in his other hand. And, as he watched with his mouth open, unable to move, his father called: "Hershele. Hershele."

"Pa. Pa."

Like a shot he was in front of his father. He flung his arms around him. His father dropped the suitcase and embraced him, then stooped down and kissed him. His face was grimy with sweat and his greenish-gray eyes were wider and shinier than Hershy had ever seen them, and for a moment both their lips were stiff with emotion.

Hershy released him as his father bent to one knee and eased the chest of tools to the ground; then he grabbed Hershy's shoulders and looked at him steadily, his eyes flooding with tears, and crushed him to his chest, just like the miner in the park with the child in his arms, but the feeling Hershy had was bigger than the whole world and it was harder in him than the granite of the statue. He couldn't talk. He had a million things to say, a million things to ask. But he couldn't talk. Then his father released him and lifted the chest of tools to his shoulders. Hershy grabbed the suitcase and, in the wake of his father's sharp familiar smell of wood and sweat, followed him to the house.

They came in the back way. His mother was in the kitchen with an apron over her long, black, lace-collared dress, stirring a pot of chicken soup with a wooden spoon, the steam clouding her face and the smell warm and deep. His mother gasped and rushed to the sink and began to wash her hands and yelled at Hershy, calling him a little devil for not warning her and frightening her to death. Then, fumbling with her apron, wiping her hands and trying to get it off, she began to yell at his father: what took him so long, did he have no regard for her, did he purposely want to shrivel her heart with worry? But his father paid no attention to her. He laid his tool chest on a chair and smothered her with kisses. In his embrace, she began to cry and beat his back weakly with her fist. She tore herself away and locked herself in the bathroom when Rachel came into the kitchen.

His father couldn't get over the way Rachel looked, after they kissed. She posed for him in her white ruffled blouse and long black skirt, turning about slowly, letting his father admire her gleaming blond hair, the fullness of her bust, her narrow waistline, her curvy hips.

"Okay?" she said.

"Okay," his father said. "But maybe you ought to eat a little more, put on a little more weight."

"No, Pa. This is the American style. Only in Europe do the men like them *zoftig*, plump."

"Anyhow," his father said, "you have grown into a regular doll. A regular Mary Pickford."

"You should be talking. Look how dolled up you are. New suit, new coat, new shoes, new hat."

"Yah, Pa, look at you." Hershy stepped to his side and clung to his arm.

His mother walked in then.

"Where did he learn to dress like that?" she said, her face still red from crying.

"People learn," his father said.

"You must have met a *shiksa*, a gentile girl. She taught you." His father smiled, pleased.

"Was she beautiful?" his mother asked.

"Like an old mattress."

"But good to lie on, hah, David?"

"Sonya, Hershy's here."

Everybody glanced at him.

"A man away from home," his mother said. "Who knows what might happen to a man away from home?"

"A woman's imagination," his father said, nodding his head. "Can you stop a bird in flight without shooting it down?"

"But doesn't he look wonderful?" Rachel interrupted.

"He looks terrible," his mother said. "Look how sunken his cheeks are. New clothes or no new clothes, he can't hide from me how terrible he looks. I'll bet they never fed you, David."

"Oh, they fed me," his father said.

"What? Pig?"

His father shrugged with his eyebrows.

"You see," his mother said. "A man goes away a good Jew. He comes home a goy."

"You mean you ate pig?" said Hershy, horrified, his mind filled with the sight of the dead pigs, with their glassy eyes and greasy bodies and sneering snouts, that hung outside the gentile butcher shop on the corner.

"No, Hershel," his father said. "Mama's only making fun."

His mother assured him with her reddish eyes that she was.

"But tonight you're going to be fattened like a pig," his mother said. "Like a king you'll eat. Gefüllte fish, chicken soup with mondelach, and a tender chicken that will melt in your mouth. So hurry. Go wash up and get ready to be fattened."

Hershy followed his father into the bathroom, where he took off his jacket and shirt, and saw how dark his face and forearms had become from working outdoors; his skin, away from his straight black hair and tanned face, was creamy white. He couldn't get his eyes off the hard, yellow-stained hands and the muscles that rippled up and down as his father washed.

"Did you wash yet?" his father asked, after drying himself.

"Yah, after school."

"Wash again."

"But I'm clean, Pa."

"Before eating you have to wash."

"Why?"

"Didn't I tell you once?"

"What?"

"That a demon strangles little children who eat food touched by unwashed hands?"

"But while you was away I didn't wash all the time and nothing happened."

"That's because my soul was here all the time, watching over you and protecting you."

"Yah, Pa? Was it?"

"Yes, my whole soul was here all the time."

Yah, Hershy thought as he washed and dried himself. Maybe that was why he wasn't killed that time last summer when he was run over by a horse and wagon. He had been playing ball on the street. Every time a horse and wagon came by and stopped the game, he threw the bat under the wheels of the wagon. But that time he didn't see the horse and wagon

· *49*

coming from the other direction. And when he jumped away after throwing the bat under the wheels he heard a scream and a yell, then he was knocked down and the horse stepped on him and the wagon rolled over him and then he jumped up and ran until his chest almost burst. Afterward, he laid down and touched himself all over. Nothing was broken. Nothing hurt. He couldn't get over it. He looked up at the sky and said: "Thanks, God. I'll do you a favor sometime, too." But now he knew what had saved him. It had been his father watching over him, his soul protecting him all the time. Gee.

2.

After supper, there was a delight in hearing his father groan from eating too much and in watching him pat his belly and smack his lips. Then he moved away from the table, picked up his suitcase, and asked them to follow him into the front room. Once past the narrow passage that led into the dining room and parlor, his father slowed down. Through his eyes, Hershy seemed to be viewing the house as though he had never seen it before. There was the stained-glass chandelier above the white-clothed round dining-room table, which was never used except for company. Off the oak, stained-glass china closet, which was empty but for a cut-glass bowl, was the daybed on which Hershy slept, and above that were three curtained windows. The walls seemed cut in half, with wood paneling on the bottom and embossed tin, painted brown, on top. The bulging stove, glowing through the charred isinglass, with its nickel highly polished, stood in a corner. His father touched the smooth surface of the wooden columns that separated the dining room from the parlor and studied the workmanship that had gone into the latticed woodwork above. Then he shifted his eyes to the starched white curtains in the front room, to the mahogany rocking chair with the leather seat that was nicked from Hershy's riding on it, to the overstuffed velours couch and the imitation oriental rug.

"What happened to the big rubber plant?" his father asked.

"Hershy, the devil, tried to milk rubber from it," his mother said. "Rubber bands he needed."

"I saw in a book how they do it, Pa," Hershy tried to explain. "But that was no rubber plant. Not even a little piece of juice did it have."

His father didn't seem to care. He laid the suitcase on the arms of the rocking chair and opened it. On top was a Spanish shawl. His mother gasped and, when it was handed to her, draped it over her shoulders.

"It's not for your back, Sonya," his father said. "It's to make the dining-room table fancy."

Then he brought out two packages which he handed to Rachel and Hershy's mother. They ripped the paper and opened the boxes and drew out two pairs of pink silk stockings. His mother looked bewildered, letting them dangle from her fingertips. But Rachel crushed them to her heart.

"Papa," she gasped, kissing him. "Oh, Daddy."

"What did you bring me?" his mother wanted to know. "What will I do with these?"

"Wear them," his father said.

"Where?" his mother asked. "To the fancy balls you always take me to? How could you waste your money on such foolish things, David?"

"Show them to your rich sister. She will appreciate them. They are the latest style."

Rachel had her shoes and stockings off and was pulling up her new stockings. She drew her skirt up to her knees and said: "Look at them, will you! Just look at them!"

The whole shape of her leg showed through. Hershy had never seen legs like that before. He turned away, embarrassed, afraid of what they meant: she looked just like the hot girls he had seen in the movies and on the stage, which the guys called *whooores.*

"Where did you learn all this fanciness, David; all this about the latest style?" his mother demanded.

"Your husband's got taste, no?"

"In your mouth only. But where did you learn about silk stockings, about such whorish delights?"

"When men are away and alone, Sonya, they do three things. They drink at night, or they go to the women with drink, or, if they have wives and children, they stay home and dream about them. But if you don't drink and you don't go to strange women and you have all night to dream, there is one thing that makes the dream better. You walk on the streets and look in store windows. You learn about the wonderful things people can buy and wear. Sometimes, with other men, I went into the stores. There, they told me you would fall in love with silk stockings."

"I'll save them for Hershel's graduation."

But Hershy knew that his mother was delighted with them. Her hands kept smoothing the stockings and her eyes closed as she ran them over her face. And Rachel, with her skirt held by one hand above her knees, her head tilted, her eyes glazed, was humming a waltz and dancing.

"And now, Hershel, let's see what we have for you?" his father said.

He dug into the suitcase and searched for almost a year, it seemed, before he brought out a ball made of rubber bands.

"Gee, Pa."

Then he handed him a large ball of tinfoil.

"From chewing gum and cigarette packs," his father said. "Like a garbage collector I was, picking up what was thrown away."

"Aw, Pa, wait'll the guys see this. Will they go nuts!"

Then he piled into Hershy's hands the colored union buttons

he had saved, of his own and of the men who had discarded them.

"What a stack! I'll be the richest lagger in the world. One of these, Pa, is worth ten corks. Nobody'll beat me, I'll have so many."

"Wait, wait." His father walked to his tool chest in the kitchen and come back with a German officer's helmet.

"Aw, Jesus, Pa. With a spear on top, too. A general's helmet, I'll bet."

"That's a present from Uncle Yussel."

A heavy silence came over them.

"He captured it, and a soldier who was his friend brought it to me," his father added. His mother looked puzzled, and was about to ask a question, but his father stopped her by shaking his finger. "You see, Uncle Yussel was a real hero."

"Yah, Pa," Hershy said huskily. "Aw, wait'll I tell the guys and they see this. A general's helmet, with a spear."

"You know," his father said, his voice trembling, "loneliness makes a man think and dream and spend money. And the trouble with thinking and dreaming is that it costs money. But now I'm finished. This is the last of my thoughts."

He drew a locomotive out of the suitcase, wound it up, put it on the floor, and away it ran, with Hershy rushing after it. The train banged into the wall and fell on its side. Hershy grabbed it, wound it up again, and saw it ride away unhurt. He lay on the floor, watching it, too overwhelmed to get up, and slowly he began to cry. These were the first real presents he had ever had. The sense of his father seemed to throb right through him. He was home at last.

CHAPTER FOUR

1.

He was the richest guy in the world. As rich as Rockefeller. Richer. At least he had a stomach, he had health. What good was all the money in the world if you didn't have them?

When the guys saw his possessions, their eyes popped and their mouths opened. There were all those many-colored union buttons which they could lag for and possibly win from Hershy. There was the largest ball of tin foil they had ever seen, which he might put up for a bet in a game of cards or in a game of follow-the-leader. There was the rubber-band ball, the highest bouncing ball in the world, which was common property, so long as he was in the game with it. But the locomotive, through which they roared over the continent as they followed it up and down the street, was a prize possession which only the favored could wind up and engineer. As for the German officer's helmet, well, through his uncle he automatically became a monumental hero, was lifted higher even than Sergeant York.

"I'll trade you. My knife for it."

"No trades."

"My boxing gloves, too."

"No trades."

"What more do you want?"

"Not even a million dollars. What do you think, my uncle

captured a German general in the war for nothing? Do you think he captured a whole German army for nothing, too? And do you think he got killed for nothing?"

"Then let's try it on."

Hands trembled to the touch of it. Faces changed under the legendary weight of it.

"Aw, Hershy."

"You lucky lucky lucky, you."

He was King of the Street.

2.

His father was also a king.

Mr. Pryztalski, the landlord, came down with a bottle of whiskey, his eyes bloodshot, his mustache bristling, standing as big as a giant, with the smell of the stockyards, where he was a butcher, stronger than the whiskey.

"Drink," he commanded. "A man is home."

But his father was not overpowered by Mr. Pryztalski's size or voice. He took a drink with him and seemed to rise as high as Mr. Pryztalski in the breath-taking gulp. Then Mr. Pryztalski studied the cleanliness of the house and said: "A Jew, in his own house, is a king." He then grabbed the bottle and went upstairs. His loud voice came back.

"The Jew comes home a king. He doesn't even own the house he lives in. He is not even a landlord. But in his own house he is a king."

Mrs. Pryztalski whimpered, her voice became shrill, then died; and in its stead came the thud of her body falling to the floor.

"He loves her," said Hershy's mother. "But what a way to express one's love, the crazy Polacks."

Suddenly, a wild kind of laughter came from Mrs. Pryztalski, as if she were being tickled.

"Oy, does he love her," said Hershy's mother, and punctuated the comment with: "Wild animals."
For a while it was quiet upstairs, then Mr. Pryztalski roared: "The king is home." He laughed, with his wife's shrill laughter rising above it.
Hershy turned away from the peculiar glances of his father and mother.
"Later," his mother said.
His father shrugged his shoulders and looked up at the ceiling, as though he were saying: certainly, later; what am I, an uncontrolled beast like a drunken goy?
Hershy tried hard to divert his thoughts.

3.

On Sunday, the relatives were coming over. Hershy's mother washed the floors, swept the carpet, rearranged and polished the furniture, baked and cooked. She was making a palace out of the house, she explained, because the king was home. A father in his home, she said, was a king. If he was the eldest son of a Jewish family he was most certainly a king, no matter how poor the home was.
"Then will I be a king?" Hershy asked.
"Of course you will."
"Am I a king now? I'm the eldest son."
"You're a prince now. Later, you'll be an emperor."
"Wow."
"Now go throw the garbage in the alley, my little prince."
In the evening, the relatives gathered to pay homage to his father. They sat around the dining-room table under the light of the stained-glass chandelier. Aunt Reva had a sparkling diamond on one of her pudgy fingers and a fur scarf round her neck. Uncle Hymie had a pinkish glow on his face, like

he had just taken a bath; his eyes blinked constantly under the lights; he smashed out one cigarette after another after taking two or three puffs. Uncle Ben, the fruit peddler, took the butts and smoked them down; one thing about the rich, he said, they always leave you something, even if it's only the remains of a cigarette; his face seemed broken up by the weather, poverty, and a tobacco-stained mustache. His wife, Bronya, and Aunt Mascha sighed and squirmed in their stiff corsets and black dresses. The lights glanced off Uncle Irving's high forehead; he smoked the butts of Uncle Hymie's cigarettes, too, and kept pulling at the lobes of his ears and his hawklike nose. But all of them paid their full attention to Hershy's father, seemed to sit almost at his feet, as though he were holding court.

Where had he (Hershy's father) been?

All over.

No!

Yes.

But where?

Maryland. Washington, D.C.

Washington, D.C.! Did he see the president?

No. The president was a busy man. What did they think, the president was a czar, with nothing to do but ride around and let people grovel on the ground before him? No, the president was always busy in the White House.

He saw the White House then?

What a question? How could a man go to Washington and not see the White House? Of course he saw the White House. A picture of a house.

Was the house really white?

Certainly it was. A white castle.

No!

Yes.

Imagine. Like going to St. Petersburg. Could anybody picture David Melov, an ordinary Jewish worker, going to St. Petersburg and visiting the czar's palace? But here, a pair of Jewish eyes looks upon the most important house in the land and nobody breaks his head for it. Ay, you live and learn. What else did he see?

He saw his congressman.

No!

Yes.

But how?

He couldn't believe it himself. But a man who worked with him said they ought to go see their congressmen. Like that, you can go in and see him? Sure, his friend said, like that. Impossible, he didn't believe it. All right, his friend said, he'd show him. After all, what was a congressman? A gross politician. A man with a face like a beet, with a cigar stuck in it. A man with strong knuckles who made a career out of shaking hands all day long. And, believe it or not, his friend was right. The congressman was in his office. And when he heard that David Melov and Walter McCoy were there to see him, the congressman came out and shook hands and asked if he could do anything for them, but they said, no, they just wanted to say hello. And the congressman said he was glad to see them, and if there was anything he could do for his voters all they had to do was ask. He shook their hands again and said they should make themselves at home in Washington and gave them a cigar apiece.

How do you like that? America, I love you, hah, David?

Maybe David, now that he was on such intimate terms with a congressman, could ask a favor from him for a friend or a relative.

Maybe.

Imagine, a poor Jew doing a thing like that in Russia. Only

in America could a thing like that happen. Only in America is a man a man. They should all be killed, those tyrants in Russia, by the Bolsheviks. It would serve them right, the *pogromniks.*

Noo, where else had David been?

Georgia, Alabama, Texas, in the South, where the niggers live.

No!

Yes.

How can one keep up with David? He lived quiet as a cat, *shah-shtill,* never moved from here to there for so many years. All of a sudden, wheeeeeet, he has become a world traveler.

A man works up in the world.

And how was it there where the niggers live?

Terrible.

How, terrible?

As terrible as in the old country. Like pigs they live. Like *mujiks.*

White people, too?

White people, too.

How do you like that? Can it be that in this country a person can live like a Russian peasant? It's hard to believe.

Believe it. He had seen with his own eyes. But even worse. He had even seen a pogrom there.

Gottenyu! who, what, how?

A nigger was killed. With his own eyes he had seen it.

Not a Jew?

No, a nigger.

Thank God.

It was terrible, like it was happening to him.

But that was life. In Russia, Jews. In America, Jews, Catholics, niggers—the Ku-Kluxers. What was life? Blood, blood. Broken hearts and fear, mixed up with the brief moments of

· 59

laughter. A baby is happy, he knows of nothing. He grows into a child learning to hide his pain. He becomes a person finally, dulled by his pain so that he can endure the broken hearts, the blood, the fears about him. Was this what people came into the world to endure? Was this the destiny of man?

Look at Yussel, may his soul rest in peace. Poor Yussel. A man who believed in living and in letting other people live. A man who never harmed anybody. A man who might have been a joy to a woman's heart and a child's life. Died all alone, a stranger in a strange land, with a bullet in his belly. For what?

A few tears, settling into sighs. The spirit of the occasion lost. The faces growing heavy with thought. The question too big to answer, for it involved settling in their minds where they belonged, what their role was in a world that had existed for millions of years and which would exist after they were gone, what place they had in a world that was not designed for them. If only they could stop the gigantic movement of the world for a moment, grasp it and then mold it for a second of its life to the time of their lives!

"Ay, how weak is man." Hershy's father quoted from a Rosh Hashana prayer. "He comes from the dust and returns to the dust; must toil for his sustenance; then passes away like withered grass, a vanishing shadow, a fleeting dream."

Hershy nudged them out of their saddened mood. He wanted them to get out of themselves and to come back to his father, the king, and himself, the prince.

"And where else was you, Pa?"

The shock of his child's voice brought laughter. It brought tea and cakes. It brought everybody's attention to himself and back to his father.

"Go on, Pa, tell them where you was."

4.

The following morning, while Hershy was getting dressed for school, his father announced that it was Labor Day. Hershy had to laugh. According to his father, he remembered, every Monday, after a restful Sunday, was Labor Day. The familiar expression made him feel good, assured him that his father was really home to stay; the homecoming was over. His mother accented the feeling, making his inward laughter warm and bubbly.

"What kind of Labor Day is it?" she wanted to know. "You don't even have a job."

"That's right," his father said. "But today I'm going to get a job. You're not looking at an idler, you know."

"And if you were idle another day or two, would that hurt? Would it hurt anyone if you slept later, rested more, got a little fatter? The way you look, David, people will think I'm a terrible cook, that I'm a terrible wife."

"Never mind what people think. It's my nature that I can't put on a pound of flesh. So, for that must I be punished with idleness: to sit around, stare at the four walls, gossip? No. A man who eats bread without replenishing it is a man who commits a crime."

"The way you talk, like we haven't a penny. Remember, you've been working steady a long time "

"But remember also the days I was forced to remain idle because there was no work, when we had to go without supper so that we could rise without debt. A workingman should work when there is a job. Work keeps a man honest and healthy."

"Talk to you and talk to the wall, it's the same thing."

"Then talk to the manufacturers, the butchers, the grocerymen. Have a picnic with them, but not with my money. The streets are lined with gold, so they think."

· *61*

"Go talk to a piece of iron."

"Besides," his father continued—once he was on a line of thought he never stopped until he completed it—"if I stay away from work too long my hands will get soft. I need hard hands and an iron back for my work. Besides, I have to pay on my insurance and we should start thinking of saving money to send Hershel to college."

"Who is arguing?"

Hershy walked into the kitchen from the dining room and stopped the playful argument.

"Hurry up, Hershel," she said. "Eat."

His father sat down with him at the table and they both concentrated on him. Eating, when food was plentiful, was the most important thing in the world. His mother served him a bowl of oatmeal drenched in milk and sugar. From a pan she poured a little coffee into a glass and then filled it with hot milk. As he ate a piece of pumpernickel bread and butter and picked out the coffee grounds with a spoon, he decided to make an announcement, too.

"I ain't going to go to college."

"We'll worry about that later," his mother said. "But now finish your coffee and go to school."

"Okay, but when I finish school I ain't going to go to college."

"What are you going to do instead?" his father asked.

"I'm going to be an explorer."

"You have to go to college to be an explorer," his father stated.

"Columbus didn't go to college."

"There were no colleges in the days of Columbus. Today, to be anything or anybody you have to go to college."

"Then I won't be an explorer. I'll go in a circus."

"And what will you do there, tame lions?"

"Maybe. But maybe I'll walk on a rope with an umbrella.

Like this, Pa." He got up and pretended he was on a tightrope, balancing himself as he swayed from side to side. "See, Pa, I'm way up in the air, a thousand feet. Yay, everybody's hollering. Everybody's clapping like anything. Hershy the Great, they're looking on, the world's champion tightrope walker."

His father shook his head as he watched. "In this country everybody wants to be a world's champion," he said. "Do they want to be a world's champion doctor or lawyer or philosopher? No. Only football players and baseball players and clowns and gangsters."

"But if you're a world's champion, Pa, you can make a lot of money; you get famous; everybody wants to know you; everybody wants to play with you; you're never left out of anything."

"It's a lively world in this America," his father continued, as though he hadn't been interrupted. "Everybody wants to be the biggest, the best, the strongest, the mightiest. It's a free country, everybody says. So what does a child want most out of all his freedom? A thick head, a steel muscle. Out of all the things to choose from, he chooses to become what nobody who grows up wants to be: a *shnook*. Go figure it out, but the world is full of them. So believe me, Hershel, if you don't go to college, if you don't learn to become a champion of the heart and the mind, that's what you'll become: a world's champion *shnook*."

"Yah, Pa? But Ty Cobb never went to college and he's no *shnook*."

"Who is Ty Cobb?"

"The best ballplayer in the world."

"See, Sonya?" his father turned to his mother. "See what I mean?"

"He'll grow over it, David," his mother said. "With them, every Monday and Thursday their heroes change."

"But why don't they make heroes out of Abraham Lincoln or Spinoza?"

"Do I know?"

Hershy interrupted: "But you never went to college, Pa. And you're no *shnook*, are you?"

His mother laughed and said proudly, affectionately: "You see, David, he has the cunning brain of a sage from Israel."

But his father went on: "Me? Don't look to me for an example. I'd have given my right arm to have gone to college. But in the old country it was impossible. One never even thought of it. A man had no chance there. A Jewish man certainly didn't have a chance. Nobody was concerned there if you could read or write. Nobody cared even if you were alive or dead. It was better that you were kept ignorant. Then you could ask no questions, you could not complain, it was easier to use one like a beast, and from this the czar and the rich felt safer and got richer."

Hershy wasn't convinced. "But Uncle Hymie never went to college, either. He can hardly read and write. And look at all the money he got; an auto, too."

"Hershel," his father said, "you'll learn later there are other things beside money. Uncle Hymie, you might learn, is a slave to his money and a bunch of machines. That's like living with your body cut in two."

"Better to be a slave to a bunch of machines and money," his mother said, "than a slave to a job and a weekly pay envelope."

"Nobody knows that better than me," his father said. "But I want more for Hershel. I want him to be of some use to this world, aside from having money. I want him to be a happy man. Wouldn't it be wonderful if he was a doctor or a lawyer, if he could keep busy without using his hands? Me, without my hands, what am I? A cripple. But a man with a brain is never a cripple; he can be useful and live forever.

"Wouldn't it be wonderful if, instead of the little things I make and instead of a boss telling him what to do, Hershel learned how to build bridges, big buildings, even whole cities? An engineer, an architect, that is something to consider. Imagine, the son of David Melov, a builder. On the bridge or building will be the name, Hershel Melov: architect, engineer. His name on something permanent, to stand for all time. Yes, for him, it is early in the morning and the sun has just begun to shine."

Hershy didn't know what to answer. It seemed, as his father spoke, that he had never really gone away, but had stepped out for a minute in the middle of a conversation and had just come back to resume it. It felt good, knowing he hadn't changed, watching his mother's rapt attention. It was like before, with himself wrapped up not only in his mother's dreams but now again in his father's.

"Noo," his father broke the silence. "Enough dreaming. It's settled. You, Hershel, will build the bridges. And I will get to work and build a cabinet that people will forget and abuse the month after they buy it."

"You hear, Hershel?" said his mother. "You hear Papa?"

"Yah, Ma."

"Remember, Hershel," said his father, "a world's champion can only give a temporary pleasure, but a man who serves humanity does not die tomorrow; he lives forever in his work. Remember, too, a champion of the heart and the mind is an explorer, but a great one. He's always discovering things."

"He is, Pa?"

"Yes. But today, to become any kind of an explorer, you have to go to college."

But Hershy wasn't fully convinced. Jess Willard, he thought, was the champion of the heart, too. He had the biggest, toughest, fightingest heart in the world. Ty Cobb had a brain like lightning, otherwise he could never figure out just when to steal a base or work a hit into a triple play. All right, say he couldn't be like them. Maybe he'd be a shrimp when he'd grow up. Then everybody'd pick on him, murder him, too. But at least if he could be like Merlin the Magician, then he'd be afraid of nothing. Not a thing could happen to him, if he only knew the right hocus-pocus. At least if he was like Merlin, then he could stop worrying about growing up big with steel muscles and he could be what his father wanted him to be.

5.

Teacher added to his confusion that day. She read from the *American Weekly* about a man called Steinmetz. This hunchbacked, gnarled little man, though a midget in size, had a brain so big that in it was contained the whole universe. Gray matter was what this man had, mountains of it, with millions of fissures flowing with knowledge. He was a wizard, this man; he was Jewish, too. Both descriptions got Hershy hunched over his desk; his mouth gaped and his whole being filled with awe before what the man had done: for Steinmetz had not only captured a bolt of lightning but had also harnessed Niagara Falls.

"Man," he said hoarsely.

Even Jess Willard, teacher said, with all his might, couldn't do a thing like that. This man, teacher said, was a great man. With these two deeds, without moving a muscle, he had turned the whole world upside down, he had shaped the world to the power of his brain, he had moved mankind two steps closer to greater perfection. "These deeds," teacher said, "are not as dead as last year's batting averages or the five-yard gains that some fullback made, nor will this man's brains go slack and fat as Jess Willard's muscles soon will; what this man has done will live forever."

That was funny, Hershy thought, teacher talking almost like

his father. She suddenly seemed less fearsome, less strange. Instead of a shriveled, forbidding woman, whose voice had always seemed like the sharp whack of a ruler striking the table and whose fierce eyes had always seemed to pinch everybody like the glasses that pinched her hooked nose, she now looked like a tired old lady. She seemed to have moved off her strange all-American street onto his own street. In a sense, his father seemed to have performed a feat of magic, to have brought their worlds closer together.

But, teacher concluded, a strong body makes a strong mind. Then she told the story of Theodore Roosevelt: a weak, puny lad, who exercised constantly to build up his frail body so that he could house the mighty, energetic mind that he was to develop, and who became the robust rough-rider and explorer as well as one of the great presidents and thinkers of the nation.

Later, when he got home, he found his father sharpening his tools. His father had got his old job back in the cabinet factory he had worked in before he left the city. Hershy told him about Steinmetz. His father patted his head.

"That's a man, Hershel. A great Jew."

"Teacher called him a wizard."

"A great wizard, with a brain sharper than this chisel."

"Can he make magic, too, Pa?"

"Can he make magic! What greater magic can you think of than to see a man take hold of a wild piece of nature and then twist it and turn it and bend it to his will."

"You think he's greater than Merlin?"

"Who is he?"

"The magician. He made magic for King Arthur."

"Steinmetz is greater. He's as great as the rabbi who made the golem."

Hershy knew the story of the golem: how this monster was created from clay to protect the Jews from a horrible pogrom and how, after he had done his duty and saved the Jews, he was made to crumble into dust.

"That great, huh, Pa?"

"That great. But remember, Steinmetz had to go to college first. Now will you go?"

"Maybe. But first I'll be like Teddy Roosevelt. I'll make my muscles big, I'll learn how to wrestle and ride horses, and I'll get real strong. Then I'll learn the magic."

"All right, Hershel." His father looked proudly at him. "Be like Teddy Roosevelt, then."

6.

Hershy couldn't explain it, but there was sufficient reason for his making a god of the Muscle; for it ordered and controlled his world just as God or the Dollar had power over the grown-up world. Not having the Muscle, he idolized and worshipped it in order to gain it; he needed it not only for his games, not only to feel that he belonged, not only that he himself might be worshipped, but also for survival. And the following day his own confusion (however small it was) and the conflict between the mind and the muscle came to an abrupt end.

Polack Kowalski, who lived on the other side of Augusta Street, where all the Polacks lived, sat next to him in the back of the room near the windows. He was always goofing around: shooting bent pins with rubber bands, flicking inky wads of paper across the room, stretching his legs and yawning while stepping on somebody's feet. Sometimes he'd unbutton his pants and say: "Hey, give me jiggers," and in the midst of doing wild crazy things to himself, a stiff smile would come on his face, his eyes would become glazed and rigid, and then he'd say in complete surprise: "Hey, look, look on a man." And because he was bigger and older than the other kids everybody was afraid of him.

On this day, Hershy made the mistake of bringing his union buttons and rubber-band ball to school. And during the afternoon recess period he produced them. Everybody wanted to lag for them and play with him. Polack, seeing the buttons and ball and resenting the way everybody ganged up around Hershy, wanted them. He rushed in and caught the ball while it was being thrown around and put it in his pocket. Nobody dared challenge him, outside of saying: "Come on, Polack, throw us the ball. What do you say, Polack? Be a good guy and throw us the ball. All right for you, Polack. All right if you don't. . . ." Then they gathered around Hershy. After all, it was his ball. What was he going to do about it? It was up to him.

Hershy confronted him.

"What do you say, Polack, you going to give me the ball?"

Polack spit out of the side of his mouth.

"You going to give me the ball?" Hershy said louder, his voice dry and tight.

Polack spit on his shoe.

Hershy's voice wouldn't work for him any more. In its stead, a raging tear crept out of his eye; it blurred the crowd that was thickening around him and Polack. Then a burning tear crept out of his other eye. The next thing he knew, Polack lunged at him and as he tripped to the ground, the union buttons spilled out of his pocket. The crowd scattered and he scurried about to pick up as many buttons as he could, but before he knew what had happened most of them had disappeared. He was lifted to his feet to face Polack again, but just then the bell rang and he let himself be pulled into line to go back to class.

There, he tried to figure out some way of getting his ball back and of getting even with Polack, but nothing he could think of seemed good. He knew that he couldn't collect a gang to go into Polack's neighborhood to get him; a bigger gang might kill them. He couldn't snitch on him to teacher; nobody'd have any use for him afterward. Could he knock Polack out and take the ball away from him? He was reduced to whispering tensely from time to time: "Give me it back, you." Immediately, he received a prompt answer from teacher: "Silence!" At which Polack got red in the face as he strained to contain his laughter.

Then Polack began to inflict more torture. Each time he was not looking directly at Polack something struck him. He did not know what it was but automatically he slapped his neck, his cheek, his ear, and the back of his head each time he was hit, until teacher yelled: "Hershel, will you *please* sit still."

This got Polack doubled up with suppressed laughter. When he turned away, bang, again he was hit. Again. Again. Again. It began to take on the effect of a shot-put dropping on him. He stared at Polack a long while to avoid being hit again. Then he turned away slowly, but jerked his head back quickly, and caught Polack in the act. A beebie, flicked out from between Polack's teeth, bounded off Hershey's nose.

"Right on the schnozz."

"I'll kill you, Polack."

"You and who else?"

"Me and me."

Polack flicked out another beebie and hit Hershy's eye.

"Right in the eye. Crack shot."

His eye seemed to explode right through his head and a ball of fire crackled through his body. He lunged over and tumbled Polack off his seat and tore at his mouth to extract the beebies. Accidentally, as they scuffled on the floor, Hershy grabbed Polack's fingers and bent them backward. Polack screamed and the beebies fell out of his mouth. Hershy put on more pressure, and as he brought his full weight down on Polack's hand, he smashed one of his knees into Polack's groin. Polack suddenly stopped screaming and squirming, and his body grew limp under him.

By this time, teacher was upon them, and with the help of a few boys tore Hershy away from him, but not before he had taken his ball from Polack's pocket. Nobody knew what had happened to Polack, least of all Hershy, who was taken by complete surprise over his quick and definite victory. But everybody had seen Polack knocked cold, everybody had seen his chalk-white face, everybody had seen how he slowly sat up in a daze and how teacher had to help him to his seat and how he looked sick and frightened. Yes, everybody had seen the triumph of the Muscle.

Teacher, of course, kept him after school. But when he got out, his pals, Cyclops and Niggy and Lala, were waiting for him. They slapped his back and punched his shoulders and jumped around him. What they felt came out in Cyclops' expression: "Boy, Hershy. Boy."

And there were no reprisals. Polack wasn't sure but that another accident might happen. Besides, Hershy always had a gang around him.

And Hershy himself? He believed that he had realized himself for the first time in his life. He believed, as he looked at himself in the mirror that night, with his hair wild, his eyes glaring, his teeth gritted, that another being had crept into him, with a secret energy that had made of him a terror.

"When I get mad," he said to himself, "watch out. Just watch out, see!"

Then a new and rich experience occurred to him suddenly. For a moment, while looking in the mirror, he idolized himself.

CHAPTER FIVE

1.

Winter was official only when the first snow fell. The sight of the soft flakes coming down brought a choking tenderness to Hershy's mother. It made her remember the old country: how the snow piled up on the ground and the trees and the bushes, and remained crystal-white all winter; how the house smelled of baked things and cooked foods; how the whole family cuddled together on top of the broad oven at night; how the bright sun reflecting off the snow almost blinded one; how the sound of sleighs and bells brought cheer to one's heart; how people gathered in the house and sat into the night spinning stories. It made her think of her parents and her brothers; and, wondering if they were still alive, she wept sadly. Winter was a time for remembering. Winter time was family time.

The father's remembrance of winter was the death of his father; a pogrom; the going to *schule* before daylight and shivering over his prayers until the warmth of the stove and the candles and the closeness of other human beings took their effect. Through the falling snow loomed the remembrance of another large city, Kiev: gray, gloomy, and fearsome, where only two kinds of people existed; those who wore boots and furs, and those who wore nothing. Wintertime there was a time for darkness and loneliness, when one welcomed hard work and fatigue.

Winter cramped Rachel's style: it was strictly an inconvenience. The only good thing about it was New Year's Eve, if you had a date. She had a date, so the winter was going to be a success. Otherwise, the only steam she could work up over it was the steam that came out of her breath. Winter was strictly for the kids.

It certainly was. (All seasons, with the wonders and new phases of life they brought, were strictly for the children.)

> *It's snowing, it's snowing,*
> *A little man is growing. . . .*

Jack Frost made magic on the windows; he made magic smoke come out of peoples' mouths; he made daggers hang from the trees and fences and windowsills; he made the milk that was left on the back porch pop right out of the bottles and gave it an ice-cream taste. It was a time for sleds and ice skates, toboggans and slides, snowball fights and King of the Hill, snowmen and igloos.

Winter was a time for cursing, too. It had no respect for a stiff muscle, a creaking bone. One could expire for a piece of daylight, the father complained. He woke up and went to work and came home in the dark. And, while waiting for a streetcar, one could almost die from the burning frost that swept in from the lake and prairies. His only comforts were a warm supper, a glass of hot tea, huddling around the stove and staring into its glowing belly, then feeling the huge warmth of the mother in bed: all of which he did not have the winter before away from home. The mother complained, too. The floors were impossible to step on in one's bare feet. The house was impossible to keep clean, what with the ashes and the coal and the snow and the slush. And the house stank and looked like a laundry with the wash hung all over to dry. Oh, for a steam-heated flat, for a home of her own with a big basement, for a maid to do all the cleaning, like her rich sister had. Only the animals lived right; they buried themselves and slept right through the winter.

Winter . . . a time for Christmas and New Year's.

It was strictly for the goyim.

2.

For Hershy, only one thing was wrong with winter: Christmas.

Everything suddenly changed, but not for him. In school, teacher smiled tenderly. It roused his suspicions; he wondered what she wanted. Then he knew. She wanted to make a Christian out of him. Fearful of being doomed forever, he gritted his teeth to keep from singing the Christmas carols in class; he bit into the nail of his forefinger so hard that it turned black and blue and he was excused from making Christmas cards when he complained that it hurt.

On the street at night, many of the houses glowed with candles on Christmas trees and the windows were decorated with holly leaves and poinsettias. On the business street, the stores were crowded, and in the red, white, and green windows were all kinds of presents. The church bells seemed to be ringing all the time. On the carline intersection, across the street from the park, there were always a couple of Salvation Army women with tambourines; with them was a Santa Claus with runny eyes and a dirty cotton beard, who heaved his pillowed belly up and down with his hands but who never laughed. Every time he went over to warm his hands over the fire that was going in a tin pail, Hershy said: "Some Santa Claus."

Once, he and his pals put rocks in the center of snowballs and whipped them at Santa Claus and the Salvation Army women; they ran away frightened when one of the women fell to the ground. Another time, they threw snow instead of money into the tambourines. And another time, they threw a shoebox full of snow into their pail of fire and put it out.

Among themselves, they fortified each other.

"Christmas is a lot of baloney."

"Yah."

"There ain't no Santa Claus."

"Yah."

"The dopes. The dumb goyim."

"Yah."

"It's all bushwa."

When they caught hold of a lone gentile kid, they said: "You believe in Santa Claus?"

"Yah."

"There ain't no Santa Claus, you dumbsock."

"There is too."

"How much you want to bet?"

"All the money in the world."

"A million dollars?"

"Yah."

"Put up or shut up."

"Yah?"

"Yah."

"Okay. Here's a present from Santa Claus."

The kid got his face smeared with snow.

Every day the snow remained on the ground, Hershy's mother cursed it and said: "The goyim live right. It's their world. God is with them. They'll have a white Christmas." Specifically, the goyim, to her, were the Polish landlord, his beefy red-cheeked wife, and their six-year-old daughter. "The snow makes the Polack upstairs a happy man."

One day, Hershy saw the Pole come home with icicles on his mustache and with the blood of the animals he killed at the stockyards still stained on his thick hands; he was carrying

• 75

a Christmas tree. When he reached the front door he stopped and touched the mezuzah, then kissed his finger and crossed himself.

"Hey, you," Hershy yelled. "What'd you do that for?"

"I'm not taking a chance. The snow has to lay on the ground. I don't want your God to be mad and spoil the Christmas."

"You'll get a sin doing that."

"*Shahkreft,* you bloody dog. Jesus Christ was a Jew, wasn't he?"

"Yah, but you took him away from us, you cheater."

"*Shahkreft,* little one, peace and good will to all men."

"Ah, bushwa."

A great puff of smoke came out of Mr. Pryztalski's mouth, the icicles dripped off his mustache, he gripped the base of the tree as though he were going to whack him one with it, and Hershy ran away.

"You little sonofabitch," Mr. Pryztalski bellowed. "I said peace and good will to all men."

For that, Hershy wanted the snow to melt, even though it was more fun to have it on the ground.

But how strong can a child be? How long can he hold out? Even his own father couldn't make it easier to bear the holiday. For once, after staring longingly at the frosty windows on the business street, at the sleds, ice skates, electric trains, erector sets, hunter's knives, guns, cowboy suits, football and baseball equipment, he said to his father: "Pa, why ain't we got a Christ?"

"Because we don't need one."

"Why don't we need one?"

"Because their God wasn't strong enough and they needed another one to help them. With us, there is only one God."

"Can our God fight their God?"

"Yes, ours is stronger."

"So why do we get beat up more than them? Why do we have to be more afraid than them?"

His father shrugged his shoulders, not knowing what to answer. In the old country you took your faith, your station in life, your very life itself, for granted. You asked few questions. The world seemed to have a definite order. There, you had your own religion, your own language, your own school, your own traditions: your whole life stemmed from the *schule*, your whole life turned inward: somehow, because you were more unified it was easier to bear the outward pressure. There was no problem there of reaching outward, of hoping to become a vital part of the community, for if you tried to poke just a little finger outward it would be crushed. So you waited, suffering, for your own Messiah. And the Jew became a symbol of eternal hope, because life couldn't be worse for them; it could only become better.

Here, well, you came here with your eternal hope; and, to a degree, it was fulfilled, for life was better. But here, you took the chance of losing your former unity; in being able to reach outward you came into greater conflict with the world about you. You had to be more careful: for there, only your life could be destroyed; but here, your spirit also could be crushed.

Here, a Jew's strength was slowly undermined in the changes he had to make. You had to work on Saturday to hold a job. You had to learn a new language and adapt yourself to the values of the new language. You didn't ask too many questions about the food you ate outside the house. In the South, where there were no *schules*, what was one to do, create his own temple of worship? His own father would have walked miles to demonstrate his piety. But he—he had grown lazy. He had even become lazy in the old country. In a sense, he had rejected his own father. Perhaps his own child might reject him. Perhaps he (Hershy) might have to reject him so that he might become a better man.

Already the foreign seeds were blooming. The child could understand Yiddish but was losing the flavor of its speech. Instead of the biblical heroes of old the child had his own: prizefighters, ballplayers, gangsters, moneymen. In one generation thousands of years of tradition had been lightly thrown away.

Even he, himself, in his daily comparisons of there and here, felt the chasm growing wider and wider. Sometimes he, himself, had asked: what is a Jew? Why shouldn't his son ask it? And how can one answer? If one is not wholly involved in a religion; if one doesn't have the language of the Jew; if one, in adopting the manners about him, doesn't even look or feel like a Jew, what can you say: that he is a part of a people, he is the carrier of a breed of oppressed people, that he must be a twentieth-century symbol proving the endurance and the greatness of a people once great, that he is a conscience, if nothing else? What can one say to a child to make him feel secure, to make him feel stronger? Could he say: We are the strongest people in the world; we prove it every day of our lives by enduring the subtlest kinds of persecution; we also prove that the world about us, with its Christ, is evil. When they stop bothering us, when they stop making us fear them, then we will know that the real Messiah has come, then all men will belong and will feel safe, all men will love each other, all our energies will be released to do good, and we will feel, for the first time since Adam, that we are fully alive? How does one put a million thoughts into the simple words that a child might understand? How does one sum up one's whole lifetime into something a child can grasp?

"When you get older, Hershel," he said, "you'll understand."

"Yah, but I still wish we had a Christmas."

"Well, we have a Hanukkah."

"Ah, Hanukkah. All you get is lotkes, them lousy dried-up pancakes, and a few pennies. But Christmas, all the things you can get."

"Don't think about it too much, Hershel."

"I can't help it, Pa. All the things in the stores."

"You'll get what you need without Christmas. If the goyim need to fool themselves, let them."

"Yah, but I wish I had a sled and a pair of skates."

His father knew that he couldn't deny him these things. He had already made many concessions to life; one more wouldn't hurt.

"All right, Hershel. You'll get them."

But his father didn't buy them in a store; he had Hershy help him build them in the basement. But Hershy was disappointed in the sled; it wasn't a real coaster. And he wouldn't wear the skates; all the guys would call him a sissy because there were double runners on them. His father tried to distract him by getting him to help build a phonograph that Rachel wanted. But when Christmas Eve arrived Hershy felt that his heart would burst. The Pryztalskis upstairs didn't help matters, either. Mr. Pryztalski shook the house with his thundering walk. Mrs. Pryztalski's giggles and high-pitched voice prickled through Hershy. He felt like killing the little girl.

"So what's Santa Claus going to bring me?" she shrieked.

"You'll see," Mr. Pryztalski bellowed.

"But when's he going to come?"

"After you go to sleep. Now go to sleep."

"First I'm going to hang up one more stocking."

"Ho, ho, ho." Mr. Pryztalski was practicing his Santa Claus voice. "Hang it up. Quick."

The pattering feet. The lumbering tread. The giggles. The excitement.

Hershy's mother sighed. "The crazy Polacks," she said.

Then it became quiet upstairs. The wind began to whistle through the passageway. The world seemed to be blowing away. A strange, drifty hush pervaded the house. Nobody was outside. Aside from the sound of the wind, only the lamppost light creaked as it swayed above the street. And then, like thunder crashed down the stairs and rumbled into the house, Mr. Pryztalski stamped into view in a red suit and a white beard, yelling in Polish, ho-ho-hoing, and calling himself Santa Claus. Hershy almost died of fright. It was not until he was lifted high in the air and had pulled away the beard that was attached to a rubber band that he came to and yelled: "See, it ain't Santa Claus. See, it's Mr. Pryztalski, the gypper." He then let the beard slap back to Mr. Pryztalski's face and, though everybody laughed, he got crying mad. As soon as he was dropped to the floor he tried to kick Mr. Pryztalski's shins, but he was held off by his long arm, and suddenly he stopped. Almost blinding him was a pair of long gleaming blades, a pair of racing skates, which Mr. Pryztalski had brought out from under his red blouse.

"Look what Santa Claus brought you," Mr. Pryztalski boomed. "Ho, ho, ho. And look what else he brought you." Mr. Pryztalski opened the door and dragged in a sled, a real coaster.

Hershy took them awkardly and stared at them. Mr. Pryztalski brought a bottle out of his pocket.

"Drink," he commanded.

Hershy's father drank from the bottle. Then Mr. Pryztalski took a long gulp, wiped his mouth with his sleeve, lifted up Hershy's mother, and kissed her with a loud smack full on the lips, which she wiped and spat away, and then he left with a roar of laughter.

Everybody stared at each other. The house had grown so quiet, like a sudden storm had struck it and passed away.

Finally his mother said: "What do you say, Hershel?"

He didn't know what to say; he was too stunned.

"What do you say when you get a present?"

"I don't know," he stammered.

"Nothing, after Papa spent all that money on you?"

"You mean Pa bought them for me?"

"What do you think? You think the Polack did?"

"But . . ."

"Papa bought them, but he wanted to surprise you. Besides, go argue with a Polack; he had to come down like Santa Claus or he'd have torn off the roof from over our heads."

"I knew it. I knew there was no Santa Claus."

He flopped down on the sled and felt himself coast a mile. He saw himself go slish-slash, zip-zam across the icy lagoon in the park, a mile on every glide. His whole world tumbled back in place.

"Live, boychik, live," his father said. "But know the truth when you see it."

3.

New Year's Eve was just another night. When the bells and whistles and horns sounded off at midnight, Hershy was sound asleep. His mother and father were drinking tea. They paused a moment and stared at each other and sighed.

"Last year I was asleep," his mother said.

"This year I'm alive," his father said.

"Next year we'll celebrate."

"Meanwhile, let there be peace."

'It's a crazy world."

They rose and went to bed.

At that moment, in an expensive night club, Uncle Hymie was kissing a young girl, who later turned out to be his secretary; and Aunt Reva, cold sober and completely out of place, sat horrified. (Later, when Hershy heard of this, Aunt Reva cried: "What good is money, if you haven't got love?" and Uncle Hymie said: "What good is money, if it can't free you to make decisions?") Uncle Irving was playing a cautious game of poker in the rear of a neighborhood restaurant, determined not to lose the ten dollars he was ahead, while his wife and two children slept at home. Uncle Ben was dreaming that he was in a world that had no automobiles and that he was a highly respected man with a flourishing harness business (a recurrent dream for him), while his wife groaned beside him. Rachel was at a house party. She had to fight off the man she was with; his breath revolted her. The following day, her comment about New Year's Eve was: "It's wonderful, if you got lots of money or if you're in love."

And so, with the holidays over, the winter settled down heavily: wheezing and whistling, creaking and crunching, biting and burning, its hard back on the streets full of crusts, its body pocked with soot and stained with refuse. Only people gave it warmth.

In the morning, Hershy's father got up first, grated the stoves, carried the ashes into the alley, came back with a couple of pails of coal, and got the stoves hot: this, his mother said, was a healthy blessing to her heart. He'd wake up Hershy's mother: "The house is warm, my queen, get up." He'd wake up Rachel: "Get up, princess." And after they left for work Hershy would be awakened by his mother: "Wake up, prince."

After school, Hershy would always have to go to the grocer or butcher to pick up something that his mother had forgotten to buy, with implicit instructions, like: "Tell him, my ma said you should give her a big bunch soup greens for two cents," or, "Tell him, my ma said you should give her a big soupbone with meat on it for a nickel." After running the errand under protest, unless he was given a penny for candy or halvah, he'd go out to the park and ice skate, flopping all over until he learned how; or he'd go tobogganing down a two-story slide in the park; or he'd settle for belly-flopping on his sled down the street; or he'd slide on the runners of ice that were made on the sidewalk. Sometimes, when it was below zero weather, he and his pals would gather in a basement that had a furnace and they'd box with open hands or with gloves on, or they'd draw lines on the cement floor and lag for buttons and corks; sometimes they'd just talk, dreaming of *someday*, or trying to relate themselves to the world and its mysteries.

"How come it's so dark so much in the winter and so light so much in the summer?"

"How come? Because the winter stinks on ice."

"Where does the winter come from, the North Pole?"

"Nah, it's the sun going away from us, teacher says."

"Where's it go?"

"What, do I know everything?"

"How come you can only see the stars on the nighttime?"

"The sun hides it from us, see."

"You mean the stars are out in the daytime, too?"

"Sure, you dope. If it was nighttime in the daytime you could see the stars in the daytime."

"Man, a shooting star could hit you, klunk, right in the eye then, and you wouldn't even know it."

"Ah, you dumbsock, a star shoots only in the nighttime."

"You think it's colder on the moon than here?"

"Colder."

"Boy, that's cold."

"You think they'll invent a rocket to go up there?"

"Sure."

"How do you know?"

"How do I know! We got airplanes, ain't we?"

"So?"

"So they can go to the moon if they want, only they don't want to yet. My old man says they got a million inventions, but they're a secret because they could either kill us or make us too happy. And who the hell wants to see us happy, my old man says."

"Your old man."

"Yah? My old man knows plenty. He reads the English paper, don't he?"

"Your old man can pitch spitballs and fadeaways, too. But if they made a rocket to go to the moon, would you go?"

"Sure."

"You?"

"And how."

Everybody was positive he'd go. Zoom, they rocketed to the moon with sound effects, and explored it. Then they talked some more. And as they did, not being able to sit still, occasionally one would punch another on the muscle of his arm. "That's for nothing, see." Somebody would walk away swimming and yelling: "The American crawl, the American crawl." Somebody would pitch like Three-Finger Brown; catch an imaginary ball like Ted Collins; bat like Ty Cobb; punt like Frank Merriwell; shoot like William S. Hart; box like Jess Willard. But the talk went on.

"Hey, punk, where do you think you come from?"

"From the Boston store."

"Who told you?"

"My ma."

"You mean you asked her?"

"Sure, what do you think?"

"Boy, what a punk."

"Yah?"

"Yah. Asking his ma. What a punk."

"Yah? So who else am I going to ask? Who else am I going to know from?"

"From us, see. From us big guys."

"So?"

So they told him.

"You bastards, I'll tell my big bro on you for that."

"Go on, tell your big bro."

"He'll kill you."

"Ah, beat it, punk."

And so, the kid in tears and kicked out of the basement, the education of a younger boy was dispensed. Then, strengthened by the younger boy's smallness, his tears, and lack of knowledge, they'd grow alive with dreams of being older. They were vague about what they'd become, there were so many things to choose from, but somehow none of them dreamed of being like their fathers. For in them was the capacity to rocket to the moon, hitch their wagons to the comets, play tag among the clouds. Even their fathers, who couldn't catch a ball or read the jokes or tell the score, believed this, or liked to believe it.

At night, now that his father was home, Hershy seldom had to read to his mother. Instead, his father read to her out of the Yiddish paper, and his mother would gasp and make tsking sounds over the news of the civil war in Germany, the perils of Bolshevism, the revolution in Hungary, the conflicts in Poland. The war was over but wars were still going on; it was hard for her to understand. But the part of the paper that absorbed her most was the problem and lovelorn letters that were published and answered. Then she would settle back with the full knowledge of the world's troubles, listen to the soft falling of ashes in the stove, and, feeling secure in her peaceful flat, would say: "People. How hard it is for them to live."

His father's being home gave Hershy greater freedom, released him for a more active life on the streets. He seldom had to go to the movies with his mother, finding much more fun there with the guys. But sometimes, when his father worked overtime, he'd have to go with her: never to a cowboy or funny picture, always to a romance. There, every time the titles were flashed on the screen, an immediate buzz of translation would rise, with Hershy's voice part of it. Sometimes, conversations would continue between parents and children over the meaning of what was happening, until those that had caught on quickly would yell: "Shut up." In some language or another the answer was always: "Shut up yourself. I paid my nickel, didn't I? I got a right." Sometimes, fights would arise between parents and children when the children would become too absorbed in the movie to translate.

"Noo, noo, what are they saying? What's happening?"

"For Christ sake, Ma, let me see the picture, don't bother me."

"Stinker, what's happening? I'll kill you if you don't tell me."

And the kid would shout out the subtitles. And, with peace attained, once again the buzz of translation would sweep the illiterate into a magic world they had never known but had always dreamed about.

Sometimes, Hershy's mother cried there, and it was hard for him to understand.

"Cut it out, Ma."

"Shut up, you devil."

"What's to cry about?"

"Everything. Everything."

Her sniffles and sobs would spoil the picture for him and he'd stop translating. Then she'd poke him hard and whisper tensely: "Read. Read it."

"It says: Don't ever darken my door again."

"No!"
"Yah."
"You mean he's throwing her out?"
"I guess so."
"Tsk, tsk, tsk." And a throbbing sob.
Afterward, she'd come out in the cold, red-faced and sniffling.
"Oy, what a wonderful picture."
"Ah, it was all right, Ma."
"So full of life."
"Ah, it was a sissy picture."
He was glad that he didn't have to go with her too often. She spoiled the movies for him. When he and the guys went they saw the pictures differently; there was more fun.

4.

During this time, something was added to the house that revealed their lives more completely than any words or gestures they could express: it was the phonograph that Hershy's father had built for Rachel. In its carved walnut splendor it stood in the parlor as a tribute to his father's skill.

When it was first brought up from the basement, there was a proud light in his father's eyes, his mother ah-ed, Rachel oh-ed, and Hershy posed beside it on his hands and knees, and, with his head cocked, began to bark. Soon afterward, Hershy discovered the remarkable charm of the instrument.

He was the only one who didn't need a record to make the machine talk and express himself. His pal Cyclops was able to make the most beautiful horses in the world: so beautiful that the sight of his Shetlands, pintos, Arabian steeds, and thoroughbreds brought a quiver to Hershy's throat. Immediately, Hershy got Cyclops to draw them on cardboard, with cowboys and Indians and jockeys to ride them; then they cut the forms out, mounted them on the green felt turntable, started the motor, and wham, a whole new world came alive for them. At the sight of the cowboys and Indians and jockeys racing on their horses, the hoofbeats of their stomping feet and the slapping of their rumps and the sound of the whirring motor was like the rhythm section of a great orchestra; and their excited shouts, grunts, screams, whistles, and cheers were the melodies and solo flights which sent them fully into the vast spaces of their imaginations.

Everybody in the house had to cover their ears to this music. When they begged for mercy, Hershy answered: "Ah, for Cry Yike, a guy can never have no fun around here." He was sure that he was putting the phonograph to much better use than they. At least he had fun. But they . . . well, look at the records they played. Rachel's were black-labeled with gold trimmings, his mother's were red-seal, and his father's had green labels printed in Yiddish.

When his father played the phonograph, he'd sit down in the rocking chair and close his eyes; through the quivering, soulful chants his throat would work along with the cantor's singing and he'd seem to go far, far away. At the end of the record he'd say: "Ay, Yussele, Yussele." Then he'd turn to Hershy and say: "You know who that is? Yussel Rosenblatt, the greatest singer in the world."

"Ah, he ain't so good as Al Jolson, Pa."

"Al Jolson? He grunts like a pig. In America there is no great singing. There is no feeling for it. There is only noise."

"Yah? Rachel says Al Jolson makes more'n a thousand dollars a week when he sings."

"What has money to do with feeling and singing?"

"I don't know, Pa. That's what Rachel says."

"Never mind what Rachel says. Just listen to a man with a great voice and learn. Listen to a man with a soul and feel the way he can make every nerve in your body tremble. Listen to him."

Hershy would listen but it sounded like Yom Kippur, a holiday he neither understood nor had any feeling for, since his brief experience in Hebrew school (which he quit as soon as his father went away) was marked by an unintelligible language and an old snuff-smelling teacher with a beard who used a stick to beat him. He'd listen and stare at his father, wondering at the way he'd rock in the chair with his sunken eyes closed and his bony face lax, watching the chanting of the cantor work in his throat, and feeling him go far, far away, deep into a life he had never known.

His mother's records were different. During the war, while his father was away, a neighbor had taken her to the opera a few times. Each time, she had come home gasping and sighing, straining to express the emotional impact of the music. Now, through the phonograph, she was able to take her part in the great tragic dramas of the opera. Caruso could make the veins at her temple throb, could make her hands clutch over her breasts, could make her face look like she was having the heart torn out of her. After playing one of his records, she'd turn to Hershy and say: "That was Caruso, the greatest singer in the world. If only you could sing like him."

"Ah, he ain't so good as Tony the bananaman."

"Don't talk nonsense. Tony barks like a dog. With his voice all he can sell is a banana."

"And Caruso?"

"When you get older, my son, you'll understand what he sells."

Sometimes she'd play a waltz. And though she didn't move, he could feel her go far away, dancing lightly through the distant mansions of her mind.

Rachel's music was less confusing, much closer, more

familiar to his ear, though what she felt about it, in her adolescent dreams of becoming a great dancer, was beyond him. Her music was more a part of the way he walked and ran and jumped and played, closer to the tissue paper and comb he'd learned to play, more akin to the plunk of a baseball in a glove, the clanking washtubs, the sticks clattering against a fence, the sharp whistles, the rhythmic train sounds, the cries on the street, and the explosive automobile noises. Instead of making one sit down and, with eyes closed, drift into another world, Rachel's music was full of motion; it made you get up on your feet and move.

Sometimes the music was close to the cantor's singing in his father's records. Blues, Rachel called them; they made her sway and twist, look hot and melty. Sometimes they were close to his mother's records. Waltzes, Rachel called them, but they did not have the sweep of his mother's records; instead, they were tight and cramped, as though laced in a corset; they made Rachel go into dizzy whirls. But most always her records were filled with plunking banjos, pounding drums, skittering pianos, thumping tubas, with a clarinet winding in and out of a growling trombone, or with a piercing trumpet shooting out fiercely from the rest of the band. Rachel called them ragtime and foxtrot numbers. His mother called them crazy. And Rachel, swaying, shuffling, whirling, would say: "Listen to it, just listen to it."

"Noise," his mother called it. "Plain noise."

"But that's the real American music. That's the real American spirit."

"It could make one go crazy."

"But it's life, Ma. It's living in a great big way."

"Do me a favor and let me live in a small way, then."

"But, Ma, if you don't like this you don't like America."

"I don't like bums, but they're a part of America. Do I have to like them?"

"Ah, Ma, you just don't understand."

Then one night the full impact of the varied music came into play. After supper, Hershy's father took the cardboard horses, cowboys, Indians, and jockeys off the turntable and, while his mother was finishing up the dishes in the kitchen, played some Yussel Rosenblatt records. Then his mother came into the parlor and played some operatic records. Hershy heard them but didn't listen; he was too absorbed in trying to get three beebies that were under a glass into three tiny holes which were punched into a clown's face.

Then Rachel came home late from work with a box under her arm. She explained that she had been working overtime. After she ate she went into her bedroom and closed the door. When she came out, Hershy looked up quickly at the sound of his mother's gasp.

"But where did you get it?" she asked.

"I made it in the shop," Rachel said. "That's why I was late."

"But what is it?" asked Hershy's father.

"A dancing dress," Rachel said.

"But you look so naked," said his father. "Where can one dance in a dress like that?"

"On the stage," Rachel said.

"And you wouldn't be ashamed?" his mother asked.

"Are the girls in the opera ballet ashamed when you see them?" Rachel said.

"No," his mother admitted. "But they're artists. Besides, you can catch a cold running around like that."

"And don't forget," his father added, "you're not on the stage yet."

"But I will be," Rachel said. "Someday, you'll see, I will be. This is my audition dress. Do you like it?"

Everybody stared at her.

"Say you like it," she begged. And, when nobody answered, she said: "Say something, will you!"

Hershy finally answered for his mother and father.

"Yowie!"

For there she stood, full and tall and graceful, like a circus queen, with parts of her showing which none of them had ever seen before. Her arms were bare and her hair was wound into a tight biscuit at the nape of her neck; her plump breasts mounded out of a tight bodice that glittered with silvery spangles; the curve of her back and hips flowed into a short ruffled skirt; and her legs, which had never been seen above the ankles, were firm and shapely in pink silk stockings.

"A regular queen of Sheba," said Hershy's mother finally.

"I'm going to give you a free show," said Rachel.

"Noo, let's see already," his mother said. "Let's see what all your dancing lessons have done for you."

"First we have to roll the rug back," said Rachel.

Hershy helped his father roll the rug back. Then he sat down on the couch between his mother and father. His mother settled back with her hands clenched on her lap. His father crossed his legs and tried to look unconcerned. Hershy shifted eagerly from side to side.

"You're sitting in the dark, see," said Rachel. "Then, when the music starts, a spotlight's going to shine on me. Like silver and gold, it'll make me look. Ready?"

"Ready," said Hershy.

"Okay, here goes."

The blare of music startled them. His mother's hands came up to her ears. His father cocked his head and stared. Hershy leaned forward with his mouth open, held by the glitter of her spangled breasts and jiggling body. On the second chorus he almost stopped breathing.

"No."

"Look out, Rachel."

"You'll kill yourself."

Rachel had gone into a cartwheel and jounced on the floor

in a full split. Then she worked from cartwheels and full splits, interspersed with taps, into a slow backward dip to the floor, from which she rolled upward to her feet, and then into walking on her hands with her legs spread horizontally. Hershy applauded and yelled while his mother and father, terrified, kept begging her to stop it. Finally, she bounced on one toe, her cleated sole tapping to the music; her other leg was raised so that her toe pointed to her face; and, as she scolded that toe with her finger, the music ended and she ran out of the room.

"Hey, Ma. Hey, Pa," Hershy shouted. "Did you see that? An acrobat. Rachel can go in a circus."

But when he looked up there were tears in his mother's eyes.

"Like Pavlowa she used to dance when she was a little girl," she said. "Now look at her, like a wild Indian, so crazy, so ugly."

His father tried to soothe her. "It's the American style," he said. "To an American, I suppose, it's beautiful."

But Hershy thought Rachel was the greatest dancer in the world. He suddenly saw her as a different being, a part of the charmed world of acrobats, magicians, and clowns. He was ready to fall in love with her, if only she would teach him all those tricks.

After that night he added her music to the music of his whirring motor, which sent his horses and cowboys and Indians and jockeys into action.

BOOK TWO

CONVERSION

CHAPTER SIX

1.

When his father first came home, Hershy used to wait for him near the newsstand at the end of the carline to meet him as he came from work. He always pretended that he was there by accident.

"Were you waiting for me?" his father would ask.

"No," Hershy would say. "I was just coming from a kid's house." Or, he'd make up another excuse.

"Oh," his father would say. He'd pat Hershy's head and then they'd walk home together, usually in silence, with Hershy carrying his father's lunch pail.

Soon, however, his father's being home was no longer a novelty and Hershy stopped waiting for him at the car stop. His father assumed his traditional role of The Man, who left in the morning, did his work, which was taken for granted and seldom discussed, and came back at night. Nevertheless, the whole order of the household was geared around his coming home each evening, and suppertime was Papa's time, during which the day was summed up, judged, and put aside for the next day. Being a man who seldom gave himself over to comparisons and who was free of pretension and envy, he was never harsh in his judgments. His dreams were small and easily satisfied, anchored by his skill as a cabinet maker, his love for his family, the weekly wage that provided for them, and a belief that what he had was sufficient. And if the end of the day yielded a hot meal, a warm stove, some bits of gossip, a few complaints, and a luxurious groan in a soft bed, then he was satisfied. What more could a man want?

Only on Sunday was the routine different. Then it was strange to be able to see him any time one wanted. But sensing this, and since he was restless unless his hand were busy, he usually spent his mornings in the basement building things for the house or for a neighbor. Then he could come up for dinner, as though he'd been away from the house that day.

The role of Hershy's mother was to order the house around The Man, despite the fact that The Man made no demands and that she complained bitterly of how boring and tiring her routine was: in the foraging for food and bargains, cooking, cleaning, washing, making the beds, doing the dishes. A man was an emperor, a woman his slave, but that was the order of things, and she found escape finally from the small circumference of her world through the movies, the stories read to her at night, through prying into Rachel's affairs, and dreams.

"Oy, if we had money," she'd say.

"Yes?" his father'd prompt her. "If you had money?"

"Oy," she'd sigh.

"Oy," his father'd mimic her, and then say: "Is your sister Reva happier with money? Does she find life more exciting?"

"I'm not Reva," she'd say. "I'd know what to do."

"What would you do?" his father'd urge her.

"Don't worry," she'd assure him. "I'd know."

"What would you do?" his father'd say. "Become a society lady, a card player, a gossip?"

"Don't worry," she'd interrupt. "With money one can do anything."

"Foolish woman," his father'd conclude. "A man works. A woman dreams. But that's life."

"Is that so?"

Life in the household was reduced to the pattern Hershy had always known, and from which, without his knowing it, he took strength.

2.

Presently, a number of things happened in such rapid succession that to Hershy it seemed as though he were a runaway kite, soaring in a great blue sky.

There was the rediscovery of Rachel. Ever since she had grown up he had been indifferent to her. She came and went, a secret behind a closed door. Suddenly, she left the door ajar. And he saw a circus queen. And, in transferring his affection to her, he began to wait for her near the newsstand at the end of the carline to meet her accidentally as she came from work.

"Cookie," she'd say. "You were waiting for me."

"No," he'd say. "I just seen you when I was coming from a kid's house, so I waited a second."

"Sweet cookie."

Sometimes she stooped over and kissed him, and the nice smell of her powder and the nice touch of her soft lips made his heart run wild.

One day he discovered that he wasn't the only one who waited for her to get off the streetcar. He began to notice that Joey Gans had taken to standing outside his restaurant, where in the back room pool, dice, card games, and betting on the horses went on. Every time Rachel lifted her skirt to her knee to keep from tripping as she stepped down to the street from the car, Joey crushed a pair of springs he held in his hands and whistled.

"Plenty hot gams," Joey remarked aloud to himself.

A strange quivery sensation came over Hershy.

"Plenty knockers, too," Joey added.

· 99

Though Rachel hurried across the street it seemed that she was pinned to Joey's eyes and changed into another kind of being.

"She could make a cowboy out of me," Joey concluded.

And when Joey went back into the restaurant, only then did Hershy feel released, as though he had been rooted to Joey, and then he was free to run across the street and catch up with Rachel. Studying her as they walked together, he remembered the clean firm length of her legs and the arch of her back and her spangled breasts when she had danced almost naked in the house. He rediscovered her again in a way that was altogether different than ever before. It sent a kind of fear and a kind of excitement through him. But then her attraction for Joey took on a different meaning for him. It brought him close to Joey. It gave him a big tight feeling being that close to him. And he almost died one day when Joey approached him.

"Hey, kid, you know the broad?"

A lump formed in his throat.

"I seen her kiss you. Who is she, your sister?"

"Yah," he managed to say.

"Put in a word for me. Tell her who I am."

"Okay."

"Tell her I like her style."

"Okay."

"Tell her to come on over. Tell her Joey Gans wants to meet her."

"Okay."

"What's your name?"

"Melov. Hershy Melov."

"What's your sister's name?"

"Rachel. I mean, Rae."

"Okay. Now tell her like I told you. I'll learn you how to fight then. I'll put you in my gang when you grow up. Okay?"

"Okay."

Hershy rushed to Rachel when she got off the streetcar. There was a guy, he blurted, nuts about her. The greatest guy in the world. He liked her style. He wanted her to come on over and meet him. Boy, if he was only her sweetheart. Boy, if she married him, Joey'd be like his big brother. Boy, to have a big brother like that.

"What, are you crazy or something?" she said, and hurried home, with Hershy chasing after her.

The following evening, Joey approached him again.

"Well, kid, what's the good word?"

Hershy shrugged his shoulders.

"Did you tell her?"

"Sure."

"And?"

"Ah, you know how sisters are, Joey."

"How?"

"I don't know. You know."

"Did you tell her like I told you, about she's got style?"

"Yah."

"Tell her again."

But that evening, when Rachel stepped down from the car, she got off with more care. She glanced their way at the sound of Joey's whistle and noticed that he was a powerful-looking man, with a tight coat over his big chest and broad shoulders. He had a broken nose, which made his eyes look small, wide apart, and crushed, and his hard face looked like it needed a shave. She carried herself differently as she crossed the street, tall and haughty, with a studied sway in the movement of her body. The chase was on. And when Hershy ran to her, she said: "I don't want you to meet me any more."

"Why not?"

"I just don't want you to, that's all."

His eyes took on a bewildered look. He felt as though he were suddenly cut adrift, both from her and from Joey. There was no pleading or arguing with her. She wouldn't listen. There was no threatening her, either. He wished he had something on her. If only he knew some secret about her, then he could have her in his power. How could a little guy get somebody in his power?

"All right for you, Rae."

"So all right for me."

"If you don't let me wait for you I'll tell everybody your name is Rachel, not Rae."

"So my name is Rachel."

"Yah? I'll tell everybody. I'll tell Joey, too."

"Tell everybody. Tell Joey, too. I give a bibble."

"Yah? I'll tell everybody you're a greenhorn."

A shadow flickered over her face. He got ready to pounce on her: greenhorn, greenhorn. But she raised her head and said: "Tell everybody."

"Yah?" He had no threat. He added futilely: "All right for you. Someday you're going to ask me for a favor, someday you're going to want me to do something for you. But you know what you'll get? *Bawbkes*, you'll get."

But nobody was going to stop him from waiting for her. Nobody was going to keep him away from his pal Joey. She didn't own the street or the corner where the car stopped. It was a free street. He could do anything he wanted on it. But the following day he waited for her alone.

See what she had done? She had chased Joey away. He wasn't coming out any more. Now Joey'd never let him join his gang. Now he could never tell the guys he and Joey were pals. A black lump lay heavy in his chest. So what if she knew Joey? Would it hurt her? She had to know some guy. Why couldn't it be a guy like Joey? Why couldn't it *be* Joey? He hated her with all his might. He was through with her. Was Joey through with her, too? Give her another chance, Joey. Don't be mad on her. Come on out and give her another chance. When she gets off the car, I'll run after her and grab her and bring her to you and you'll meet and it'll be like you're my big brother. Ah, Joey, come on out and give her another chance.

He stared anxiously through the restaurant window for Joey. A man sat at the counter drinking coffee. Through the door that led into the back room he could see a few men playing pool and some men were at a table playing cards. But he couldn't see Joey. He was in front of the glass door, peering through it, when he heard an auto skid to a screeching stop. He turned about and his mouth hung open as two huge men with beefy faces got out with a little redheaded guy. The little guy was Red Doyle, whom Hershy recognized from a picture he had seen in the papers as the Father Protector of the Racketeers: he looked like a rabbit, with pink eyes and a pocked, hard-lined, reddish face, crammed between two bulls. They pushed Hershy out of the way when they got to the door.

Hershy watched them sit down at the counter near the cash register. They began to talk to Joey's brother, Louie. The man drinking coffee got up and went into the back room. Then Joey came out and stood near the door, his eyes dead, his body big and tight, while Louie talked with his hands. Then Louie took some money out of the cash register and gave it to Red Doyle. Everybody smiled except Joey. Everybody was pals. Nothing was going to happen. Then Hershy's heart leaped. As the men got up to leave, one of Red Doyle's boys stepped on Joey's foot and pushed him aside. Joey grabbed the guy's coat, pushed him through the swinging glass door, and hit him. The guy fell to the sidewalk, right at Hershy's feet, with a broken jaw, and Hershy stared down at his glazed eyes and the raw mouth that was twisted out of shape. At the same time, he saw the flash of a gun. He fell against the wall of the building and shut his eyes and tensed himself for the sound of the shot. Instead, he heard a tight, level voice.

"It's okay, Jerry. Put it away."

"Okay."

Hershy opened his eyes to find Red Doyle talking.

"Hey, Joey, you got no respect?"

There was a wild gleam in Joey's eyes, like when he looked at Rachel.

"Nobody pushes me around," Joey said, his voice high and hoarse; it didn't seem to belong to his body; the pitch of it made Hershy shiver.

"You ready to push up daisies for that?"

"Nobody's pushing daisies."

Red Doyle looked down at his bodyguard.

"Jerry," he called his other bodyguard. "Put him in the back seat."

The other bodyguard dragged the beefy man with the broken jaw into the car.

"Well," Red Doyle said. "I need another boy now."

Suddenly, like a deep sigh, everybody relaxed. Hershy felt a dry thump when he swallowed.

"You know," Red Doyle said. "I like you, Joey. You don't say much, but you talk a mile a minute when you move. You got style. You got the kind of style I like. Let me feel the arm."

Red Doyle felt Joey's shoulder and bicep and pursed his lips.

"You push plenty of muscle, Joey."

"I do okay with it," Joey admitted.

"I could use you, Joey. A brain needs plenty of muscle around it. Maybe I could use Louie, too, with that angle he's got on prohibition."

Louie found his tongue. "Yah, Red. The way I look at it, a law ain't going to stop a man from drinking. A man, he puts in a hard day's work, he needs a place to relax, a place to get away from his ball and chain, his kids, his troubles; he needs a drink, a man does. And who are we to say no to a man? Like I said before, Red, live and let live, that's my motto."

"See me tomorrow," Red said. "We'll talk about it. Bring Joey."

Hershy tried hard to remember every word, every action. He never wanted to forget this scene. He wanted to report it as accurately as possible. This had the movies beat a mile. He watched Red Doyle drive off, then Louie slapped Joey's back and said: "We're in, kid." Just like that. That was exactly how he was going to end the story when he told it to the guys: "We're in, kid."

But he wouldn't be able to tell anyone what happened afterward. He'd have to remember it for himself, a delicate secret, as a private victory. For afterward, Joey didn't go back into the restaurant with Louie. He began to wait for Rachel.

This time he didn't whistle when she got off the streetcar. She fluffed her hair and glanced his way and lingered a second before crossing the street. Joey crushed the springs that he had been working on in his hands and stepped over to her. She glanced at him and turned her head away, then hurried along with Joey chasing after her.

"Where's the fire?"

She didn't answer, just jerked her head and shoulders, as though a fly had disturbed her.

"Where you going?"

"Home."

"Okay, I'll take you home."

"Thanks. I can find my way."

"I said I'll take you home."

"You get away from me. I'll call the cop on the corner."

He seemed to suddenly loosen up in his tight coat. He put the handsprings in his pockets, and, as he laughed, he placed one of his big hands on her shoulder and turned her to face the cop on the corner.

"Call him," he said.

"Don't. Get your dirty hands off of me."

"Call the cop. Go ahead, call the cop."

She hesitated.

"What's a cop?" he said. "A tin button you can smash like that." He tore a button off his coat and crushed it to bits on the ground with his heel. He tore another button off his coat and put it in his pocket and jingled the money there. "I got him in my pocket, see. Loose change."

"So you got him in your pocket."

"But you, I got you here." He pointed to his head. "It's got me walking in circles. And I got you here." He punched his heart. "Big as a basketball."

He put his arm through hers. And, in the powerful bulk of his muscle moving like a life force against her as they walked, she felt her throat grow hot and dry, kindled by fear and fascination.

Hershy, in seeing them finally together, leaped high in the air and wrapped his arms about himself.

Afterward, through Rachel, as she was seen again and again with Joey, Hershy became the link between his pals and the bold, powerful, heroic lives of Joey and his gang. His favor was always sought. No game was played unless he led it. No stunt was done until he could view it and approve it. And whenever a kid got in trouble, or was hit, or was threatened with a fight, he'd say: "I'll tell Hershy on you."

Perhaps for the first time in the lives of his pals they wished they had a big sister. Those who did have a big sister sometimes stopped Joey on the street.

"Hey, Joey. I got a big sister. A beaut." Then they'd roll their eyes and describe her curves with their hands. "Want to meet her?"

Joey'd pretend to slug them with the back of his hand "Go on, beat it, punk."

Hershy, the kids said secretly, must have put a hex on Joey. They said, when Hershy wasn't around, that Rachel must be a whore. Sure, they argued. She was a dancer, wasn't she? All dancers were whores. Sure, once Cyclops had seen her practicing in Hershy's house. Man, did she have legs, like a whore. And tits, with beads on them, like a whore. She was bow-legged, too. And that wasn't from riding horses. Then, whop, he had seen her jump way up in the air, and she came down, kerflop, in a full split, right on it, whoppo, right on it. A contortionist, she was, too. And everybody knew what a contortionist was. Nobody had to tell them. And was she *zoftig*. With beads on them, yah.

No wonder, then. Hershy could have her for a sister, then.

But still they approached Joey: "I got a sister, Joey. An acrobat. *Zoftig*, too. Want to meet her?"

All this bewildered Joey. What the hell was happening to these kids? he wondered.

But still they paid tribute to Hershy. After all, you couldn't afford to let a guy like Hershy get mad on you now. He might tell Joey. It wouldn't be healthy. Besides, Joey might become Hershy's big brother for real. That lucky Hershy. It called for tribute.

3.

Though Hershy was overjoyed at the prospect of having a big brother like Joey Gans, he didn't quite know how to feel about the prospect of having a baby brother or sister. For one was surely on the way, and it was hard to admit the truth of it to himself, especially since nothing definite had been announced.

His father suddenly began to sit prouder at the supper table. He ate heartier, had a stronger light in his eye, seemed to swell as he flexed his muscles, and was more tender to Hershy's mother than Hershy had ever known. His mother seemed to grow softer and fleshier. Something happened to her posture;

she seemed to stand taller, with her chin tilted up and her shoulders arched back. Something happened to her eyes; they seemed to glow inward, as though they were searching for something within herself, and, as though finding something pleasant, they became soft and warm.

Men felt his father's arms and slapped his back and poked him slyly, and looked with wonder at his mother. Women admired his father, made his eyes shine, gave him a kind of glowing manhood, and groaned and sighed and looked pleased with his mother. Everybody was a part of what was going on with his mother except himself: the child, until his time came, was cast out of the universal social experience of conception and impending birth, and it confused Hershy.

There were peculiar allusions to the food they were eating. What kind of spice had his mother discovered suddenly, after all these barren years, that radiated the pure, necessary heat to thicken the blood and make it pound with a life force? It was a wonder that Rachel hadn't been affected, and if they weren't careful Hershel might become a man before his time. Perhaps his mother had changed icemen lately, or surely milkmen, or the coalman for certain. Or perhaps his father, in his travels down South, had done some strange things to change his luck. Or perhaps it was her powerful prayers over the Friday night candles, combined with the wonders of her baked choles, whose braids were the finest anybody had ever seen.

Hershy knew about the braids. He had heard Aunt Bronya, his mother's oldest sister, talk about them once. In olden days, before Moses and before there was One God, women offered their hair to the goddess of fertility. Later the Jewish women adopted the pagan custom, but instead of hair the braids on the Sabbath bread were offered. Maybe it was a foolish thing to do, Aunt Bronya said, but who could it hurt? He remembered then how his mother, just before putting the chole into the oven, pinched off a piece of dough from the braid and threw it quickly into the oven and muttered something mysterious. And he remembered recently the charred crusts of dough that came out of the oven when he watched her clean it. Sometimes he dreamed afterward that her long black hair caught fire and she went up in a screaming flame and then drifted down through a cloud of smoke all charred and as big as two people, and the dream woke him up choking and trembling.

In a few months, however, the cruel truth struck him on the street.

"Hey, Hershy. Your ma's getting fat."
"So what? When you get older you get fatter."
"She ain't getting fatter from getting older."
"Then what's she getting fatter from, wise guy?"
"You know."
"You sonofabitch. She's getting fatter because my pa's home."
"Sure she is. Ha, ha, ha."
"Because we're eating more to get him fatter, see. My ma eats a lot, that's all, to show my pa how good she cooks, see."
"Yah, yah."
"My pa didn't eat good for over a year, that's why. So to make him eat like a horse she's eating like a horse."
"Yah, yah."
"I'll kill you if you don't believe me."
"Okay, okay."

A shocking image, gained from the dark alleys and the basements and the streets, over which he had reveled and laughed in other cases, formed in his mind. He tried to hide from it. In doing so, he felt himself cringing from his mother and father, Rachel and Joey, and his pals. They changed suddenly, seemed to rise as enemies. He dreaded being with his pals for fear of their talking about *it*. He tried to avoid thinking about his mother and father, and Joey and Rachel, for fear of the grotesque things they did in his mind. Nobody, somehow, knew what was happening to him. And, helpless before the fact, he brooded.

"Why don't you go out and play?" his mother wanted to know one Friday.

"I don't want to."

"Why, is somebody after you?"

"No."

"You sick?"

"No."

"Then what's the matter with you?"

"Nothing, see."

"Go turn a somersault, then. Let what's bothering you fall out."

The kitchen smelt of the boiling chicken and the gefüllte fish that was cooling off and the baked chole that rested on a clean dish towel. As the light dimmed, his mother lit the white candles, which rested in brass holders. Then, with her hands almost touching the flames, she made strange symbols while muttering a prayer over them. Her bulkier back and broader hips were facing him, and the flickering candles gave her shadow a grotesque look on the wall and ceiling. He began to mimic her mumbling and from the shadow of his hands he made an eagle fly on the wall; but to his mother it looked like a bat. She stopped her prayers suddenly and looked at the flickering wings in terror, then gasped as she saw the bat quickly jab its beak into the shadow of her throat. She reeled back and then saw that it was he who had made the shadowed bat. She rushed over and slapped his face and swore at him.

"Ah, what'd I do?" he yelled. "What'd I do?"

She paid no attention to him and went back to her prayers. He formed a hopping rabbit on the wall from the shadow of his hands. His mother saw it just as it took a bite out of the shadow of her nose. She stumbled back, cursing him, but he rushed past her and dived under the bed in Rachel's room and crawled into a corner. He lay there awhile, the dark like a hand pressing him against the wall and crushing out all thought. When he thought it safe, he came back into the kitchen.

"*Dybbuk,* you."

She was sitting at the table, huge in the dim light, and he glared at her.

"What kind of a devil are you?"

He didn't answer.

"Why do you twist your face like that? What are you mad about?"

"For nothing, see."

"I'll give you, for nothing."

"Yah?"

"I'll hit you so hard you'll turn over three times if you're not careful."

"Yah?"

"Yah."

"Why, what'd I do?"

"You almost frightened me to death, you black cholera, you."

"What'd I do? I only made some magic on the wall, that's all. For that you got to hit me?"

"It's a sin to do it when I'm praying over the candles. Do you want something bad should happen to us?"

"I don't care."

"I'll give you an I don't care."

"Why do you have to *bench licht?*"

"Because I have to."

"You didn't always."

"I have to now."

"Why?"

"So you won't get sick, so Papa will be in good health and keep working, so nothing will happen to Rachel, so I might be strong enough to care for all of you."

"It ain't not why."

"All right, you tell me why."

"You do it to make you fat."

"Who told you?"

"You eat like a horse, too, to get fat."

She stared at him with her mouth fumbling for something to say. "What do they tell you on the streets?" she said finally.

"Nothing."

"Snots, and already they know the secret of life."

"Why'd you do it, Ma?" He felt his throat get fuzzy.

"What?" Her eyes opened wide, horrified.

"Get fatter."

"It's nature."

"Can't you get skinny again?"

"No."

"All the guys on the street, they know."

"Let them know. I don't know what they say on the street, but let them know I'm proud. Let them know Papa's proud. Let them know I am carrying a gift from God. Let them know you're proud, too, Hershele." She leaned toward him. "Maybe you'll have a brother. A little brother, who will grow up and play with you and be your best friend. A little brother, who will be to you what Uncle Yussel was to Papa. Wouldn't it be nice to have a brother like Uncle Yussel?"

"Yes," he had to admit. "But what if it's a girl?"

"Then she'll be like Rachel, the blood of your blood, who will be like your own life. I don't know what they tell you on the streets, but remember this: life comes from God, and no matter how life comes into this world it has to be good because God made it. Remember that."

The talking subdued his tension. She reached for him, and, in finding himself being drawn to her, he felt his whole being flood over with a need for her. It was nature, he told himself. It came from God. It couldn't be dirty. It came like a present. It came from magic, like he could suddenly form an eagle or a rabbit, from out of nothing.

In a few days, he accepted the fact and then ignored it. The coming of the baby was something ordered. It might just as well have been ordered at the Boston Store.

4.

In the midst of all this, the spirit of Uncle Yussel appeared on a Saturday morning, heralded by a shrill whistle and hidden in a thick official-looking envelope. Hershy rushed to the front door, with his mother behind him, and the mailman handed her a piece of paper and a pencil.

"Sign here," said the mailman, pointing to an x. . . .

Hershy watched his mother stare blankly at the small print.

"Here, where the x is. Sign."

"What does he want from me?" she asked Hershy in Yiddish.

"He wants you to sign the paper," Hershy said.

"Why?"

Hershy turned to the mailman and said: "My ma wants to know why she got to sign."

"Tell her it's a registered letter. Say it's an important letter, see. If it's an important letter you've got to sign that paper so the other party knows it was delivered to the right party."

Hershy translated but she couldn't understand why this letter was so different from all others. A letter was a letter, she wanted him to tell the mailman. All of them were important. What was so special about this one?

The mailman knew that all letters were important, but this

one was very special, it cost extra money to get it delivered, and for the extra money the other party wanted to get a signature.

The talk and the insistence upon a signature got her suspicious and frightened. With all that importance attached to that letter there could only be one meaning: bad news, perhaps tragic. Was the mailman sure the letter was for them? Yes, the mailman was sure. Perhaps he had made a mistake. No, he hadn't made a mistake. He was sure the letter was for them. Was she going to sign or was he going to take the letter back to the post office?

"He wants you to sign, Ma," said Hershy.

"Tell her there's nothing to be scared of," the mailman said to Hershy. "Tell her the post office is like the United States government. Tell her the government don't pull no phony tricks. Tell her it's safe to sign. Tell her, for Christ's sake, to sign."

Hershy translated. She nodded her head, punctuating: "Yah, yah, yah, yah." She understood, but she wanted him to tell the mailman that it was Saturday, it was a holy day, and that she couldn't write on a Saturday, it would be a sin to do it.

"It's Saturday," Hershy said to the mailman. "My ma can't write on Saturday. It's a Jewish rule, see."

"Holy Jesus," said the mailman.

"A rule's a rule," Hershy said appeasingly.

"Then you sign. Just write your father's name, David Melov, and take the goddam letter from me, will you?"

"The man," said Hershy to his mother, "wants me to sign for Pa."

She thought about it a moment.

"All right," she said. "If you sign, nothing bad can happen then. If it's a trick they can't hold us responsible. We'll prove an infant signed it. Go ahead, sign, Hershele."

"But, Ma," he said. "Won't I get a sin if I write on Saturday?"

"Don't worry about it, Hershele. Until your thirteenth birthday you're forgiven everything. God keeps you pure. It's after *barmitzvah* that you have to be careful and thoughtful. Sign."

"Well—" the mailman said.

"I'm signing," Hershy said. "My ma said it's all right."

"Thank Christ," the mailman said.

Back in the house, suspicion and fear filled his mother. A letter was an uncommon event in her life. Who would want to write to them? Why was it so necessary that the letter be delivered in person by the mailman, that it require a signature? From whom could it be and from where did it come? Since the war and the revolution in Russia she had never heard from her family. Nobody knew if her parents and brothers were alive or dead. But the letter couldn't be from Russia. There was print in the upper left-hand corner of the envelope, looking very austere and formidable, and there was type from a machine in the center. Letters from Russia came with small, curlicued, timid handwriting on the envelope.

"It isn't from Russia," she announced.

"No, Ma. It's American writing, from a machine."

"So where is it from? Who could want to write to us?"

"In the circle here it's printed Washington."

"Where the president lives?"

"Yah."

"But Papa says the president is in Europe making peace."

"This ain't from the president, Ma. What do you think, he's got nothing to do but write letters to us?"

"Who knows what a politician can have in his crazy mind? Papa says the president wants to talk to the people in person to make a good peace so it will last forever."

"It ain't from the president, Ma."

"Don't shout at me. Then maybe it's from the congressman Papa saw there, the one who shook his hand and gave him a cigar."

"It ain't from nobody. On the top here it says in-sur-ance company."

"Insurance company? But Papa just paid his insurance, the bloodsuckers."

"Maybe he didn't. Maybe they want more money. Maybe Pa didn't pay them right."

"Oy, the bloodsuckers. But maybe it's a nice letter telling Papa what a good, fine, honest, dependable man he is, always paying on time to the penny."

"How about we open it and see?"

"But it must be bad news. Otherwise, why should they want us to sign the paper? Good news you receive with no trouble. But bad news—they make the heart fall out of you before you get it, and then, when you do get it, you haven't the heart left to grieve over it. Noo, open it already."

Hershy tore the envelope and studied the contents.

"Noo, what is it? What does it say?"

"Wait a minute, will you?"

"Lamebrain, don't they teach you anything at school?"

"The print's too small."

"All of a sudden the print's too small. Print is print. How can it be too small?"

"There's big words, too. I never seen so many big words."

"Dummy, you. What's a big word? If you can read you can read, that's all. On the street you know everything. But when it comes to something important in the house your brain turns to stone."

"Give me a chance, will you? What do you think, I'm in high school already?"

"All right, I'll give you a chance. . . . So read. Read."

"Like here, it says, benny . . . benny . . . benny . . ."

"From somebody named Benny? Who do we know called Benny?"

"It's a word, Ma, not a name. After it comes fish. Benny . . . fish . . ."

"Benny the Fishman, hah?"

"It's a word, I'm telling you, not a name, not nobody. Then it says, yary. Benny . . . fish . . . yary."

"What kind of word is that? What does it mean?"

"See, I told you. That word's too big even for a giant. You got to be a doctor or a professor to know it."

"So what will we do?"

"Wait'll Pa comes home."

"No. If it's bad news we should know first so we can help Papa. Read some more. Try, Hershele. Try."

"For Cry Yike, all right."

After puzzling over the letter at great length, he said, "It's about Uncle Yussel."

"Yussel," she gasped. "What did he do? What do they want from his poor soul?"

"It says he's *diseased.*"

"*Diseased! Gottenyu!* He's dead, may his soul rest in peace."

"That's what it says. And it says Pa is the benny . . . fish . . . yary."

"What can they want of our poor lives?"

"We got to fill out forms, too."

"Forms? What is that?"

"I don't know. Form, I thought, is what a baseball player or fancy diver has got."

"Oh, dummy, dummy, dummy."

"It says something about a check, too."

"What is that?"

"That's what Uncle Hymie talks about all the time. You know, he says, in this country a businessman never pays with money, he pays with a piece of paper from a bank that he has to put his name on. You buy this paper from a bank with money, he says. That's a check."

"So now I know everything. Give me the letter. I'll go to the groceryman. Maybe he'll tell me. Or maybe his son, who is studying to be a lawyer, will be home, and he'll tell me."

Hershy tried to duck when she came back, but he wasn't prepared for it, so he couldn't escape. She grabbed his head and pulled his hair and kissed him hard on the lips. Only when she began to cry did she release him. She stumbled into a chair and covered her face with her hands.

"What's the matter, Ma? Was it bad news? Was it, huh?"

"No, sweetheart. No, dearest."

"So what's to cry about?"

"Everything. Everything."

He stepped toward her, his throat hard. She clutched him and he felt her tremble in the embrace. And then, through her choking gasps, he heard her say:

"We're rich, dearest. We're the richest people in the world."

5.

They were going to collect ten thousand dollars from the government insurance Uncle Yussel had carried as a soldier.

What could one do with all that money?

It was bewildering. It was staggering. It was like climbing a steep mountain. For a lifetime all you can see are the lofty peaks above, disaster below, a small crevice here and a jagged rock there to gain a foothold. Finally you reach the top and look around. There is a new world to behold. You don't know what to make of it. It takes your breath away.

What does one do with all that money?

There were a hundred things they had yearned for and needed, practical things and luxurious things; but suddenly, as though an avalanche had struck them, they were buried under the weight of the money and couldn't name a thing they wanted. And when they did finally express their desires they sounded utterly fantastic. It was an art, they concluded, to know what to do with money.

Of course, they could buy a house and never have to pay rent again. But to buy a house only for themselves would be selfish and Hershy's father couldn't see himself buying a large house because he couldn't see himself in the role of a landlord. They could buy an automobile, but for a person who did not need it in business that was a luxury which only the absolute rich could contemplate. They could buy diamond rings, too, and a houseful of new furniture, and closets full of clothes, and fur coats, but who would see them: the moths, the dark corners of a drawer, the envious eyes of their relatives and friends? If they were going to waste money to make a finger glitter or to enrich their backs, they might just as well buy Hershy the speedboat and racehorse he wanted.

All right, Rachel could have a few dresses and a fur-trimmed coat, and Hershy's mother could have a new tapestried chair instead of the leather rocking chair, and Hershy's father hoped that nobody would mind if he got some new tools, and Hershy could have a pair of cowboy shoes. But they'd still have thousands and thousands of dollars. What could they do to secure their whole future?

Well, they could go in business. What kind? There were so many, too many to enumerate. It would require some heavy thinking. Ay, what to do with money, said Hershy's father, was an art that took a lifetime to learn.

So what were they going to do?

Ah. Hershy's father had it. The true meaning of their good fortune had finally worked through his stupid head. Last week he had had a dream about Yussel, but not knowing the meaning of it then he had said nothing. They were in Russia, little boys, and Yussel had earned some money for helping a *mujik*. Afterward, Yussel gave him three kopecks, three cents, and said: "What will you do with this, David?" And he said: "I don't know. Buy something sweet, maybe." "No," said Yussel. "Don't waste the money. I did not kill myself for you to waste it. Guard it well. Save it for a time when you will need it. Use it wisely. Money, if it can't do good, is bad. So use it wisely."

Yussel, he concluded, had risen from the dead to counsel him. And this was his interpretation: Yussel meant the money to be for everybody. He loved Rachel. He wanted her to marry well. He (David) would make sure of it. He would lay aside two thousand dollars for her dowry. Maybe Rachel might meet a struggling student who would soon become a doctor or a lawyer or an engineer. The man will want to open an office, he will need a start. Rachel, with this two thousand dollars, will be able to help him. She will marry fine. All right, two thousand dollars to Rachel.

Yussel loved Hershel, too. He wanted Hershel to grow up into a man of great resources, a man with a mind, so that he would never know a lonely moment, a man who would be able to pick up a book with his hands and be able to hold it, a man who would be useful and do good. In short, Yussel wanted Hershel to go to college someday. So, for Hershel's future education there must be put aside another two thousand dollars.

Now, Yussel couldn't have known about the new child to come. But had he known he would have wanted the child born in a hospital with a doctor and a nurse in attendance. For the mother, then, two hundred dollars would be laid aside for her care and delivery. And for the new child, another two thousand dollars, to be used for education, if it's a boy, or a dowry, if it's a girl.

And what about him (David) and his wife? Well, there

were thirty-eight hundred dollars left. But they'd never touch it for themselves. No, they'd use it to help the children along, for he was a man, with strong hands and a skill and simple tastes, and so long as there were jobs and he was able to work they would need no more than his weekly wages to get along. So, thirty-eight hundred dollars would be put aside for any emergency; it could last a lifetime.

"And that," said Hershy's father proudly, "is what you do with money. You see, it wasn't hard to get rid of it at all."

CHAPTER SEVEN

1.

How much was ten thousand dollars?

In the old country Hershy's father had worked for ten rubles a year. If he had stayed there, he would have had to live a thousand years to earn that much. Here, in the twelve years since he had arrived, he hadn't earned that much. Here, he could stop working and live like a retired gentleman for at least ten years. As for Hershy, he could have a dollar a day for ten thousand days or a penny a day for a million days. That's how much ten thousand dollars was.

Hershy slapped his forehead with the heel of his hand. A penny a day for a million days. Holy holy holy Moses.

"Then we're millionaires," he said, staggered.

His father smiled gently. "Here," he said, handing Hershy a dollar. "Celebrate. Learn what a dollar means."

"It's all mine?"

"It's all yours."

"I can do anything I want with it?"

"Anything."

"I can spend it all?"

"Yes."

He slammed out of the house, shutting off his father's laughter, and ran into the street, singing:

My father gave me a dollar
I shouldn't holler
I shouldn't wouldn't holler
I bought some chewing gum . . .

"Hey, Hershy. Let's see."

"Don't grab." He snapped the bill and held its edges tight. "Just look."

"A whole dollar. A real dollar."

"I'm a millionaire."

"Yah." Husky, awed.

"Because my Uncle Yussel was a hero the government gave us ten thousand dollars."

"How much is that?"

"A million pennies. A penny a day for a million days."

"Holy Moses. What are you going to do with all that money, Hersh?"

"Anything I want. I can have anything I want. See that Pierce Arrow. If I want I can have it. Get out of my way, I'm a millionaire."

He made off he was smoking a cigar and that he had a big belly.

"If I want I can take all you guys to the show."

"That where you're going?"

"Yah."

"No kid? You're taking us?"

"Yah."

"Make way, make way for the millionaire."

They stopped in a candy store. The way they ganged around him, the way they yelled and slapped his back and looked at his money, made him suddenly realize that money, too, had a value, as great as having the muscle to win a fight or having a big brother who was a star ballplayer or having a guy like Joey Gans for a pal. It bought all the things you needed, even people. Was that what his father meant: learn what a dollar means? Or did he mean it made you happy and made all your pals happy? Or (after the movie and the candy-buying spree for himself and four guys, he found that he still had fifty cents left) did he mean that a dollar was so much money that you couldn't even spend it all at one time?

Boy, but a dollar was a lot of money. Man, but it could buy a lot of things. Jerusalem, but it was hard to spend all of it. Jesus, Pa. Oh, Jesus, Uncle Yussel.

2.

At first, the insurance check was hidden in the lining of an old hat, along with the family savings, which was kept in a bedroom closet. Each night the doors and windows were locked and the shades drawn as the check was taken out and placed on the kitchen table. Everybody stared at it and their throats got dry and they wet their lips: the check contained so much promise.

At first, it was enough for Hershy's mother to say: "We're rich." For Hershy to add: "We're millionaires." For Rachel to sing: "I'm waltzing, I'm waltzing." For Hershy's father to conclude: "Know what this means. Know that a man of our blood died for it."

Actually, they were afraid of the money, and they had to conquer the idea of it. Then the check slowly changed in appearance, became a vacuum of desire through which they were sucked.

Hershy wanted to join the YMCA. Then a kid had given him a booklet describing the muscle-building course of Earl Liederman, with shocking poses of men dressed in muscle, jockstraps, and leopard skins, and with text asking him if he was a real red-blooded American and if he'd like to make his girl proud of him and if he was a man or a mouse; he begged for this course. He also wanted a real live horse and a racing automobile and a speedboat and a league ball and a first baseman's mitt.

"All right, then. Give me a dollar."

"What?" his father said. "Do you think dollars grow on trees?"

"No, but what's a dollar?"

"A fortune for a child."

"Why, what's a dollar? Ain't I got two thousand dollars you said Uncle Yussel wanted me to have?"

"That's for later."

"Now I want it. Who wants it later?"

"You'll get it later, when you need it."

"I don't want it later. I need it now."

"Go outside and play and don't bother me."

"Yah? It's my money, ain't it?"

"No, it isn't."

"Yah? But you said it was."

"I was only talking."

"Yah? You cheap skate."

His father glared at him. Hershy backed away, afraid.

"I promised the guys I was going to take them to the show."

"Don't promise."

"But I did."

"Then be a child without honor for being a braggart."

"Yah? They'll be mad on me."

"If they're real friends they shouldn't care if you don't have a penny."

"Yah? Then what'll I tell them after I promised?"

"Tell them the truth, that you have no money."

"Yah? Then what'll we do?"

"What you always did."

"I can't no more. It ain't no fun no more."

"I see." His father shook his head sadly; he turned away and looked up at the ceiling. "Yussel, Yussel," he said. "You're making me a very lonely man."

"Yah?" said Hershy. "Yah?"

Outside, he explained:

"Ah, my old man's Scotch."

"So what'll we do?"

"I don't know. Mope around."

"Ah, the Scotch cheap skate."

He realized that it was not he who had said that. It was the first time he had heard something bad about his father. For a moment it paralyzed him. Then he wanted to fight. He got mad at everybody. What'd they do, what'd they do? They had called his father a Scotch cheap skate. Well, hadn't *he*? Yah, he had, but his pa was his pa, he could call him anything he wanted, but nobody else was going to call him a name. What the hell was the matter with him, was he going nuts or something? Yah, he thought, what the hell was the matter with him? He wished he knew. It got him scared.

3.

Like a tyrant, the thought of the money began to dominate the household. It loomed over the supper table, sat with them in the parlor, crawled into their beds. All because Hershy's father had a fixed notion that if once the check was cashed the money would disappear quickly, just as one feared that if you broke a dollar or any part of a coin larger than a penny it was always squandered as though there were contempt for anything less than a round denomination. He tried to live as before to keep the check intact, but gradually the cash savings diminished. It was nice to be kind.

"Here, Rachel. Fifty dollars for a new coat. Say it's your birthday."

"But the one I want cost a hundred."

Slowly: "All right, a hundred. Be happy."

And: "Here, Sonya. For a new chair in the front room. For a new dress, maybe. For Hershel, too, things he needs. A hundred dollars."

"*K-nocker,* don't do me favors and don't dole me out money. I know where it is and I know where to get it."

"But be careful, Sonya."

And, looking at Hershy: "Mama knows what you need. You'll get it from her."

"Yah? She's Scotcher than you are."

But Hershy's father had to be strong. It took great strength to be able to harden your heart and say no. It took iron. "Until the eye is buried desires never end," he said.

It was hard for Rachel to understand him. She could understand a guy like Joey Gans: power, drive, a guy ready to knock over mountains. Oh, what excitement. Like dancing on a balloon. Didn't Hershy's father ever want anything?

Yes. He wanted nobody to mix him up. He wanted to be left alone. He wanted the hardest thing in the world to get: peace. He didn't want to hear about a small-time gangster, with a leer for a face and a piece of iron for a brain.

Rachel didn't want to be brought into a fight. No matter how hard and sharp she tried to become, she was always readier to yield; you could feel it in the way her body was shaped, in the way it moved, in the way her soft full lips fumbled for the right thing to say. But she knew what she wanted. She was going places and doing things. That's what she wanted. But it was hard to do it right feeling like a slob, an orphan. The styles were changing, the skirts were getting shorter. She needed a whole new wardrobe. She was looking like the last century. She was ashamed to be seen. All her life, she was neither here nor there. Now that she had a chance she wanted to be *there*. She was going to a big affair at a big club. Judges and lawyers were going to be there, even the Mayor.

"Yah?" said Hershy. "If you buy her new clothes you got to join me in the Y."

"You shut up, Hershy," said Rachel.

"Yah? Who do you think you are?"

Hershy's mother interrupted. "What, do you think we have nothing better to do than put our wealth on your back? You should live so."

"But what am I asking for?" Rachel said. "A few measly dollars?"

"Peace," said Hershy's father. "Please, a quiet moment."

"Papa, Papa, Papa," Rachel pleaded. "Please. If Uncle Yussel was here he'd give it to me."

"Not to go out with that gangster, that bum."

"He's not a gangster, a bum."

"What is he then?"

She tried to describe Joey Gans, but only her hands worked, and finally she said desperately: "What have you got against him? What's wrong with him?"

"What's wrong with a rotten apple? Only a worm."

"Listen, Pa . . ."

Hershy had seldom seen Rachel angry. It was strange to watch the confusion in her face, with her eyes growing cold and hard in her soft face.

"He'll like you without new clothes," Hershy's mother interrupted, "if he really likes you."

"But I don't want him ashamed of me. A girl needs things. Lots of things. Once in my life I see the moon. And what is it? A cold face. It got no heart."

"If he'll be ashamed of you, let him do something about it," said Hershy's mother. "He's got plenty money, a car, a business. What hasn't he got? So let him."

"Sonya!" Hershy's father looked at her, shocked.

Rachel yielded completely. She ran into her bedroom. They could hear her cry. A tear formed on his father's eyelash and slid down his bony nose. Hershy could feel it slide down to the pit of his stomach. It made him forget what he wanted.

4.

David was really a hard man to understand, said Hershy's mother. How could he want so little out of life?

A hungry man, a man with great appetites, claimed Hershy's father, was always easy to understand, for he dictated how the world should live, what it should strive for. But the contented man was always hard to understand.

The contented man was a dead man, said Hershy's mother.

No, his father countered, only the contented man was alive, only the contented man could live at peace and be happy, because he didn't eat himself alive with envy and jealousy. A man content with what he has, only *he* is a rich man.

Ah, his mother was disgusted. Go talk to a Talmudist. He could go bury himself in the ages, with the dead, but she was going to stay alive with the living.

What was she going to do?

He would see.

Please, had he ever let her starve?

No, she had never starved for food. But she was starved for other things, for the beautiful things in life.

For rich things, she meant.

All right, he could call them rich things. But they were the beautiful things.

Oh, but she was a foolish woman. Oh, but she had a bulging eye.

Bulging, *shmulging*, she was going to show him who was foolish.

What in the world was happening? He was being treated like a miser, a criminal, a man not to be trusted. Why? Hadn't he worked all his life to win trust, to be looked up to, to be a man for his family and a man among men? All his life he had protected them, thought only of them. It broke his heart to deny them anything. But one had to think of tomorrow, For he was a man whose life was in his hands and whose family was dependent on them. All their lives were bound up in his two hands. What would happen if he should get crippled by a saw, if he were killed by a falling two-by-four, if he should get sick, God forbid? Didn't she realize that in his hands rested the future of their lives? (He lifted them, and Hershy saw the hard calloused fingers tremble.)

His mother ignored them. To put one's life in a man's hands, she said, could lead to only one thing in the end: being choked. One did it out of desperation, there was no choice. But now there was a choice. Business.

Business, business. His father didn't want to hear of it. He was a worker, not a boss. He thought and felt like a worker. To trample upon his whole life and become something else. He couldn't do it. He'd be a failure and be deeply hurt for trying and failing and still being gnawed with want; and his hands would never be the same again.

There was silence for a moment, in which they wandered through a wilderness of loneliness. It gave Hershy a funny feeling. He had always taken sides. Even in cops and robs, though he never wanted to be a cop, if he was put on that side he accepted it and played the part fully. But here, not being able to take sides, he felt like an indifferent spectator, and it made him lonely: for in his life, to watch was to be out of life, to play was to be part of it; watching was like dying, it made you go far away.

His mother walked away. She'd take matters in her own hands, she said.

Hershy saw how she had. He saw the Overland touring car outside the house. It belonged to the *landsman* who had been in love with his mother in the old country. He sneaked quietly into the kitchen, his heart hammering, then hid in the pantry, so that if he was caught he could pretend that he was rummaging through his drawer for his rubber-band ball or his marbles. Their voices came to him from the front room: his mother's high and clear, pitched to the ceiling; the *landsman's* low and guttural, like waves gurgling through a cave.

She needed his advice.

Anything, he assured her. From him she knew she could have anything.

Yes, she knew. He was good. He was loyal. He was a man she could trust. He could have made a woman and the children she bore him rich with happiness. Ay.

What was the trouble? Wasn't she happy?

Silence. Hershy strained his ears. What were they doing? Were they close to each other? Where were they sitting? If he could only take a peek. Should he make a sound, let them know he was there? Should he? The big noise of his heart shattered the silence, stifled his breathing, pulled him to his toes. His mother's voice broke the tension.

Happy? she asked. A moth, beating itself to death against a lighted window, was it happy? Better it should have remained in a dark closet.

Aye, if she had only married him, said the *landsman*.

Aye, if she only had. But what could she have done? For he, the *landsman*, was nothing in the old country, the son of a poor ignorant tailor, with no promise, no promise; while David, the son of a *sofer*, commanded great respect, had great promise. But who could have seen into the future, who could have gone against one's parents?

He could have made her so happy.

Why were people born with hearts and voices and minds? she said. Oh, why? Better a person should be an animal. He fills his belly and goes to sleep. He's happy. But a human being . . .

Hershy felt as though a hand shaped like a talon was clutching his throat. He could hear himself yell: Mama, Mama. His breath muffled the sound. His ears bolted his lips.

Money, the *landsman* was saying. Ah, money. The foolish spend it. The smart bold ones, like himself, go into business. The timid put it in a bank.

But what if you had a man who hated to think about business?

You suffer then. You spend it slowly until it dwindles to nothing. You die a pauper without the price of a stone for your grave. But the least one can do is draw interest from a bank.

What was interest?

Interest? It was three pennies for a dollar the bank gave you for using your money to make more money.

No!

Yes. A bank, it's made of stone and steel, but it knows what a dollar is.

Could anybody put money in a bank?

Anybody, if they knew how to write.

Why did one have to know how to write?

In America, nobody trusted a face, only a signature. Give a bank money, but to get it out the bank demanded a name on paper.

She was trapped. But perhaps the bank would let Hershel sign for her.

No, he was a child. You couldn't trust a child. He could go to the bank and draw out a thousand dollars and squander it or lose it. What does a child know about money? So a bank couldn't do business that way. Besides, what if the bank should, and what if the child, in anger or to please some friends, took the money out and ran away, then what would she do?

She was thoroughly trapped. What could she do? Whom could she trust? Oh, if only she could control the money. Oh, the curse of her ignorance.

Perhaps he could discuss it with his lawyer.

Would he?

Certainly, he would. Perhaps the lawyer could find some way of taking the money from David and putting it in her hands.

No, that frightened her. It would break up her family. David might kill her. Who knows what a man, even one so gentle as David, might do in great anger? No.

Whatever she wished.

But she would think about it. She hoped her head wouldn't burst. Now, he'd have to go. It was getting late.

Hershy heard them get up. They were walking to the frontroom door. The *landsman* sighed. His mother sighed. He peeked out. The way was clear. He sneaked out through the kitchen and sat down on the stairs off the back porch. He couldn't get himself to move any further. He even had to hold his head in his hands.

5.

Supper that evening was a glum affair. It consisted of limp boiled beef and potatoes, with red horseradish, and cabbage soup. Rachel was complaining about her foreman. He was the roaming type, but for him her body was the world over which his hands liked to roam. One of these days she was going to spit in his face and quit the job.

· *133*

Before, Hershy's father thought, he was a nice man, so she had said.

"Before, before," Rachel said angrily. "Can't a person change?"

His father glanced at her and retreated to a bone he picked out of the soup and began sucking out the marrow.

"Noo," his mother said. "What are you going to do with the money?"

His father didn't answer. He sucked the bone and wiped his teeth with his tongue. Then he pushed the plate away, cleared his throat, and said, as though everyone were relaxed:

"Well, what's new? What happened today?"

Hershy looked up startled and glanced at his mother. Nobody answered.

"I see," said his father. "The tyrant is still with us."

"Look who is talking," said Hershy's mother.

His father paid no attention to her. He turned to Hershy.

"A riddle, my son?"

"Yah," said Hershy eagerly.

"Why is a man born with his hands clenched, but when he dies his hands are wide open?"

Hershy concentrated hard, but he couldn't think, he couldn't think at all.

"Noo?"

"I don't know, Pa. Why?"

"Because on coming into the world man desires to grasp everything, but when leaving it he takes nothing away."

"That's a good one, Pa."

His father smiled triumphantly and continued: "Even as the fox who saw a fine vineyard and lusted after its grapes, but being too fat to squeeze through the only opening there was, he fasted three days before he could get in. When he did get in, he ate until he almost burst. But he could not get out until he fasted three more days. What does it mean?"

"What, Pa?"

"A man enters the world naked and naked does he leave."

"Yah, Pa?"

"Yes."

"Got another riddle, Pa?"

"Who is a hero?"

"Who?"

"He who conquers himself."

Hershy knitted his brows, trying to understand.

"That's you?" said his mother scornfully. "A conqueror?"

"That's me," said his father.

"Another one, Pa."

"Who is wise?"

"Who?"

"He who can foresee the future."

His mother interrupted again: "Philosopher!"

"Quiet," his father said. "I'm teaching from the Talmud."

"Teach him from something else. Teach him how to face life."

"Show me where there's more knowledge, more wisdom."

"In a bank. Teach him what goes on in a bank."

"All right." His father's voice rose. "Tell me, Hershel. What makes more noise: a bag with two coins or a bag filled with a hundred coins?"

"I don't know. What?"

"A bag with two coins." He glared at his mother and shook a few coins that were in his pocket. They did make a lot of noise.

"Teach him how to cash a check, how to make money out of money."

"When it's time, I will."

"But when will the time come?"

"When I find it."

"But you never have time. When you leave in the morning the banks aren't open yet. When you come home the banks are closed. You have to make time."

"But what can one do if he hasn't the time? I can't come late to work or leave the job just like that. I have to tell the foreman and then he has to see if he can let me off. And if he does let me off, I still have to lose a half-day's wages. But what's the difference if the money is on a check or if it's a figure in a bankbook? It's still paper."

"Go argue with a stubborn fool like that." She turned to Hershy and Rachel for support, trying to draw them to her side with her eyes. "What if something happens to the insurance company, then what have we got?"

"What if something happens to the bank?"

"Can one move a mule?" she complained to Hershy and Rachel. "Did you ever see a mule like that?"

"Ridicule me. Make me nothing in front of my children. All I know is this. The check is money and we don't need it now. Once it's changed to another kind of paper we will be tempted and we'll be poor again."

"Why, why did I ever marry a stubborn mule like you? I could have married anybody I wanted, men who are rich now, rich! But my mother and father had to pick on you. Why?" She turned to Rachel. "You see, Rachel, in the old country a woman had no choice. If your family said yes to a man, then you had to obey. In the old country, what was he? A poor *shnook* who had a father who was respected. Who did you marry, the man? No, you married the respect people had for his father. Here, he has no father, he has nobody. A man has only himself. And what is he? Still a nobody, begging for respect. But me, for his being so stubborn I'll give him a *fig*, that's how much respect I have for him." She closed her fist and inserted her thumb between her first two fingers, its obscene forcefulness sending a shudder through Hershy. "*Na*, here," she said, then turned to Rachel again. "Remember, Rachel, here you have a choice. Don't let any pair of pants fool you. Make the man promise you the world and hold him to that promise. Remember."

Hershy felt his father shrink, his face taking on a stunned look.

"I should have been firm," she said. "In the old country, the way he looked at my *tochas*, I should have known. I could have had anything I wanted. I could have gone to America, like I wanted, with the promise of marrying him here. And I could have carried out my plan, to go to work, pay him back for the ship ticket, and marry whom I pleased. But I was so young then, so young and afraid."

His father stumbled for words but his astonished ears held him speechless. Rachel's lower lip quivered.

"Papa means well, maybe," she said.

Yes, Hershy wanted to agree. Yes, yes, yes.

"Sure he means well," his mother said. "Everybody means well. But it's knowing what to do that's important. It's knowing how to be a man that's important."

The blood seemed to go out of his father's lips and filled the veins of his eyes. He pounded the table with his fist.

"Am I not a man?"

"No."

"Look at your belly. Feel the man I am."

"Any stupid fool can fill a woman's belly. But it takes a man to satisfy her."

He bit his lower lip and left the deep marks of his teeth on the flesh. He left the kitchen and came back with the lining of his old hat torn out. He dumped the check and all the savings on the floor.

"Take it. Spend it. Kill yourselves with it. But leave me alone. Leave me alone."

He stormed out of the house and left them looking at the money strewn on the floor. Hershy's mother sighed deeply, staring at the floor.

"Papa left without his hat and coat," she said. "He'll catch cold."

CHAPTER EIGHT

1.

That night, in his sleep, Hershy saw the silver bike roll up from nowhere, its gleaming frame and spokes so bright it hurt his eyes. In mounting it, a strange thing happened. His hair changed to orange tufts; his lips began to bulge and his nose, sticking way out of his face, got thick and red; and two black lines down his cheeks made his eyes droop. A crowd collected and began to laugh. He started to ride the bike. Though he pumped madly, the wheels spinning so fast that the spokes turned to silver disks, he hardly moved. The crowd laughed harder. Slowly, he rode up a pole, high, high, high. A silver wire stretched to another pole, a silver ping of sound shimmered up when he began to ride on it, high, lonely and far away, like the steady night whistle of a popcorn stand. Then the crowd burst into bellyaching laughter: for he began spinning like the wheels, as though they had taken control of him, with the red of his nose and the orange of his hair and the black of his cheeks and the pink of his flesh splashing through the silvery gleams of sound and motion. Suddenly with terrific force he was hurled outward, whirling, whirling, whirling, and, as the spinning slowed, he began to fall. He tried to clutch a spoke of the wheel but his hands closed upon a black void. He reached for the shimmery wave of pinging silver; it burst into fragments of black silence. He fell and fell and then leaped up in terrified fright just as he was about to hit bottom.

He stood at the doorway of his parents' bedroom, staring through the dark at their sleeping forms. They were on their sides, facing each other, with their mouths open. He wanted to get in with them and feel the warmth of their bodies, but he was afraid to wake them. A chill crept through him and he walked back to his bed. Under the covers, he heard the clock in the kitchen tick. He heard the wind in the passageway and the squeak of the swaying lamppost light. He heard the snoring of the Pole upstairs and somebody muttering in the next-door flat. From far away the bell of a streetcar clanged. A burnt coal from the stove dropped through the grate. But the stove had no light in it. There was light only from the lamppost outside; it made great shadows swing through the street.

But the following night he slept soundly. For earlier, his father came home from work and laid a bankbook on the kitchen table, just as he laid his weekly pay envelope on it victoriously every Saturday night.

"A man has to be smart," his father said. "Now, not only is our money secure, but it's also making money."

"Yes?" said his mother innocently. "And how is that?"

"The bank pays me for the pleasure of being able to look at that insurance check. Interest, they call it. Three hundred dollars a year they'll pay, just so I'll let them hold the money. Go know a thing like that. But if you live, how can you help but learn? You see, money is a responsibility. You have to learn what to do with it and then you have to learn how to live with it, otherwise you will get headaches, stomach trouble, ulcers, even a cancer, God forbid."

Hershy saw his mother smile.

"One can live like a king with three hundred extra dollars a year," his father continued. "So let's eat. Afterwards, we'll celebrate. We'll go to a nickel show. A treat from the bank."

His mother's smile broadened. It was a smile of victory.

2.

The news spread fast.

"Who, the Melovs?" people said. "Millionaires."

Neighbors stopped Hershy on the street. What was his father going to do with all that money? Hershy didn't know. Why, didn't he listen to his father's plans? Sure, he listened, but he didn't know. Ah, he was ignorant, too involved with himself, a child. But how did he feel, being the son of a rich man? He shrugged his shoulders: all right, he guessed.

Some people expressed a hollow joy over the Melovs' good fortune, but nobody really meant it; in fact, they resented it. Imagine, a dummy like David, having had a brother smart enough to insure himself and not knowing what to do with money. But what could you expect from a common worker? Oh, if they had had David's luck. Oh, what they wouldn't do. Oh, how they would make the world turn handsprings. Oh, if they only had an insured brother lying deep under the earth.

Only Uncle Hymie was sincere in his congratulations, for David was still no threat to his being the richest and most respected member of the whole family; besides, though Hershy's father had never asked him for a dime, he was now eliminated as a prospective borrower or job-seeker; Uncle Hymie could afford to be generous in his good wishes.

People were funny, Hershy's father decided. Suffer with them and you're all right. But if there's a chance that you will leave them, even if it's for a new kind of suffering, then suddenly you're a grafter, a conniver, a *no-goodnik*. Aye, people.

The talk, however, scared Hershy.

"Jesus, Hersh, you could be kidnapped."

"Ah, what are you talking?"

"Yah. They could hold you for ten thousand dollars ransom."

"Ah, they only kidnap rich kids."

"Well, ain't you rich?"

"Ah . . ."

"And then they kill you."

"Ah, shut up already."

The nights became full of shadows. In each passageway lurked a kidnapper. When alone, phantoms made him run through the streets at night, brought him heart-pounding and pale into the house, made him close the windows before going to sleep. He wished he were poor again.

He wished it harder when his mother said: "After Pesach, in the spring, we're going to move."

"Why?" his father asked.

"We'll move to the other side of the park where my sister Reva and Hymie live," she stated.

"But why?"

"Should I make you pictures? It's a better neighborhood, isn't it?"

"Sure, but better neighborhoods cost money."

"So?"

"So! Rent costs more. In the fancier stores food costs a fortune. You'll want to dress different, be like the high-tone neighbors. On my wages we can't afford it."

"We have to afford it."

"Why do we have to?"

"For our children. We have to give them a better life."

"Why? Do I hear them complain?"

"Oy," she groaned. "Do I want to move for myself?"

"For who, then?"

"For Hershel. He should be meeting nicer friends. He should know children like my sister's Manny—polite, refined, gentlemen, not the wild ruffians he knows."

"I don't want to move," Hershy said. "You think I want to live with sissies?"

"You see," she pointed out to his father. "Everybody who isn't a bum is a sissy. Is that a way to bring up a child?"

"Yah, but I won't know anybody there," Hershy argued. "I'll be all alone."

"Shut up." She glared at him, and, as he backed away, she continued: "We should move for Rachel's benefit, too."

"How is that?"

"She's getting old enough to get married. Can she bring a suitor in this house without shame?"

"Why not? We live in it, don't we? If it's good enough for us, why shouldn't it be good enough for a suitor? I don't believe in pretending. Let a suitor know who we really are—that we're plain, honest people."

"Fool, why do you think Rachel never brings a boy friend home?"

"Why?"

"Why do you think she wanders around nights, God only knows where and with whom?"

"Why?"

"Because she's ashamed of us, the house."

"It's hard to believe."

"Oh, blind one! How you love to stay blind! But a woman knows. Even a woman without a brain in her head knows so many things that a man can never hope to learn."

Hershy watched his father stare at his mother.

"In a better neighborhood," his mother argued, "she'll meet better people. Two thousand dollars you want to give her for a dowry. Doctors, lawyers, engineers, you'd like her to meet and marry. Where can she meet them: on her job, here? Only in a better neighborhood. Here, she can only meet a bum like Joey Gans. And even he's too proud, so he thinks, to come into our house."

"All right," his father said. "In the spring, we'll see."

"All right." So far as his mother was concerned, it was settled.

But for Hershy it was not all right. He didn't want to move. He didn't want to leave all the guys. He didn't want to go to a new school with sissies. He bet they didn't even know how to play ball. They were too sissy for football. He wasn't afraid of the fights he might get into. He could murder them one hand lefty. But it wouldn't be any fun fighting a bawling sissy. He would be the loneliest guy in the world. His mother was going to ruin his life. And his father, who wasn't a fighter, was going to help her. Don't let her, Pa. Be strong, put up a fight, don't let her, Pa. But he knew his mother'd win, especially now, for as she got bigger with the baby it seemed to give her more power. Gee, but he wished he was poor again.

The only thing good about being rich was a certain magic that surrounded him when he ran an errand, or decided to treat himself, at the grocer's. His mother had developed a habit of saying: "Tell the groceryman he should give it to you without money." She herself said to the grocer: "I'll buy it without money."

"For the Melovs," the grocer said, "anything."

So whenever he felt like it he went in and bought candy, fig newtons, chocolate cookies, or halvah, "without money."

At the end of the week, though, his father yelled bloody murder. He'd add up the butcher and grocer bills. He was sure that they were tacking on the debts of other people to his account.

"Cash," he'd say. "From now on, buy with cash. I don't ever want to owe anybody a penny, you hear. And you, Hershel, if you don't stop eating so much sweets you'll get diabetes."

"What's diabetes?"

"Never mind what it is. It shouldn't happen to one's worst enemy, that's all." Then, turning to Hershy's mother: "You see how money suddenly commands respects, the lowlifes. But you see, also, how people suddenly want to bleed you to death, the leeches."

But then Hershy got to hate going to the grocer's, even though he could buy things without money there. The grocer was a bowlegged little man with sharp eyes and a jerky way of moving, so that he looked like he was always ready to chase him out. His wife, who was short and fat, with thick legs and fleshy arms and the most amazing bulge of breasts he had ever seen, used to ignore him completely. But now the grocer began to swarm all over him, tousling his hair and pinching his cheeks and slapping his face tenderly, and his wife sometimes laid her heavy hand on him to draw him to her huge belly and breasts.

"Is it true your sister Rachel is going to get two thousand dollars for a dowry?"

"I don't know."

"It's what your mama said."

"If she said it she said it."

"Your papa's an angel. A man, a man."

"Yah, I guess so."

"And he wants Rachel should marry a lawyer, doesn't he?"

"I don't know."

"Our Benny is studying to be a lawyer."

Benny was a four-eyed guy, with kinky hair and a greasy face full of pimples. His studying to be a lawyer was supposed to mean something.

"So what?" he asked.

But Hershy's mother, he found out, couldn't escape them. She invited Benny over after supper one night.

"But, Ma, how could you without Rachel saying okay?" he said.

"Shut up. It's not your business."

"But she's got a guy, Joey Gans."

"Who knows about him? Do I ever see him? All he is to me is an automobile horn that makes Rachel run."

Rachel went wild when she learned of Benny's coming to meet her. "Why didn't you tell me first?"

"Because I knew you'd say no."

"If you knew I'd say no, why'd you say yes?"

"Because it's not easy to get a leech off one's back."

"Jesus Christ!"

"It won't hurt you anyhow. Maybe you'll like him."

"But I got a date tonight."

"You'll have it another night then."

"Oh, Ma. Go to the grocery and tell them I'm busy. Tell them to peddle their kid someplace else."

"No."

"Tell them I got no dowry. It was only talk from Papa anyway. And if it wasn't only talk, then here and now I give it up. Imagine, me paying off a guy to marry me; me, a girl with style. A guy wants me, *he's* got to have it. What am I, a fathead, a broken-down bum?"

"You tell him."

"All right, I'll tell him."

But Rachel didn't tell him. It seemed that Benny had just come over and had sat down in the front room, with Hershy's mother trying to get Hershy to stay in the kitchen with her and his father, when the horn began to blow. Rachel got up and said: "I'm sorry, kid, but I got a date. My mother got her signals mixed. Some other time, huh, kid?"

Hershy burst out laughing. Benny was left sitting alone, digging at the skin around his fingernails and looking at his shoes. The laughter suddenly burst into tingling stars from the slap Benny had given him.

"The bitch," Benny said, and walked out.

He opened the window and yelled after him: "Wait'll I tell Joey Gans on you. He'll kill you for that."

Benny walked on with sloping shoulders and bobbing head. Looking at him, like an empty sack, Hershy began to feel sorry for him. In the kitchen his mother cursed Rachel, but his father said it was her own fault, she shouldn't be a matchmaker, a meddler, even if the grocer and his wife had plagued her to death; this should teach her a lesson. Afterward, Hershy was glad of the incident. He was able to walk into the grocer's without being bothered.

The insurance man who had sold Hershy's father his first and only policy and who came around twice a year to collect the premium, was overjoyed at the news, but it was hard to believe his sincerity. He had a tight thin mouth set in a long dry face. When he tried to laugh or express good cheer, his high stiff collar seemed to choke him, his mouth jerked to one side, and his whole face seemed to crack from the force of the emotion. Besides that, Hershy and his father associated insurance with death; it made them feel solemn in his presence. And though the insurance man insisted that he dealt primarily with life, Hershy's father didn't believe it; a man had to be solemn in the presence of one who dealt with the bereaved and the dead. But now the insurance man was armed with a big selling point. He was not going to be done out of it. He pressed home his arguments with pinched, believe-you-me eyes, a piston-like arm, and a pointing finger. He wanted Hershy's father to take out more insurance at once, not only for himself but for the whole family.

"You see what insurance can do for you," he said.

Hershy's father saw, solemnly. He could see where insurance was important for him. His family was dependent on him and if, God forbid, something should happen, well . . .

Nothing was going to happen to him, the insurance man was confident. Why he was sure that Mr. Melov would live to be at least a hundred, a strong hard-working man like him, and he'd collect on his policy, every cent, plus interest, plus dividends, plus the money he had put in. That was the way to look at things. That was the bright way.

No, Hershy's father couldn't see it. He would feel funny if he took out insurance for Rachel and Hershy and his wife. He would feel like he was dependent on them. It was not a good way for a man to feel. He didn't like to think that their lives were being valued in dollars and cents.

But, the insurance man argued, a man didn't take out insurance against death. He took it out for life. He could save through insurance. That's why it was called life insurance.

What was wrong with saving in a bank?

Well, a bank, the insurance man was contemptuous. Money there was like money in your pocket. It was too easy to take out, too tempting. But insurance was something you paid for, something you kept, no matter what. It forced you to save money.

Hershy's mother interrupted. She had a superstition about insurance; it could put evil into one's head. If David wanted, he could take out another policy, but she wouldn't hear of having policies taken out for her or Hershy or Rachel.

Nothing else the insurance man was able to say could convince them. Hershy's father said he'd let him know later about another policy for himself. To pay money with the thought of death involved gave him the shudders.

"Did you ever see a leech like that?" said Hershy's mother after the insurance man left.

"You see," said his father, "how money doesn't let you alone."

"Holy man," said Hershy, glad to be released from the presence of death. "Everybody's got an angle. Everybody."

Peddlers, with I-should-drop-dead-if-this-isn't-an-honest-to-god-genuine-bargain, had angles, too; only Hershy felt sorry for them because his Uncle Ben was a peddler. And Hershy's mother began to wonder where all the bearded Jewish beggars had come from, asking for one donation or another; it seemed to her that they had gathered from every part of the city to her door.

And one night a neighbor, Mr. Finkel, whose wife was a friend of Hershy's mother, came over with a man to talk to Hershy's father. Hershy knew Mr. Finkel as a man who played cards in Joey Gans's place; he had sad slanting eyes, looking like he was always being gypped. The man he brought over had a tight suit on. There was a scar on his chin and a tic twitched one side of his face. He was carrying something under an oilcloth and he placed it on the kitchen table.

"Sport," he called Hershy's father, making him wince. "Call me Joe."

He wanted to talk alone to Hershy's father. What he had to say was very important, very hush-hush, strictly personal; he was going to let Hershy's father in on something he had never dreamed of. Hershy didn't want to leave the room; he was fascinated by the man's twitch and the thing under the oilcloth. Hershy's mother wouldn't leave, either: whatever the man had to discuss was for her ears also. The man shrugged his shoulders.

"Okay. Kiddies love it and ladies scream," he said. "Watch it, sport."

He removed the oilcloth and a machine something like a cash register came into view.

"Watch it carefully, sport."

Then he did the most amazing thing. He inserted a dollar through a slot, punched a few knobs, and the machine began working and buzzing like a gum slot machine. Then a bell rang, and from the bottom popped a ten-dollar bill.

"How do you like that, sport?" the man said.

"What is it?" asked Hershy's father.

"What is it!" the man laughed. "Money, hey?"

"Yes, yes, I know," said Hershy's father.

"What's the matter, ain't you never seen a ten-dollar bill?" said the man. "Here, touch it, feel it. Nice, hey? Real nice, hey?"

Hershy's father stared at the bill.

"Here, let me have a tenner," the man said. "I want you to match it. I want you to see it ain't fake. I want you to see it's the McCoy."

Hershy's father fumbled in his pocket and took out a ten-dollar bill. He looked at both of them carefully. They were exactly the same.

"From the one dollar came the ten?" he asked.

"Exactly, sport." The man slapped him on the back.

"It's really real?"

"Strictly McCoy, sport."

"David," said Hershy's mother, her eyes bulging. "Do you realize . . ."

"Man, oh man," said Hershy. "Some magic, huh?"

"I told you, sport, kiddies love it and women scream. Yep, missus. Yep, sport. Five thousand gets you fifty thousand. One dollar gets you ten, every time."

"How, what do you mean?" said Hershy's father.

"How? What do I mean? The machine, sport. The machine. What'd I do, give you a demonstration for nothing? The machine talks, I don't have to. You seen with your own eyes, didn't you? Okay, I'll show you again. Give me a dollar. I'm going to show you with your own dollar."

Hershy's father handed him a dollar. The man inserted it through the slot, and bang, out popped another ten-dollar bill.

"Now here's the pitch, sport. I understand you got ten thousand dollars. All right, I got two of these machines, but I got no money. Now this machine eats money, but before it produces ten for one you got to feed it one. So, in order to make this machine work for me, too, I need some ready cash.

150 ·

So I'm willing to part with this gold mine for five thousand. That leaves you five thousand. Right? And five times ten gets you fifty. Right? So both of us stand to make fifty thousand on this little invention a great scientist dreamed up and all our problems are over. See? Here, give me another dollar bill."

Hershy's father handed him another dollar and watched the machine with his mouth open. The man continued talking, spieling like a barker at a circus, his face twitching, his hands working, his body getting tighter and tighter. Suddenly, Hershy saw his father's mouth close and his eyes flare.

"Get out," he said.

"What do you mean, get out?" the man said. "What, are you nuts or something, giving me the shag, me, who's willing to let you in on the hottest thing man ever invented?"

"Get out, I said."

"What, have you got holes in your head or something?"

"Get out, you hear!"

Hershy's father picked up the machine and the oilcloth, thrust them into the man's hands, and pushed him out of the house.

"You, too!"

Mr. Finkel, the neighbor, lifted his eyebrows, his face looking more than ever like he had been gypped, and walked out.

Alone, Hershy's mother said: "But David, you saw with your own eyes."

"Yah, Pa," said Hershy. "It worked. Like magic, it worked."

"Shut up," his father said. "Do you want me to spend the rest of my days in jail?"

"No," said Hershy's mother. "But if it was real, who would know?"

His father dismissed her with a wave of his hand. He slumped into a chair. He said: "Do I look like an idiot, a complete idiot? Tell me, do I?"

· *151*

"No," said Hershy's mother.

"Then why do people come to me with their wild, greedy schemes?"

Hershy didn't know. His mother didn't answer.

"The two connivers. Imagine what they must think of me. Talk to him fast, Mr. Finkel must have told this man. The less sense you make the better it will be, Mr. Finkel must have told him. It hurts that I should be taken for a complete fool. It hurts hard."

What hurt more was the night Uncle Ben, the fruit peddler, came over with his wife Bronya, the oldest sister of Hershy's mother.

Uncle Ben had been a harness-maker, but when the automobile came he lost his job and couldn't get another. One day, in a rage against the machine that had made him obsolete, he took a sledgehammer and broke up an automobile on the street; as a result, he spent thirty days in jail and came out a baffled man, with the wrinkles of his forehead seeming to form in curious question marks. Logic finally came back to him, the logic of a desperate man: since he knew about a horse's equipment he should also know something about a horse, and since he came from a village that was surrounded by farms he should also know something about fruits, so he decided to get a horse and wagon and go into the fruit business. The horse, he found, became another mouth to feed and house and care for; and the wagon, he learned, became something that always needed fixing; and fruit, until he discovered the cheating ways of the men at the market, was something that turned rotten as soon as he touched it. The only pleasure he got out of the business was handling the harness, but even that got old and worn and its rough texture became an irritant. Recently, his horse had slipped on the ice and broken a leg. He had stood silent over the animal, looking into its blood-streaked eyes, pitying himself more than the horse, while somebody ran for a policeman. The horse was shot and dragged away and he had left the wagon to rot with the fruit. He was strictly a *shlimazel;* the fates were against him. Perhaps he was made to suffer, he reasoned, just so that his being might reassure those who made the world move that they were great. People said you could weep for Uncle Ben. And perhaps you could, looking at his sparse sandy hair and his tangled eyebrows and his runny gray eyes and the unkempt mustache that was wedged between the two long grooves of his cheeks; and the way he sat, as though a weight had settled on him, crushing the baffled wrinkles out of his forehead, made one squirm. His wife complemented him, her folded hands resigned in her lap, her long pale face shrouded in a shawl of tightly combed hair that was pulled into a thick biscuit, her head and shoulders rocking steadily as she sat; from time to time she sighed.

Hope, which had led Uncle Ben from one agony to another, was gnawing at him again. He knew of a newsstand he could buy; it brought in between thirty and thirty-five dollars a week.

"No!" said Hershy's father. "You mean, from little penny sales a man can make all that in a week?"

"It's the truth," said Uncle Ben. "I saw it in black and white."

"Imagine that."

There was a long silence, filled with sighs, throat clearing, and the sullen sounds of their clothes rubbing against the chairs. Uncle Ben was working hard to gather his forces and Hershy could feel his mother and father begin to retreat. It seemed that his father had suddenly assumed for Uncle Ben the position of Uncle Hymie, the one you catered to, came to for advice or for a loan; mixed with all this was also a sense of envy and contempt. His father tried to relax, make Uncle Ben comfortable, but didn't know what to do except look away from him.

"The man," said Uncle Ben finally, "is making a sacrifice. He's a sick man. He can't stand the cold. So he has to go away to a warmer climate. He is making a real sacrifice." Uncle Ben paused, trying to focus his eyes on somebody, but getting no contact (not even from Hershy, who kept identifying him with the crippled horse that was shot) he stared at his stubby calloused hands. "The man wants twelve hundred dollars."

"That's not bad," Hershy's father admitted.

"I could make that in less than a year. I figured it out in black and white. Even if it's only thirty dollars a week I could make fifteen hundred and sixty dollars, three hundred and sixty more than I'd pay in, and then the stand would be mine, all mine, all my life."

"You mean you'd pay the twelve hundred dollars back in a year and live on only three hundred and sixty?"

Uncle Ben studied the question; it seemed to bewilder him. "No," he said. "I mean . . ." He got all mixed up in his calculations, then cast them away with an incestuous curse in Russian. "But I could pay it all back, in one year or five years: what's the difference?"

There was a pause again, with everybody straining as if they were standing on their toes. Hershy had some marbles in his pocket. He picked one and flicked it against the pile. He said silently: give it to him, Pa; aw, give it to him. Then his father cleared his throat, as though there were a bone in it.

"Couldn't you get it for a thousand?" he said.

Uncle Ben seemed to leap up: "Maybe I could. The man is desperate. He is making a sacrifice. Maybe I could, maybe I could."

"A thousand dollars is a lot of money, you know."

"The man will take it. He's desperate."

"In fact, I put aside a little more than a thousand for Hershy's education."

"You have to think of the children, I know."

"Rachel has to have some money for the day she gets married. She's a big girl now. Who knows? Maybe tomorrow she'll come home with a boy and say: Pa, meet my future husband."

"I hope so, I hope so."

"Things here aren't like in the old country. It costs money to get married. Everything costs a fortune."

Uncle Ben nodded his head. Slowly, he was losing the enthusiasm he had worked up. Hershy could feel his spirit droop. His father, without realizing it, because he wanted to be kind and because he couldn't be abrupt and say no, had a need to explain his situation further.

"The new baby also needs money. If it's a boy I'll have to put some aside for his education. If it's a girl she'll need money to grow up and then more for her marriage."

"I know," said Uncle Ben dryly. "The children are very important. All we live for is the children."

"And then there will be hospital bills and doctor bills for Sonya and the new baby. What's left?"

Uncle Ben shrugged his shoulders.

"Have you asked anybody else?"

Uncle Ben nodded. "But you know what everybody thinks of me. Like in the poem by Abraham ibn Ezra:

> *"If I sold shrouds,*
> *No one would die.*
> *If I sold lamps,*
> *Then, in the sky*
> *The sun, for spite,*
> *Would shine by night."*

· *155*

Aunt Bronya stopped her weary rocking and sighing a moment to say: "True, true. Once a *shlimazel* always a *shlimazel.*"

"Words, everybody is willing to give me," said Uncle Ben. "Even my silent horse, who didn't have any words, told me what he thought of me. Once, when I was washing him he spread his legs and peed on me. Another time he lifted up his tail and farted right in my face. At least, he was honest."

"Did you ask Hymie?"

"You know Hymie. He's so stuffed with money, his guts should only turn green with it, that he can't even get his finger in to pull any of it out."

"Then what can I do? You know I'm not a rich man. All right, I have a few extra dollars now to protect me and my family, should anything happen. But all I am, really, is a hard worker who lives only on his wages."

"But I'll pay you back, David."

"Yes, but how? To put so much money, twelve hundred dollars, into a business and get so little in return seems scandalous. Money goes, nobody knows where. And if you don't pay me, can I become a tyrant and demand it, can I take it out of your mouth and the mouths of your children? What if I should need the money before you can pay it up? Can I ask you to sell the stand? Can I force you to do a thing like that? And if I could, would I be able to? Would I be able to see you and your children go hungry? It's such a hard thing you ask of me."

"But what can happen? You're working. You and your family, may God protect you from any evil, you're strong and healthy. What can happen that you might want to need the money suddenly?"

"Who knows? But I remember the days when I wasn't working, when we almost starved from hunger and couldn't pay the rent, when I walked the streets trying to make a penny while swallowing my own bitter gall. Look what's happening in the world: revolutions, strikes, maybe a depression, the papers say, even the cost of a piece of bread makes it almost a luxury. And what if something happens to me? Will you work and earn a living for me and my family?"

"Then you won't give me the money?"

"If I were a rich man, I'd say all right. But what have I got, a little security, through the heavenly grace of my poor brother? Even I, with a little money, am I thinking of business? What is it with this business-business? Can't a man be happy without a business?"

The contempt finally came out of Uncle Ben: "Don't talk about you and me. We're two different people."

"Oh, how you confuse me."

"I should be so confused."

"Look, Ben." Hershy's father leaned across the table and put his hand on Uncle Ben's shoulder. "Buy another horse and become a fruit peddler again. It made you a living before and it's something you know about."

Uncle Ben shrugged the placating hand away. "No. Never again."

"I could give you the money for a horse, even for a wagon and your first load of fruit. But twelve hundred dollars, that's a fortune."

"Don't do me any favors. I don't want the rest of my life harnessed to a dumb animal."

"Don't dream so big, Ben. You got along before with a horse, why not again?"

"Don't tell me how to dream. Because you have some money, it doesn't make you a boss over me. Remember, you're still David Melov, a common worker."

"Listen to reason, please, Ben."

"Go to hell with your reason."

Hershy's father began to show anger. "Do me a favor and

go to hell yourself if you won't listen to reason. Do what millions of other men have to do to live: go get a job."

"Don't tell me what to do. Don't forget, I'm not used to taking orders any more. The horse taught me how to give orders. Remember?"

"How can I talk to a man like you?"

"Then don't talk to me. I don't care if we never talk again. But if you should want to talk to me, talk to me with money. Come, Bronya." Uncle Ben rose, took Aunt Bronya by the hand and pulled her to her feet. "And may your insides, too, turn green with the money you're stuffed with."

Hershy watched his mother and father stare at each other after Uncle Ben and Aunt Bronya left.

"Gee," he said, feeling he had to say something, "I'll bet if we ever go to their house, their kids'll never play with me. They'll be mad on me."

"Don't worry," his mother said. "You have plenty of other bums to play with."

His father paid no attention to him. "Sonya," he said. "Did I do wrong?"

"No."

"But maybe I should have given him the money. He'll pay me back."

"That *shlimazel?* Never."

"But it's for your sister, too."

"I don't care. We have to think of ourselves first."

"The money feels like a bone in my throat."

"If you had agreed to give him the money, I'd have killed you."

Hershy's father looked up at the ceiling: a habit, Hershy noticed, he was getting into lately.

"Ay, Yussel, Yussel," he said. "You meant good, but look what it's doing to us."

158 ·

3.

Hershy's mother couldn't let the matter about Uncle Ben rest. She was afraid that Uncle Ben and her sister Bronya might gossip to all the *landsmen,* that they might create the impression that she and David had hearts of stone. She was certain that she and David had treated Uncle Ben right, but she needed assurance; she needed people to stand up for her good name. She took Hershy along to the West Side to visit her sister Mascha and Uncle Irving, who lived on the same street as Uncle Ben. Hershy's cousins, Louie and Charley, were at a movie, and he moved about restlessly as his mother explained her plight.

Uncle Irving said: "Poison, I'd have given him."

Hershy watched his mother agree eagerly.

"What right does a man have to ask for all that money?" Uncle Irving said. "What does Ben think—you owe him a living, you have nothing to do but squander your money on him? He's crazy."

Hershy's mother patted Uncle Irving's hand. "Irving," she said. "You're a man with sense. I knew you'd understand."

Uncle Irving went on. "What if you should want to go into business yourself? Then what would you do?"

"Yes," said Hershy's mother. "What would I do?"

"Is David thinking of going into business?"

Hershy's mother shrugged her shoulders.

"He should take his time," said Uncle Irving firmly. "He should know what he's doing. He should be careful."

"Sometimes a man can take too much time."

"Now," said Uncle Irving, rubbing his hands, his eyes lighting up. "If a man should come to David with a proposition where he could make a lot of money, then he'd really have something to offer, hah?"

Hershy's mother placed her hands on her belly, as though protecting the baby within her.

"If a man, say, like myself," Uncle Irving continued, "were to come to David and say: 'David, I have a proposition that will make you a fortune—' that would really be something, wouldn't it?"

Hershy saw that though his mother nodded she wasn't convinced. Uncle Irving smiled and patted her knee.

"Don't worry about Ben," he said. "I know your heart is bleeding for him. He had no right to ask you for all that money. He had no right to torture you. He should go to work."

Hershy was glad when Uncle Irving's kids, Louie and Charley, came home from the movie. He went outside with them and played run-sheep-run with a gang of other guys.

After the game, since his mother hadn't called him yet, he went over to one of the lampposts with Louie and Charley to watch the crap game.

"Jiggers," said Louie. "There's Itzik."

Itzik was Uncle Ben's oldest son, who was a couple years older than Hershy. He had a soft down of hair on his face and pimples were beginning to break out. He had lost a dime in the game. He was broke but still he watched the game anxiously.

"So what?" said Hershy.

"He'll cockalize you."

"Yah, for what?"

Itzik saw him. "What are you doing around here, punk?"

"Nothing. My ma's by Aunt Mascha."

"Beat it, you cheap sonofabitch."

"I won't."

"Then give me a nickel."

"I ain't got it."

"Yah? You and your cheap kike of an old man."

Itzik hit him and knocked him down. Hershy got up and

160 ·

rushed at him. Itzik hit him again and knocked him down. Hershy got up, bursting with rage, but Louie and Charley and a few other kids held him back. They dragged him away from the crap game. When his mother saw him she yelled: "I told you not to go outside."

He didn't answer her.

"Why'd he hit you?"

"You know why."

"I'll kill him, that bum."

On the way to the streetcar they approached the crap game. Hershy's mother walked over to Itzik and slapped him full across the face. Itzik felt his cheek in amazement, then laughter broke out from under the lamppost, and, as Hershy and his mother hurried away, Itzik broke out into a volley of curses. But Hershy didn't feel any better over his mother striking Itzik. He still wished he was poor again.

4.

It was important, of course, also to get Uncle Hymie's reactions, solace, and advice. Uncle Hymie rose to the occasion.

"To a bank you should have told him to go, that *shlimazel*," he said.

Hershy's father had dealt with Uncle Ben exactly right. After all, he (Uncle Hymie) was a man who dealt with banks. He dealt with a loan association and countless insurance companies and manufacturers of all sorts; he had a hundred people working for him; in short, he was a man who ought to know about such matters. Even the way he lived was proof that he ought to know. Look at the way he dressed. A sport, everybody called him. Look at the way his wife dressed. A society lady, everybody called her. And the children, Manny and Shirley; did one have to ask about them? Off the fat of the land they lived. And look at the house he lived in. It was his own. But would he have risen to where he was today if he had let himself cry over every *shlimiel* and *shlimazel* who had come to him with a greedy hand and a tale of woe? "You bet your life, no," he said.

Uncle Hymie paced the floor. A discussion of finance always brought him to his feet and made him move; it charged his wiry body and reddened his blunt face and intensified the nervous blink of his eyes.

"Hymie," Aunt Reva said. "You'll wear out the rug."

"Shut up. A man is talking."

"Don't aggravate yourself, please, Hymie. You'll go to sleep with a bellyache tonight. The doctor said you have to be careful with the ulcer."

"Shut up already."

Aunt Reva retreated to a corner of the couch. Uncle Hymie breathed deeply, unfettered at last, and continued.

When he needed money, where did he go: to David, Ben, Irving? He went to a bank. (Of course, he didn't say that his partner, whom he was planning to get rid of now, had a capital investment in the laundry and that he was able to borrow money on the strength of it; that was ancient history.) And he had to pay back every penny with a heavy six per-cent interest right on time.

What was money: something you found on the streets, something you tore up into confietti to make hula-hula on a holiday? People sailed around the world and discovered new lands in search for it; that was how America was born. People lived like beasts and suffered untold hardships to dig it out of the earth, so that they could become free men and do anything they wanted. People even killed for money, even themselves. It was a curse, sure. It was evil, too. It could even make a slave of you, all right. But a man without money was always a slave. With it, he had a chance for freedom.

But there was a secret to money. The secret gave it life: power. Without knowledge of the secret, money was useless. What was the secret? Very simple. Something the banks, the merchants, the manufacturers, and the landowners had learned long ago. The secret was so simple that he was afraid everybody was going to laugh. Here is what it was: money had to be used; its only value was in making more money; like a magnet, it had to draw everything to itself or it was nothing. The secret was that simple.

"You hear, David?" said Hershy's mother.

"I hear."

"Listen to a man who knows."

Uncle Hymie smiled, pleased. Aunt Reva, looking worried, was about to open her mouth. Uncle Hymie knifed her with his eyes and said: "Shut up."

Uncle Hymie was really wound up. He continued. "Can a hungry man go to a bank and say: 'Lend me a dollar so that I might fill up my belly?' The bank says: 'What is your security?' And if the man says: 'Me; if my belly is filled, I'll be able to work, and then I'll be able to pay you back . . .' do you think the bank is interested in the man's belly? No. Because what's a belly? The man might go and poison himself with food, who knows? So where will the bank get its dollar back with six cents interest, from the stones in the pauper's grave? But if you ask a bank for money to build a factory or a building, or if you need a loan to buy machinery, then, if the bank knows that if you can't pay up it will profit more by your misfortune, then you're a good man, you're a gem, you're a regular *allrightnik*. Bellies, nobody is interested in. But a building, a business, securities, a piece of machinery, everybody is interested in. That's the world. A piece of iron is more important than a man. Go change it."

"All right, my *allrightnik*," said Aunt Reva. "Stop talking before you wear out both your belly and the rug."

On the way home, Hershy's father said: "It's a funny thing about a man in business—he thinks he knows everything."

"Doesn't he?" said Hershy's mother.

"I don't know. Sometimes when I look at him now I can hardly recognize him. He used to be a socialist. Now look at him. The sweat has dried out of him and he appears like the iron that has become more important to him than a man. Money, he says, gives you freedom. But I see him as a man who is in a deep dungeon, chained to a dollar."

"I should only be chained like he is."

"What do you think, Hershel?" his father asked.

"I think Uncle Hymie stinks," said Hershy. "He never lets me drive his car. He only lets me sit in it and turn the wheel. He's full of hot air."

5.

The conversation didn't end there. It continued after Hershy got into bed. Their talk came to him from the kitchen. He listened intently, afraid to fall asleep. He was afraid that if he fell asleep he'd wake up in a strange world where everything had changed. Even now, nothing seemed the same any more. He lay hard against the bed. And yet, though he felt the whole surface of his body against the mattress, he felt himself dangling.

Uncle Hymie was right, his mother said. Money had to be used. Money could make you free. It could release you from the drudgery of the kitchen; it could free you from being a slave to a landlord and a boss and a piece of bread; it could open up your life and fling you into a world you never dreamed of; it could make a waltz of life. She'd be the happiest person in the world if she knew that she wouldn't be on her hands and knees scrubbing the floors a few days after the baby was born, if she was sure that she was going to have some help, if she knew that she was living in a larger flat with steam or furnace heat, if she knew that she wouldn't have to kill herself hunting and fighting for bargains. What was a person without money? He was a nothing. In the old country, if a man could read or write and had a trade, he was respected, he was an important man of the community, he was a somebody. Here, you could be a philosopher, but if you didn't have money you were a nobody.

"Talk, talk, talk," Hershy muttered.

Here, said his father, a woman got into a man's pants and never left him alone. What was it with the air here that made a woman go crazy with the desire to become a man?

Here, said his mother, a woman got into a man's pants to put a fire in him. Here, a whole new world had opened. A woman grasped the importance. A man, however, could continue to stumble blindly from his job to his bed.

Oh, what happened to a man here! said his father. He is pecked, pecked, pecked. Instead of being stronger with the security of money he had grown weaker, he was slowly being undermined. He had become like a wounded chicken. . . .

Hershy shut his eyes tight against the image that flashed through his mind. It was of himself, on his hands and knees, looking through a basement window, watching the *shochet* slaughter chickens. Zip, the throat was cut. Splash, the blood shot out. Whop, the chicken was flung away, regurgitating as it ran about, growing weaker and weaker and finally dropping in a pool of blood. Next. The *shochet's* razor flashed. Blood spurted out of the chicken's throat. Suddenly, the cackling and the flapping of wings became furious: a chicken tore free from its coop, pounced on the wounded chicken, immediately pecked it to death. The sight, when one of the wounded chicken's eyes was punctured, made him turn away with nausea.

"Leave him alone," he yelled inwardly. "Leave him alone."

The image remained as the talk went on.

There, his father said, a woman had her place. She wore a skirt. A man raised his hand and there was silence. A man beat the woman and she whimpered with pleasure. Here, a man became nothing. A woman tried to take away the very thing that made a man a man. What was she trying to do to him?

She only wanted to make him a greater man; a man of importance; a man, who, with a glance, would command respect; a man who would give his children every chance to grow into powerful figures in the land.

So what did she want of him?

A man, she continued, who did not make a place in the world for his children would never be remembered.

All right, what did she want of him?

She wanted him to use the money.

He had already spent it.

How? In small dreams, in a future that belonged to nobody and that would amount to nothing?

He thought he had spent it wisely, unselfishly.

He had spent nothing, she said. He had only talked. There was no future in holding money in a bank. If he lost his job or got sick the money would be gone before they could look around.

What was the matter with her? his father wanted to know. Didn't she sleep well at night any more?

No. She could feel the baby stirring in her. Feel, she said. Feel the baby in her belly.

A little life, he commented.

It will want a big life.

Everybody wants. Doesn't anybody ever want to give?

Not in this world.

Yes, he admitted sadly.

"Aw, go to sleep already," Hershy said, not loud enough to be heard. But his mother was far from getting ready for bed.

They had to start thinking about using the money, she said. God had taken away a life and had given them a gift. If life and death had meaning, if there was an order to God's world, then it was up to them to find it. The meaning she had discovered was that God had taken away a life in order to make room for a new life. God, in his kindness, to make up for David's grief, had made his seeds potent after all these years and had given her body the strength to make them grow. A new life was coming, growing bigger and bigger every day, making more and more demands. Soon it would burst into the world to make more demands, and she wanted to be able to give it more than a breast full of milk and a kind pat on the head. Not only that, God had suddenly given them the means to make a new life for everybody. It was up to them to fulfill God's graciousness.

What else had she discovered in her sleepless nights?

How, she countered, does a man make a new life if suddenly he finds money in his hands?

He doesn't spend it, that's certain.

No, she agreed. He uses it. He uses it to make more money. He buys his freedom with it. He creates a bigger and richer world for himself and his family. He goes into business.

What kind of business?

Any kind, so long as it was good.

What was good?

A cabinet-making factory. After all, he was a cabinet-maker, wasn't he?

He wanted her to talk sense. A business like that took heavy heavy thousands.

What about being a contractor? He was a carpenter. He was a builder. What more did it take to be a contractor?

· *167*

Oh, but he wished she'd talk sense. What was he, a millionaire?

All right, a dry goods store. Did one have to know much to own a dry goods store? Goods was goods. Everybody knew about goods.

No, he knew nothing about goods.

Did he know anything?

Yes. He knew that he was getting sleepy.

"Yah," Hershy said silently. "Go on to sleep already. Leave him alone already, will you, Ma? Will you leave him alone?"

Look, his mother said. What about a delicatessen store? What did one have to know to handle that?

Nothing, his father admitted. But he would not be chained day and night to a sawdust floor, with his children living out of a pop bottle.

A laundry.

No, he knew nothing about that.

Hershy saw his father become smaller and smaller, his mother larger and larger, himself crushed between them.

But look at Hymie, she said. He was an ignoramus. Like David, at one time he knew about nothing but a saw and a piece of wood. But when he lost a job in his trade he looked about him and said: No, if a man spends his life learning a trade only to find that he can't work steady at it, then it wasn't for him. It took a man to make a decision like that. So what did he do? He took a job as a laundry driver. He saw it was a new business. It was growing. It was being a maid for people who couldn't afford to hire a human being to slave for them but who could afford a dollar for a bundle of wash. He saw all that. And then when the opportunity came he bought into a laundry and became a success. Did that take a great wisdom, a great brain?

No, his father admitted.

Did Hymie have more brains than he?

No.

Why, what he had in his little finger, Hymie could never hope to have in his whole head. So what did it take? Only a little courage. Only a little.

But Hymie didn't have a heart.

She was convinced that even a man with a heart could become a success.

But what if he went into a business with a heart and then had it cut out of him? How would people be able to bear him? How would he be able to bear himself?

That was not a thing he had to concern himself with. His job was to look to the future. His job was to change his world.

But what if he should fail?

Why should he fail? Why should he even think of it?

But people had failed. People do fail.

Oh, his mother groaned. Why hadn't she married a man with the heart of a lion.

Oh, his father answered, what a burden he was carrying. A beast was on his back.

Hershy felt the beast pounce on his father. It was a life and death struggle. He tried to help, but the beast flung him away. He had to stand on the side and watch. Kill him, Pa. Oh, kill him, Pa.

"Yussele, Yussele," he heard his father say. "Help me."

CHAPTER NINE

1.

Hershy's mother, with her frustrations growing deeper during this time, turned to Rachel to find release. She suppressed her own envy and watched the excitement filling up Rachel's life.

"Rachel doesn't know from nothing," she said. "Oh, to live, and not know from nothing."

"I'm floating," Rachel said. "Floating."

"Rachel's in love," Hershy's mother announced.

"Love," said Hershy's father. "What can a girl of seventeen know about love?"

"More than a woman of twenty-eight," Hershy's mother answered. "I assure you. After all, how old was I when I was married?"

"That was different," his father said. "In the old country people grew up faster. A man was a man when he was thirteen. A girl was a woman before she could look around. People were more responsible there."

"Is that what love is: responsibility?" his mother asked.

"Why not? Is love more than that? Can it be more?"

"Don't talk like an idiot."

Hershy's comment was: "I'm going out and play on the merry-go-round."

Love, for him, was mush. It had no body. You could put your heel in it, and when you lifted your foot it made a squishy, sucking sound. Love had no muscle. It made you fall apart.

Love, for his father, was not a dreamy eye, an empty song, a veil of sighs, a melted nerve. Romance was something he didn't understand; that was for people with leisure; he had never had any time for it. Love was responsibility, a belief in people, loyalty, respect. Love was giving without expecting anything in return. Perhaps there was romance in memory. But love was always reduced to feeding and being fed, to living in a house that was clean and warm and weatherproof, to having children and caring for them, to respecting those who live with you, and to bearing the full responsibility of your life and those you surround it with. Everything else was sham, bubbles in a vault of pins.

But love, for his mother, was something sacred. Like God, it was something you couldn't describe, it was something you couldn't name. Like God, she knew what it wasn't and evoked images of what it was. It wasn't obedience or duty or bearing children or having worries or being responsible. It had to give one a sense of being transported to a new world, where the heavens lifted and a star was given to you for a jewel, and you had to feel that you were conquering and being conquered all at once. That was love. And for a moment of this she was willing to endure torture the rest of her life. For her, Rachel expressed all this, in the dreamy sway of her head, in the way she seemed to flow through the house, in the songs that vibrated from her.

"Rachel, where were you last night?"
"In a night club."
"No!"
"Yah."
"Imagine."
"Yah, Ma. All the people there, dressed to kill. All the music.

All the soft lights. All the fun. Ah, Ma, you should have been there."

"Ay."

"I could have danced all night long."

"Is he a good dancer?"

"I get dizzy, he's so good."

"Ay, Rachel, Rachel. I never danced."

"Everybody knows him. Everybody says hello to him. Even judges, big lawyers, people with diamonds on their fingers. He makes me feel like nothing can ever happen to me. I feel like a baby with him, so safe."

"A strong man, hah?"

"A power. A real power."

"Oh, to have a man of strength."

"But he's soft, too, Ma. I'm his soft spot."

"Imagine, strong and soft."

"He asks me what music I like to hear. 'Angel music?' he says. 'Angel music,' I say. He tells the orchestra to play. 'Play for my doll,' he says. 'My baby likes angel music,' he says. 'Play,' he says. And they play. For me, they play."

"And then?"

"And then I come home."

"Does he try to kiss you?"

"What a question!"

"I only ask, Rachel. But you want to be careful. A kiss can lead to tragedy."

"Don't worry. I'm careful."

"Is he in love with you?"

"I hope so."

"Are you with him?"

"What a question, Ma!"

"I only ask. What does it feel like?"

"Aw, Ma, the way you talk, like you never been in love. You know: you can't even breathe."

"But how does he express his love?"

"In the way he looks, in the way he can hardly talk, in the way he says: 'Say the word, baby (that's what he calls me: baby). I'll make the world shove over. I'll put rocks on your fingers. I'll cover you with mink from head to toe. Say the word, baby.'"

"What kind of word do you have to say?"

"It's just an expression, Ma."

"So why don't you marry him?"

"He didn't ask me yet."

"Oh."

"Someday soon, he says, he's going to get me on the stage. He's working on a connection."

"If he wants to marry you, why should he want you on the stage?"

"Because I want it."

"Where do you think you are now, if not on a stage?"

"You got something there, Ma."

"So when are we going to meet him?"

"Later, later."

"What's the matter? Are you afraid I'll steal him from you?"

"No, Ma."

"I'd like to meet him. It's only right that he should meet your family."

"Later, Ma. Later."

She looked at Rachel, nodding slowly, and a great gap seemed to open in her, leaving a bleakness in her glazed eyes. But Hershy's father reacted differently. "What a fool you are, Sonya," he said, "throwing yourself into the world of a child. You should be grown up; but, really, you're like a child."

For he had met Joey Gans one day when walking down the street with Hershy. Joey was leaning against the building of his restaurant, his face tightening and relaxing as he worked on a pair of springs in his hands.

· *173*

"There he is," said Hershy.

"Who?"

"Joey Gans."

"Hyah, kid," said Joey. He spit through the side of his mouth, a gesture which Hershy had been practicing, and rumpled Hershy's hair with his big thick hand.

"Okay," said Hershy, looking up.

"That's a kid, kid. And how's Rae?"

"Okay, too."

"That the old man?"

"Yah, that's my pa."

"How's the boy, kid?" Joey put the springs in his coat pocket and shook hands with Hershy's father. Hershy watched his father wince with pain from the pressure. Then, released, Hershy sensed that his father wanted to say something, in the way his throat was strained and in the way he groped for his (Hershy's) hand as he stared at Joey.

"Want to shoot a game of pool, a bite to eat?" Joey asked.

His father shook his head.

"Any time. It'll be on the house. It'll be on Joey Gans."

His father began to move away.

"See you, Pops," said Joey.

His father came into the house as though suffering from a blow. He had got it from a golem, a man with no soul, whose head was stuffed with a fist instead of a brain. What could a man like that know about love, about such a sensitive thing? What could Rachel, spawned from his own family, see in a man like that? Could it be that he didn't know Rachel at all, that he had seen her grow up only to feel that she was a stranger? The thought was shattering. It shook him with great fears for Rachel. He wished he could do something. He wished he could have threatened the man. But as he had stood before him he knew that if he had opened his mouth the man would have pushed his fist into it; he was a frightening man. He wished he could say something to Rachel. If he could only threaten her. But he had nothing to threaten her with. Besides, he was a man who was incapable of doing such a thing. But he didn't want Hershy's mother to encourage Rachel any more; he didn't want her to go into the silly dreams and emotions of a child. Meanwhile, he would talk to Rachel.

Hershy had seldom seen him so disturbed. Even his mother, sensing it, remained silent.

But when his father did talk to Rachel that night he only antagonized her.

"So what do you want me to do?" she said.

"Find someone else, an honest, upright man."

"You mean a working stiff? You can have them kind a nickel a dozen. Remember, this ain't the old country. Here, you don't match people up before you ever see them and then wind up saying until death do us part. Here, a girl's got a choice."

"But make a good one, Rachel. This bum is no good. All he'll ever give you is trouble."

"That's for me to decide."

"Listen to me, Rachel," he pleaded. "For your own good."

"For my own good, leave me alone."

His father, not knowing what else to say, grew tense. "If I could only pound some sense into your head," he said.

"Don't try it. Remember, you're not my real pa."

Hershy saw his father reel back. His eyes became glazed and he sat down limp. It was a blow, he said after Rachel left, he'd never recover from.

2.

The following day, Hershy's father didn't come home for supper. Waiting for him, Hershy had seen the men

· *175*

come home from work and the kids go into their houses to eat. He had seen the day die and the lights on the lampposts go on. The street was quiet and the houses seemed to have retreated in shadows. A terrible fit of loneliness came over him. Then his mother called him.

"All right," she said. "We'll eat without Pa."

Rachel was sitting at the kitchen table in a kimono, her face glowing from a bath. His mother began to serve him and Rachel: a *milchidige* (dairy) meal; pickled herring, boiled potatoes with sour cream, and spinach borsht.

"Maybe Pa'll be mad if we eat without him," Hershy said.

"Eat," his mother said. "Let him be mad enough to burst when he comes home, but if he can't come home on time I won't feed him. I'll teach him a lesson."

He turned away from her, hardly able to recognize her, not only because she was getting bigger with the baby but also because she was so stirred up.

"Maybe Pa ain't home because he's mad on Rachel," he said.

"Why should he be mad on me?" Rachel asked.

"You know why. You know plenty why. You made him hurt."

"Who? Me?"

"Yah. You."

Rachel looked at his mother.

"Did I, Ma?" she asked. "Did I?"

Hershy's mother didn't answer.

"Ah, Pa ain't the kind of guy to stay mad," Rachel said. "He's too sweet a guy."

"So why'd you make him look like he was punched in the nose?"

"Ah, shut up. I feel bad enough as it is." Rachel turned to Hershy's mother. "Pa ain't mad, is he?"

His mother didn't answer.

"A girl's got a life of her own, ain't she?" said Rachel.

"Eat," said Hershy's mother. "The food will get cold."

Hershy looked down to the food. What was she talking about? The food, except for the boiled potatoes, was served cold.

"What'd I do, stand up for my rights?" said Rachel. "What do I have to do: say excuse me for living? All right, excuse me for living."

"Maybe," said Hershy's mother, placing a glass of milk and a plate of chocolate-covered cookies in front of him, "Papa's working overtime."

"Yah," said Rachel eagerly. "Sometimes a rush job comes in. You have to stay until it's finished. That's a job for you."

"Yes," said Hershy's mother. "A man's time, unless he's in business, is never his own. A workingman never belongs to his wife or his family, not even to himself: he belongs to a boss, a factory, a piece of machinery, a tool. Remember that, Hershel."

Hershy nodded. All right, he'd remember. If he had to remember everything he'd have to have a head bigger than the moon.

Rachel pushed away from the table and stood up.

"I have to get a move on," she said. "I got a date. But when Pa comes home tell him I'm sorry and tell him not to be mad. Okay?"

"Tell him yourself," said Hershy's mother.

"Tomorrow, I'll tell him. Tonight, I've got to rush."

"Can't you ever stay home?"

"Aw, Ma."

"Like a wild Indian you live. Night after night, rush, rush, rush, *hoolya, hoolya, hoolya*. You'll go crazy living like that."

"Aw, Ma."

"But what do you do night after night?"

Rachel didn't answer.

· *177*

"Are you careful, at least? Papa'd go crazy if anything'd happen to you. That's why he worries about you. It'd kill him if anything happened."

"Yah," said Hershy, as though for his father, "Whyn't you stay home sometime?"

"You shut up, Hershy."

"It's not your business, Hershel," his mother said.

"It is, too," he said. "People talk."

"Who?" his mother wanted to know.

"People."

He didn't know exactly who. The kids shut up when he was around. But he felt that they talked. His father's fears disturbed him. If Rachel shamed him and his family he'd kill her. But he wanted her to go out with Joey, too. It made him important. It made him feel safe. But his father's fears mixed him up. He wished everything was easy. He wished everything was like before.

"Let people talk," said Rachel. "I know what I'm doing."

"That's the trouble," said Hershy's mother. "You know too much. These days, a girl knows too much."

"Aw, relax, Ma. I wasn't born yesterday."

"That's the trouble. Now you're old enough. And with men now it's *tochas aufen tisch*, you can't hide behind long bloomers and a corset made of bone, they don't stand for monkey business."

Rachel looked steadily at her. "I thought you were on my side, Ma," she said.

"I'm on Papa's side, too. I'm on the side of respect. We have to live with our name."

"A name, a name. You live and die and who remembers you?"

"But until you die people talk."

"Talk is cheap. You can buy it for a nickel in any phone booth."

Rachel's eyes filled with tears. She seemed to fling herself out of the kitchen. She shut the door of her bedroom. When she came out, dressed in a red taffeta gown with a low hipline and a silver spangle shaped like a flower above her plump breast, Hershy watched his mother's face soften, as though, after relenting, she had moved into Rachel's position. Looking at her, Rachel's set face relaxed and her eyes began to sparkle. Women, thought Hershy. Go understand them.

Just then an automobile horn began tooting and the sparkle in Rachel's eyes seemed to fizz out like a roman candle.

"Be careful, Rachel. Be careful."

"I will, Ma. I will."

Rachel rushed out of the house. Hershy and his mother watched from the window as she got into the touring car. After it sped away, his mother said:

"She'll freeze to death."

3.

Back in the kitchen, waiting but averting the thought of Hershy's father not being home, his mother began to question him about Joey Gans. She knew that he owned a restaurant with his brother and that it had a poolroom in the back, where gambling went on, and she warned Hershy that if she ever caught him in there she'd kill him. She knew also that Joey's father was a melamed, a Hebrew teacher. That was in his favor. He had money, too. That was more in his favor. And he was respected, too. But was it true that the goyim stood in holy terror of him?

"Yah," said Hershy.

"Like a king? Like a Samson?"

"Yah."

"Then how could he be bad? He protects people, he doesn't kill them."

"Joey ain't a bad guy. Only Pa's afraid he is."

"Papa doesn't know everything. But if I could only see his face. If I saw him, I'd know. What does he look like?"

"Big. Strong. A giant. He got a fist like a sledgehammer. Muscles like a horse. A face so strong it always needs a shave."

"You call that a description? What does he really look like?"

"I told you, for Cry Yike."

"His eyes, for instance. What are they like?"

"I don't know. Maybe like William S. Hart, the cowboy, or Tom Mix."

"Like them, God forbid? It isn't possible. What could Rachel see in a pair of stones like they have? Are you sure Joey hasn't a pair of eyes like the moving-picture stars, Charles Ray or Wallace Reid?"

"Who? Them sissies?"

"Ach, go out and play and leave me alone. From you I'll find out nothing, absolutely nothing."

"Okay. So I don't know. So I'll go out and play."

He didn't have much fun playing. For the first time in his life he became conscious of not being wholly involved in a game. He couldn't name what was bothering him; it was something; it made him feel very peculiar. Before, when he went into a game reluctantly because of some anger or irritation, the magic of the street, through the guys and the game itself, would lift him up and hurl him right into its spirit, completely absorbed. Now, he couldn't feel it, he couldn't get lost. What was happening to him? he wondered.

"Hey, what's a matter, Hershy?"

"Nothing."

"Ah, come on, it's your turn."

There was a ball. There were two guys. One was the catcher at home plate; the other was supposed to be the third baseman. He was supposed to steal home but they had trapped him, were closing in on him as he shuttled between them, the ball that was to tag him being tossed back and forth, whirling in a yellow orbit of light under the swaying arc of the lamppost, its whacking sound accenting the excited voices surrounding him. For a moment, scuffing and scampering back and forth, his eyes as intense and wary as the hunted, the ball seemed to lift him away from himself and socked him right into the game. Suddenly he felt that he himself had become the ball, being tossed back and forth over a crazy crouched shadow, and he stopped and was tagged out.

"Hey, what's a matter, Hershy?"

"Nothing."

"Just when you was ready to slide into home plate, zippo, you stop and get tagged out."

"I know."

"Just when you was going to be safe, zingo."

"Yah," he said.

He left before the game was finished. His mother was looking at the clock in the kitchen.

"Pa home yet?" he asked.

"No. Where were you?"

"Playing."

She had the bankbook in her hand and drummed it on the table. "Where could he be?'" she asked.

"Maybe working overtime, you said."

"God, I hope so."

"Why? You think something happened?"

"Don't say that."

"Why? What'd I say?"

"Don't even think it."

"I didn't think nothing."

"Then shut up."

He shut up. The clock ticked loud. The minute hand hardly moved. The hour hand was still, so still in the ticking sound. His mother had her eyes on the clock, but her eyes

· *181*

looked blurred. She shuddered each time the minute hand jerked a space.

"He never worked so late before," she said.

Hershy didn't know what to say. He hardly knew what to think. He had a superstition that if you thought about anything steadily it would become real. He didn't want what was trying to get into his head to become real.

"Where could he be?" she asked. "What could have happened?"

"Don't worry, Ma. He'll be home."

"Certainly, he'll be home. Where could he go? But what if something happened?"

"What, Ma?" A hard lump suddenly formed in his throat. "What could happen?"

"Shut up and go to sleep. Take a glass of milk and go to sleep."

She rose and brought a bottle of milk out of the icebox and poured a glassful. Then she cut a slice of pumpernickel bread.

"Here," she said.

Hershy dunked the bread in the milk, and, as he ate and swallowed, without being able to wash down the lump in his throat, his mother, as though answering the ticking of the clock, said: "Nothing happened. He'll be home soon. Nothing happened." It was exactly what he was saying to himself; it had to become real; he was saying it often enough in his head.

Then, thinking out loud, with woeful creases bunching up her face, she said: "If something happened, what would happen to the money in the bank? It's in his name. I can't read or write. To get money from a bank you need a signature. Who could sign? Only David. The bank then will keep the money. I'll be left penniless. Oh, oh, oh."

"What are you talking, Ma?"

"I know what I'm talking. Oh, the curse of being ignorant, of being married to a workingman. The curse of being bound to a man and his job. If there is no man for the job, what is there left for the woman, a woman with a child: the street? What can a woman do with no skill, no education: beg, steal?"

"What do you mean, Ma? What's Pa's is yours, ain't it?"

"Who knows? In this crazy world, who knows anything?"

"Let me see." He took the bankbook from her hand and looked at the small print inside.

"Well, what does it say?"

The print and the words were a blur. He read out loud. Nothing in it made sense to either of them.

"You see?" she said. "The banks, the smart banks, they make it impossible for anybody to understand anything."

"Yah."

"They'd like nothing better than to cheat us."

"Maybe a lawyer can tell us what to do?"

"Maybe."

"Maybe we should see Benny by the grocery. He's going to be a lawyer. Maybe he'll know."

"Shut up."

He looked at her frantic face in astonishment.

"Nothing happened yet," she said.

"Who said something did?"

"Shut up and go to sleep before I go crazy."

He left reluctantly, got undressed slowly, and crept under the covers on the couch. But he couldn't fall asleep. The clock ticked too loud. His heart beat too hard. The coals in the stove were making too much noise. The wind outside made him shiver.

Nothing happened yet, he told himself.

A man suddenly reared up with a hammer in his hand. It came down with terrific force, but instead of driving the nail into a board it struck the hand that was holding the nail in place. The shocking pain made him gasp for breath. The hand

· *183*

had suddenly become a bloody pulp. He shuddered away from the image.

Nothing happened. Nothing happened.

He heard the whir of an electric saw. A man put a plank of wood to it. The saw bit into the wood, made the sawdust fly, made the wood scream. The saw suddenly loosened from its mooring and whirled right at the man. He closed his eyes tight, trying to blank out the scene, but the saw ripped through the dazzling white dots of tight blackness and cut the man in two.

Nothing, nothing, nothing happened.

He was utterly alone. Rachel was gone, married, living far away. He was utterly alone with his mother. He had to fall asleep. Oh, sleep, because tomorrow he had to go to work. He had come home so tired he couldn't eat. Oh, sleep, because he needed rest to work. Sleep, sweetheart, sleep, his mother was saying. You are the man now. You have to sleep if you are to earn a living for us. Sleep, *babele*, sleep, so that I won't have to go out in the street. No, dearest, you can't go out and play. You'll never be able to play again. You will have to make new friends. They will be men. You will have to be a man. No, no more play. You'll have to sleep to work hard. So sleep, sleep.

A tear dried into a stone. It welled up in him, so big it began to choke. No, Pa, he yelled without sound. Don't let nothing happen, Pa.

His face was set with sweat and tears when he heard the kitchen door open and shut, and his heart leaped at the sound of his mother yelling and his father trying to quiet her down. He ran to him and wrapped his arms around him and felt the cold outdoors against his clothes and smelled the familiar odor of wood and sweat that was part of him, as his mother called his father every black name he had ever heard.

There had been a union meeting. The men were going out

on strike. It was going to be a big strike, a general strike in the trade. It started first in New York. The New York carpenters wanted support. So the Chicago carpenters were going to give them support. And they were going to get what the New York carpenters wanted: a dollar an hour and a shorter work week.

For that, shrieked Hershy's mother, he had almost made her go out of her mind with worry? What affair was it of his if crazy people wanted to go out and have their heads broken?

His father tried to calm her. It had to be his affair. He'd have to do what the union decided. Imagine, he said. A dollar an hour. That would really be something. No other worker in industry got that much. Not even Henry Ford paid that much. Why, a wage like that, with a shorter work week, would make a man out of a worker. Why, the world would begin to belong to the worker.

His mother laughed at him. A dollar an hour, she sneered. Cold beets, they'd get, a club on the head, a good jail sentence, they'd get. What business did he have anyhow to think of going on strike? Him, a greenhorn, a man the government could send back to Russia on the next boat. Was he crazy or something?

No, he insisted, he wasn't crazy. He wasn't a greenhorn, either. He was a citizen. He'd like to see the government send him back to Russia.

Oh, she groaned. Suddenly she was blessed with a hero for a husband. Suddenly a Bolshevik was in her house. Suddenly a striker. Over her dead body was he going on strike.

What would she have him do: scab?

He wasn't going to scab, either.

What was he going to do? Not an honest job was open to him.

She knew what he was going to do. She knew that he had no business allying himself with common workers. Imagine, a man with money, tying himself to a dollar an hour dream. Imagine, a man with money, deciding to go out to get his head broken. Not on her life. No, he was going to find a business and make a man of himself.

His father shrugged his shoulders.

She knew what she was saying. This was an example of a worker's life. He never knew where he was. If the boss didn't fire him or lay him off, then the union took him off a job. Like a dog, he was between his mouth and his tail, chasing himself in circles. But a man in business, he knew where he was all the time. He was his own boss. He made the decisions. He had control over his life. He came home on time for supper; he had time for his children and his wife; and he never drove his family out of its mind with worry. One thing she had learned about America: each man had to make his own fortune or else he had no business here. And he, if she had anything to do with it, was going to make his own fortune, he was going to stop thinking about strikes. If he didn't she'd leave him. She'd take Hershel and leave him.

A strange look came over his father's face. It reminded Hershy of a kid he once hit. The kid just sat down and looked up at him in amazement. It made him walk away.

4.

The news of the strike caused a flurry of excitement in the neighborhood. Most of the men on the street belonged to unions and, through Hershy's father, saw their own battles being fought.

Mr. Pryztalski, the Pole upstairs, who had been in the stockyards strike the year before, stopped at the back door on his way home from work each night.

"Well?" he asked. "How goes it?"

"So-so," said his father.

"Don't give an inch." Mr. Pryztalski curled up his beefy fingers and pounded his thick fist against the door. "Be strong like the stockyard workers. If you lose, maybe my bosses will take away everything we won. If you win, we will be stronger. So be strong."

His father nodded with determination.

"If you give in I'll chop you up in little pieces. I'll kick you out of my flat."

"I won't give in."

"That's good talk. I talk funny for a landlord, huh? But I'm a worker, too. If you win a dollar an hour and a shorter work week, maybe later I'll get it, too. I'll live a little. Imagine, a dollar an hour and a forty-four hour week; it'll be a worker's world."

Hershy's father agreed.

Mr. Pryztalski, who considered himself an authority on strikes, since he had been in one which was won, concluded: "Give them hell."

Mr. Bromberg, the cigar maker who lived next door, claimed a great stake in the strike. Impressively smoking an expensive cigar he made, which was his only link to wealth, his bronchial cough hacked away at his whole body and his dried tobacco-leaf face seemed to crack apart as he said: "Listen, Melov, my union just gave your union a lot of money. So don't lose, you hear."

Mr. Greenberg, the dress cutter who lived in the flat above the Bromberg's, loosened a piece of phlegm from his throat, then raised his stooped shoulders and pointed a gnarled finger at Mr. Bromberg. "Look who's talking. And do you think my union, the garment makers, are cheap about a dollar? I'll have you know the garment makers buy and sell the cigar makers. Without us, no strike can be a success."

"What's the difference?" said Hershy's father. "So long as we win."

· *187*

Even Old Doc Yak, a machinist in the nearby railroad yard, who owned a house across the street and who was considered a madman because he worried more about his garden and the fence that surrounded it than a human being, called Hershy over one day and glared at him from his broad face and bushy eyebrows.

"I wasn't on your fence, Mr. Peterzak. Honest."

"Who said you was?"

"Then what do you want?"

"How's your pa?"

"Okay."

"Here, give him this."

It was then that Hershy noticed the red flower sticking out of Old Doc Yak's rough hand; it came out of one of the many pots that lined his windowsill.

"For good luck," he said.

The sentiment embarrassed Hershy but he felt proud in taking the flower and handing it to his father, who, in turn, and with great dignity, presented it to his mother.

"From an admirer," said his father.

"Who?"

"From all the neighbors. They think well of us. They respect us."

"Respect won't bring a dollar in the house. Remember."

"No, but it brings a good feeling. It makes you feel you belong."

Hershy's mother accepted the flower and put it in a glass of water; no matter what she felt about the strike, she couldn't help but feel pleased at the gesture and its meaning.

Among the kids, of course, who saw only danger in a strike, Hershy's father was lifted to a pinnacle: Tough Guy. It was hard to see him in that role, but it was a fact that he went out to the picket line every day to brave the threat of a broken head. He was not a yellow scab like Jo-Jo's father who had scabbed on a job the year before and as a result couldn't find anybody to talk to him afterward. His pals made Hershy feel proud of his father, but in school he sat in fear, wondering what might happen and praying that nothing would.

For all that year, in a period called Current Events, teacher had dedicated herself to the duty of educating her pupils to the American way of life. In her missionary zeal, she attacked directly the roots of their lives, since, in her opinion, all of the world's ills, from bobbed hair to bolshevism, converged in one word: foreignism. Pinched by her rimless pince-nez glasses, her bony corset, the pins in her hair, and the very wrinkles of her flesh, she turned into a battleground, it seemed, upon which raged the forces of destruction that were running riot in the world.

Hershy felt personally indicted. It seemed, when she talked, that her eyes flared out at him and that her bony forefinger pointed right at him: for on his school records it was stated that his mother and father were from Russia, where the winds of death were gathering; even he was born there. It seemed, as she made him squirm and slink in his seat, trying to hide from her steady accusations, that he had turned dark and evil. It was he who wanted to make of America the burning hell that was Europe. It was he, the fomenter of strikes and revolutions and disaster, who was the impure element of America. It was he who was crucifying humanity on a barbed-wire fence and who made mankind stalk the Earth with a gun in its hand. It was he who forced the Four Horsemen of the Apocalypse to thunder through the sky.

America, which teacher represented, reared up like a wild horse, crashed down upon him, and trampled all over him. And now, with his father on strike, her accusations pierced deeper; his whole being shrunk with fear before them.

In defense, Hershy wondered who she was talking about: the dark, evil bomb-thrower, his father, who turned the other way when he saw a cockroach so that he wouldn't have to kill it? Mr. Pryztalski, who talked loud and looked big, but who had a childlike belief in Christmas? Mr. Bromberg, the cigar maker, who looked more dead than alive? Mr. Peterzak, who looked fierce, but who spent all his spare time trying to raise flowers? Uncle Ben, the *shlimazel?* Uncle Irving, who would rather play cards than eat? Uncle Hymie, the big businessman?

Outside, completely rejected, the un-American children talked.

"Ah, teacher. Yap yap yap."

"Yah."

"If you want to know, she ain't even American. Nobody is American. Only the Indians are American, if you want to know."

"Yah. *Mayflower* or no *Mayflower*, she's a foreigner. So what's she yapping about?"

"You know what she needs?"

"Yah."

"One good one. One real good one. That's what my big bro says. That's what they all need. By a Russian, too."

"Wow."

"She knows what she's talking about like I know French. *Parley-vous*, that's all the French I know."

Thus they dispensed with teacher, in order not to be whirled completely out of the pattern of their lives.

"Don't worry about a thing, Hersh."

"No."

But Hershy worried. And each day he came home and saw his father alive he'd exhale with relief. Because teacher was not the only one who talked.

There were the restless big guys on the corner who dreamed of getting their hands on a wobbly or a Bolshevik. A newspaper wrote about a striker out West who was taken out of jail and lynched. A story came to him of an I.W.W. who had his testicles crushed, and then, begging to be shot, was thrown out of an automobile. Uncle Hymie came over to warn his father: if he wasn't careful he might find himself in jail, he might find his money taken away, he might find himself deported to Russia, where he could starve for a piece of bread like the rest of the Bolsheviks there, citizen or no citizen. Uncle Hymie, with his warning, terrified Hershy's mother.

She cursed the men on the street, with their flowers and their heroic stances, and she cursed the union and the men who worked with his father, and she cursed her own lot. Others could pin their hopes on him, could make him feel like he was doing something important, but in the end it was the woman, who brought the man into the world, who did all the suffering. What would happen to her and Hershel if anything should happen to him? Who was he to suddenly want to turn the world upside down? What if he did win? What would he have: a dollar an hour, a job he couldn't call his own? What was he striving for anyhow, a piece of dung, when in the shop windows were steaks for the asking? What kind of flaw was there in his character that made him endanger his life for a future that nobody in his right mind wanted? When was he going to stop this nonsense? When was he going to put his time and energy to better use? When was he going to start looking for a business?

Later, he said. Later.

Hershy worried more the night Rachel came home and said: "Pa, don't go picketing tomorrow."

"Why?"

"There's going to be trouble."

"How?"

"Some scabs are going to try to get into the plant."

"How'd you find out?"

"Never mind how. I'm telling you."

"Will your sweetheart be there?"

"Never mind. I warned you. Don't go."

Hershy's mother tried to prevent him from leaving the house the following day, but he left despite her. Hershy sat tense all through school that day. When he got home his father was there. He wasn't hurt but he looked tired. He looked like something in him had been destroyed. Some gangsters, he said, tried to make trouble, but nobody had got into the plant. The bosses, however, got what they wanted as a result; they got an injunction against picketing; and the union officials had decided to honor the injunction for reasons he didn't understand. The strike, he felt, was practically broken.

"Good," said Hershy's mother. "Good."

But, though men were free to scab, it did the company no good; for nobody with the necessary skill to make cabinets could be had. The strike settled down to a siege, with the strikers' only weapons being their patience and their skills.

Hershy's father continued to go to union headquarters every day, but somehow his heart wasn't in it any longer, and each day he came home looking depressed. He was not used to being idle; it made him feel lonely and useless. Being with men who quickly became demoralized when not working, as though all their life and vitality were bound up in their hands, began to take its toll. Being around the house more often, with Hershy's mother nagging him to start looking for a business, began to undermine him.

It was strange for Hershy to find him at home when he left for school in the morning and to see him again when he came home from school. It seemed, in the way his father carried his head and body, that he was waiting endlessly for something to happen, like a sick man impatient to get out of bed to start functioning again. In his waiting, he took to moving the furniture about, building new shelves for the pantry, and a new phonograph for the house. The day he drew some money out of the bank for living expenses he seemed to come home with a hole in him.

"You see," said Hershy's mother. "You see what I mean?"

"All right," he said. "I'll start looking for a business."

Hershy wished he could do something for him. It was strange that he should feel sorry for an older man, for his father. He could never let him know he felt this way. He wanted to make him feel strong again, very sure. He wished he could understand why his father was afraid of a business.

"What's wrong with a business?" he asked his father once.

His father tried to make him understand. "Nothing," he said. "But for me, it doesn't seem right. You see, Hershel, there are three kinds of men in this world. The ones who dream but who never realize their dreams, they are the very unhappy ones, the destroyed ones; the ones who dream and who are able to grasp their dreams, they are the successful ones, the dictators of the world; and the ones who think they understand themselves and who try to live inside their understanding, they are the happiest ones. Maybe I am the last kind of a man, if I could only be left alone. Being in business for me would mean giving up the whole of my past, and I don't know if I have the courage to do it. Perhaps the past is an anchor; it can either drag you down or make you feel secure; it all depends how you look at it."

Hershy thought he understood: his father wanted only what he had, he was afraid to reach for more. All right, he defended his father to himself, so his father didn't have guts; but he didn't hurt anyone, did he; he wasn't yellow, was he? But he knew that his father's anchor was slipping away. For each day he made a pretense of looking through the newspapers for a business and each day he said he was going to look at a business he had seen advertised. But as he was greeted eagerly by Hershy's mother when he came home, he shook his head hopelessly and said: "There was nothing there."

"Why? What was the matter?"

"Everything. A good business nobody wants to sell, but everybody wants to get rid of a bad one."

"They can't all be bad, can they?"

"Those that are advertised are."

"Look again, David."

"All right. But if somebody wants to sell a business there must be something wrong with it."

"Look again and see."

But Hershy knew that his father was doing nothing, really, but keeping peace in the house, for he had seen him a few times sitting idly in the park. Once Hershy approached him.

"Hello, Pa."

His father looked at him in surprise. "What are you doing here, Hershel?"

"I was playing ball with some guys."

"Oh."

"Was you down by the strike today?"

"Yes."

"They still striking?"

"Yes."

"When they going back to work?"

His father shrugged his shoulders; his hands seemed lifeless.

"Did you look on a business, too?"

His father avoided the question. "Let's take a boat ride," he said.

There were a couple of boats on the lagoon for the first time. The snow had melted for good, the winds had died, and, in the longer and warmer days, there was the wonderful surprise of buds and sprouting grass. They rode out on the lagoon silently. First, his father rowed, then Hershy rowed; then they rested and drifted over the calm water, with the landscape seeming to flow about them.

"We used to have fun in the old days, huh, Pa?"

His father nodded sadly.

"Remember, we used to go on a picnic and Ma'd take off her shoes and stockings and she'd run on the grass and scream when it tickled, and we'd go on a boat ride with a mob of people bumping us all the time?"

"Ay."

Silence. Remembering.

"How is school, Hershel?"

"All right."

Silence. Hershy trying to think of something to say. His father still remembering.

"In the old country, what was wealth for a Jew? What did houses, money, property mean? It was always something that shriveled your life, something that made you live in fear, for in a moment all of it could have been taken from a Jew. That's why education, knowledge, was so precious. It was something nobody could take away from you. It was something that could make you feel immortal. I wish I had known that then."

"You mean, like that, somebody could take what you had away from you?"

"Like that, if you were a Jew. Here, it couldn't happen. But there are a hundred other ways of losing what you have. To spend a lifetime grasping, only to be able to lose it, is senseless. What is it in the end: another possession? But what you have in your head you can never lose. Remember that, and perhaps you'll do better in school."

Silence. His father seemed spent. An oar slipped away from him. He roused himself.

"Pretty soon it's going to be Pesach."

"Yah."

"Pretty soon you're going to be a man."
"Yep, pretty soon."
"You'll have to start going to Hebrew school for your *barmitzvah*."
"Will I have to?"
"You'll have to."
Silence. Drifting.
"Pesach used to be a nature festival. It was to observe the beginning of spring."
"Yah?"
"Later it meant the deliverance of the Jews from Egypt."
"Oh."
"Still, it's a happy holiday. In the old country it was a big holiday. People went crazy getting ready for it. Happiness came with it. Here, it's like a trouble, like a business affair, get done with it fast."

The sun began to sink over the western slope of Bunker Hill. Hershy looked at the gentle slope sadly. He saw a kid tumble down to the bottom of the hill.

"We used to play cowboys and Indians there," he said, pointing to it.

"Don't you play there any more?"
"Sure. But it used to be more fun before."
"That's because you're getting older."
"Yah? Is that why?"
"Yes. Slowly, with the years, the fun works out of you. Something else takes its place. Something more endurable."

His father started to row back to the boathouse, whose shadows were rippled in the purple water. In the wake of the boat, Hershy felt his world lap slowly away, and it made him feel sad, as though a good part of him were washing up against the rushes on the shore. Holding his father's hand, as they walked home, feeling hard and close to him, he felt like a grown man.

"I won't tell Ma I saw you," he said.

His father squeezed his hand and smiled at him.

The next time he saw his father in the park, playing with a blade of grass, he ducked quickly and avoided meeting him. He didn't want to embarrass him or make him think he was spying. At home, now that he appeared to be looking for a business, his father tried to assume his role as the positive man. He was tired, he complained. He had hunted hard that day. One would think that there'd be hundreds of people jumping at him from every corner to get at his money. But it was hard to find something good.

"You sure you're looking?" Hershy's mother asked.

"What a question! But I'm beginning to realize that it's as hard to find a good business as a good job."

Hershy's mother had no way of knowing anything different. She fed him and treated him as the positive man.

5.

Uncle Irving came over one night, like the spring, bursting with enthusiasm. There was a high shine in his eyes. Even the dandruff from his scalp had disappeared and there was a luster to his receding hair. Everybody's troubles would soon be over, he claimed. Nature was changing to celebrate their good fortune. Call him the Messiah, a new day was being born. Because he had come across something on his laundry route that could happen to a man only once in a million years: a real buy, a steal, a giveaway.

Well, well, what was it? Hershy's mother wanted to know.

Everybody knew that he wasn't Ben, the *shlimazel*. Everybody knew that he had never come begging for a penny. Everybody knew that he had an eye like a hawk and that his word was as good as the ace of spades. Everybody had always said of him: "Irving is a man who never blows hot and cold. Give Irving a chance and he will do wonders."

All right, all right, but what was he so excited about? Everybody knew that he was a hustler, a man who knew a good thing when he saw it. Well, he had seen it: a beauty, a gem, so cheap that it was a steal. What was it? A laundry. And how much? Fifteen thousand dollars. A diamond of a buy.

Hershy's father leaned back in his chair, practically disinterested: who had all that money? But Uncle Irving said: "Listen, listen." With almost a force, he brought them leaning over the dining-room table, perhaps fascinated by his Adam's apple that bobbed up and down his scrawny neck, or by the overhead lights that gleamed off his high forehead, or by the shadows of his hawklike nose on his face, or the quiver of his long hands on the table. Whatever it was, he had Hershy's mother folding her hands tightly and his father listening patiently.

The plant itself, said Uncle Irving, was worth more than fifteen thousand, much more. He ought to know. Not a dime was being charged for good will. That itself was sometimes worth a fortune. But the man's health was broken, and, as a result, he had let the business run down, and now was willing to sell at a sacrifice.

Hershy's father shook his head. Somehow, he said, every business put up for sale involved a man's health and was being sacrificed. They ought to face it. These propositions were no good. To succeed where another had failed took a crazy kind of hope and confidence. He would like to see a business where the owner was still in good health with a plant that was running good. But he knew that a solid business was never put up for sale.

That was true, Uncle Irving admitted. But why should a man let an idiot's failure govern his future? One man fails, another succeeds. That was human nature. Life, the scientists said, crawled out of the sea: the strong ones adapted themselves to the land, the weak ones died. That was life. In the end, life went on. Thousands of Jews crawled out of their holes in Europe and went to a new land: some of them crawled back into new holes, but others, the ones who counted, adapted themselves to the new land, and they saw the sun, they lived. That was life, too. He had a motto: Never look at a failure, always look at a success. And if one has an opportunity to succeed where another failed, why not, why not?

Hershy's mother liked the way Uncle Irving talked. Talk, she said. Talk.

All right, Uncle Irving was willing to talk. Sense, too. Now he knew that Hershy's father had ten thousand dollars. Well, he had fifteen hundred dollars saved up. Yesterday, he had gone to a loan association. First, he told them all about the laundry. Then he said: if he got a partner to put up half the money, and if he put up his fifteen hundred dollars, would they loan him six thousand dollars? And they said, yes. All they needed for security was the laundry. Now, if the loan association saw it as a safe risk, that was all he needed to know, that was all the guarantee for success that anybody needed.

Would they really lend him the money? Hershy's mother wanted to know.

Yes, said Uncle Irving. He didn't come with any idle prattle. He had investigated everything.

Who had ever known a loan company to throw a dollar away? said Hershy's mother. For them to give money, the laundry must be as good as gold.

Absolutely, said Uncle Irving. And what he wanted was simple. He wanted to go into partnership with Hershy's father. It was the opportunity of a lifetime.

But what, pleaded Hershy's father, did he know about a laundry?

What was there to know? Uncle Irving argued. Did one have to be a genius to operate one? Even Hymie, a man who could hardly sign his name, operated one. The operation was so simple even a Chinaman could do it. In the plant he was talking about there were six washing machines and two ringers. One man, in Hymie's laundry, took care of six machines, and got fifteen dollars a week for it. That was a workingman for you; if he didn't own the machine, he got nothing for his work. Each machine had four pockets. In one operation, then, with twenty-four pockets, at a minimum of a dollar a bundle, you could make twenty-four dollars. Now, a laundry can handle at least seven loads a day, close to two hundred bundles in the one he was talking about, and with loads like that on Monday and Tuesday, the heaviest days, you could make nearly four hundred dollars to take care of expenses; the loads on Wednesday, Thursday, Friday, and Saturday become sheer profit. The only wages they'd have to spend would be for an engineer to take care of the boilers and the machinery, and a girl to handle the books and the phone calls. Hershy's father would be on the inside, tending the machines, and he would be the driver on the outside bringing in the business. And he was a master salesman, that Hymie could tell them; once he had brought in so many customers that his route had to be split three ways. How could they fail?

It sounded good. Everything sounded good in talk. Hershy's mother could hardly contain herself. She wanted to speculate more on the profits. Uncle Irving made the business look like a gold mine. He had Hershy's father, with talk about his skilled hands and brain, willing to admit that he could handle the inside of the plant much better than the dumb laborers Uncle Hymie hired at a slave wage. And with both of them looking after the business details, with both of them being able to read and write and talk, what else was there to know, how could they fail?

The talk went into other aspects.

Look, said Uncle Irving. Hershy's father was on strike. Already, he was eating into his savings. How long could money last if he kept that up? And supposing he went back to work soon? What could he look forward to: wages? Was that a life, living off wages? And supposing, after he did go back to work, the season got slack? There'd be a layoff. Other factories would slow down then, too. Where does a man turn then? Back into his savings? A workingman can be rich only if he doesn't eat. Now, he was still young, he was valuable. But in ten years, when he got to be forty could he keep up with a younger man? And then, who is the first to be laid off in a slack season, the younger or older man? Then what does a man of forty have? His savings, if he's fortunate? And how long could that last? But in business, a man of forty is just beginning, he is in his prime.

Hershy's mother nodded: true, true. Hershy's father wondered if he hadn't been happier as a child, an apprentice. Sure, he was a slave then, but he always knew that he'd get food and shelter. Freedom mixed you up. Would he want that kind of life again? No, he was just talking.

If, continued Uncle Irving, a worker is a greenhorn and a Jew on top of it, he is the first to suffer in bad times. But one thing business does: it puts you on an equal basis with all people who deal with you; in fact, it makes you superior to the people who come to you for service. Are equality and independence bad things to hope for? It's what people kill themselves for. Why does a Jew always want to open a business, even if it's a little candy store that enslaves him? Because it gives him independence; he has people come to him; and no matter who it is, if they want something you have, you're a king, even if you're a little candy-store owner. After all, why had they come to America? Sure, for equality and independence. Here, there was the promise for a man to build a dynasty. There was the promise for a man to do wonders, not only for himself and his wife, but for his children. And after all, what does a father live for if not for his family? How nice it would be in one's later years to be able to say: "Here, son, here's an empire." How nice it would be in one's later years to sit back, a gentleman, a man to be remembered, a man who has kept his family together, a man who is deeply respected by his children and his neighbors. Ay, what a successful business can do for a man.

For a moment there was silence. Then Uncle Irving shook himself.

"Well," he said. "What do you say?"

"I'll think about it," said Hershy's father.

"Don't think too long. Somebody else might grab it from under our nose."

"Pesach is almost here. I'll look the laundry over, and then come to a decision after Pesach."

"I warn you, David. It's the opportunity of a lifetime. Don't wait too long."

"All right, Irving, all right, but don't rush me. A business at a sacrifice is never grabbed up in a hurry."

After Uncle Irving left, Hershy's mother couldn't wait to see Uncle Hymie. He would know. She had to get his opinion immediately. And the following day they went to his house.

Uncle Hymie listened carefully, his eyes blinking rapidly, as though catching every word and storing it in his mind; then, as from a great height, he said:

"David, if you were another man, I'd say, yes, go ahead, take a gamble, good luck. But you're a man who is not suited for business. Business isn't only dreaming and hoping, like your wife likes to do. It's hard work."

"Am I not used to hard work?"

"Yes, but this is different. It isn't like a job, where somebody orders you around all the time. In business, you have to do the ordering. You have to give up your soul for it. You have to make your heart become a rock at times. You have to make decisions that don't let you sleep at night. To be a success, you have to give up your whole past. You can't let a thought enter your head or a feeling enter your heart if it hasn't a dollar sign on it. I know.

"Besides, I don't trust Irving. What has he got to lose: fifteen hundred dollars? What will happen if he can't pay the six thousand dollars to the loan company? You're a partner. You'll be responsible for it then. And if you can't pay, what do you think will happen? The loan company will come in and take over the laundry. Where will your seventy-five hundred dollars be then?"

"Can they do a thing like that?"

"What do you think? Irving can talk like a fiend. He can almost make one believe anything."

"But he was a good driver, wasn't he?"

"Sure. Once he got so much business I had to split up his route three ways and hire two extra drivers to handle his customers, but that was when the business was young. Now there's a fierce competition. You have to offer real service. Nothing can go wrong. You have to woo customers. That's the way it is today. And if you go in business you'll soon find out. Every other laundry will be ready to cut your throat, remember that. Even I, your friend, your brother-in-law, will have to be ready to do the same. That's business."

"Then your advice is no?"

"For somebody else: yes. For you, David, no."

Hershy's mother contained herself until she got outside. "He's jealous," she said.

"Why's he jealous?" said Hershy's father.

"He's afraid you might become a success, more successful than him."

"Why?"

"He's afraid you'll give him competition. Maybe with you in business he'll make a dollar less, the greedy swine. He's afraid to lose Irving, too, his best driver."

"Maybe you're right. Who knows what can go on in a man's head?"

"And the way he talked down to you, I could have torn his eyes out. David, listen to me. You go and look at the laundry. You make up your own mind. What have we got to lose: seventy-five hundred dolars? It looks like a fortune but it can become nothing. But look at what we have to gain: a whole new world. Let's have courage, David. Let's have courage."

The day Hershy's father looked at the business he came home looking very depressed. The place, he said, looked like a hole. When he saw the man who owned it his heart almost caved. The man was old beyond his years, with a drawn face, a stoop, and a stiff arthritic leg. He was able to understand why the man wanted to make a sacrifice. He wondered, as he talked to the man, if he would soon look like that. He wondered if it would be worthwhile sinking not only his money but also his life into a business like that.

But was the machinery all right? Hershy's mother wanted to know.

Yes, it looked all right.

Was everything else all right?

Yes, he supposed everything else was all right.

Did it look like it had a chance?

It had what a human being could put into it.

Well, the man was probably old and dead before he started and had let it go to pieces. But he was young and energetic. He could expand it. He could make it so good that later he wouldn't have to work inside; he'd work in an office, like Hymie.

He would have to think about it.

He suffered, trying to make a decision, for a week. Hershy had the feeling, during the time, that his father was engaged in a great wrestling match and that it was slowly wearing him out. Finally, on the first day of Passover, his father abruptly came to a decision.

6.

On Passover, the first Seder, was always held at Uncle Hymie's house. The whole family gathered there, not only to celebrate the liberation of the Jews from Egyptian bondage, but also to pay homage to him. Each family dreamed of having an opulent Seder at its own house. They said: "Next year, with luck, it will be at my house." But when the time came, it was held, without question, at Uncle Hymie's. As a result, mingled with the joyous meaning of the holiday was a sense of defeat.

On that day, Hershy's mother left the house early in the afternoon to help Aunt Reva. Toward sundown, Hershy and his father got dressed in their new suits, which they hadn't worn since the homecoming.

"Look, Pa, the suit fits me better. It ain't a big bag on me now."

"Yes, Hershele."

"Boy, but I must of grown."

"You certainly have."

Hershy measured himself against his father. He came up to his mouth. He didn't have to look up very high to meet his eyes. The thought of almost being as big as him was overwhelming.

"Pretty soon I'll be as big as you, huh, Pa?"

"Bigger."

"Boy, I hope so."

"Why are you so eager to be big?"

"I'll be able to do anything then. I'll be strong. I'll know a lot. I'll be able to help people in trouble. Even you, Pa."

"Why, do I look like I'm in trouble?"

"No," he lied. "Only in case."

"Yes." His father studied him. "Before you know it, you'll be a man one day; you'll look back and wonder what happened to the child. But you'll have a childhood to remember."

Yah, he thought. He was sure he'd remember. It was strange: his father seemed to think of his childhood only on a holiday, as though on all other days he was never a kid and never played a game. It was strange also that he had never been able to picture his father as a child. Could he have come into the world as a grown man? Did all Europeans get born old? He wondered if his father had ever had any fun.

They went off to the synagogue. Hershy had his pockets stuffed with nuts and his bull's-eye knick. His father carried a dark-blue velvet bag under his arm, containing *t'fillin*, a prayer shawl, and a Hebrew prayer book. When they got there, a change seemed to come over his father: of peace, safety, belonging, as though coming out of his indecisions and fears from a world he was trying to know into a world he did know. Other men from the neighborhood, who usually acted as though there were a threat in every sound and speck on the street, now seemed to be at one with everybody, bearing themselves with strength.

Some of his pals were there, too, their pockets bulging with nuts; they were impatient for the evening services to start so that while their fathers prayed they could play. They paid a reluctant tribute to the holiday and their fathers by going inside the synagogue when the services started. Though many of them could read Hebrew very few understood it; their teachers seldom taught the language, only the symbols of the alphabet for reading. For most of them, without a rabbi to order their whole culture, the synagogue stood for a completely foreign symbol, which they rejected in their efforts to integrate themselves into the broad stream of American life. So, with little or no understanding of the prayers or of the rituals taking place around the Ark and the Torah, they soon became bored with the hurried mumblings and the swaying rhythms of their fathers' tallith-draped bodies; and one by one they left their fathers' sides and came outside, yelling, mocking the rocking and chanting figures of their fathers, and then settled down to playing for nuts.

Hershy got into a game of odds-and-evens: first one up, then two up, then five up, and then, frustrated by his inability to guess right the odd or even number of fingers that were flicked out, ten up. Suddenly, all his nuts were gone. And the kid he was playing with, both overwhelmed by his winnings and frightened that Hershy might start a fight to take them away, ran to his father's side in the synagogue. Hershy tried to borrow some nuts but nobody would loan him any.

"What! And then give you a chance to win with my nuts? You crazy or something?"

"Ah, be a good guy, will you?"

"No."

He wandered around, watching the games of odds-and-evens, lagging, and baby-in-the-hole. His spirit was broken, not because there was any value attached to the nuts he had lost but because he had been beaten; something in him, for not being a winner and for not being able to play any longer, was destroyed. Finally, to get away from this feeling, he walked across the street into the park.

A new moon was out, a bright white slit in the deepening

blue sky. It didn't look real. Then he saw a star break through. That didn't look real, either. There was no breeze and the trees stood tall and still, their twigs swollen with buds. It was so quiet that he could hear the chants from the synagogue. He walked away slowly, hard with loneliness.

Presently, across the boulevard, near a group of bushes, he saw a man and woman stretched out on the new grass. He stooped low and ran across the boulevard and crept into the bushes behind them. At the edge he dropped to his belly and peeked out. The girl was lying on her back, staring up at the sky; the guy was on his side, propped up on his elbow, looking down at her. Hershy was sure that he hadn't been heard and that he couldn't be seen. He felt that he was as good as a big-game hunter, as good as any Indian with moccasin shoes. He strained his ears, trying to catch their voices.

"What do you say?" the guy said.

"It's early."

"Pretty soon it'll be dark."

"All night long it's dark."

"So?"

"So what's your hurry?"

"Listen, I been in a hurry ever since I met you, even before. I ain't made of iron, baby."

"But you are, you are. That's what I like about you, the iron in you."

"Yah?"

The guy dropped off his elbow right down beside her and pulled her to him, and, as they both began to squirm against each other, Hershy yelled inwardly, with a strange sensation in his stomach: "Wow! Wowee!"

They separated, breathing hard.

"Don't," said the girl. "What if somebody's looking? What if somebody comes by?"

"To hell with them. One crack and I'll kick their teeth in."

"But we better go."

"Where?"

"I thought we were going to the *Frolics* later."

"That's later."

"Well, I still have to get dressed."

"I'll help you."

"Not yet. Please not yet."

"When?"

"Sometime."

"Now. Nobody's at your house. We'll have a quiet time."

"No."

"What's to worry about? You said your mother's at your aunt's, helping with the Seder. Your father's in *schule* and he's going to your aunt's from there. If I know Seders, they last a century. So what's to worry about?"

"Nothing."

"What's a matter, you ashamed of bringing me in your house?"

The girl stared at the guy and shook her head.

"Parties. All you know is parties. I'm so busy showing you around I forget what I want. Sometimes I like a quiet time. Say the word, baby, I'll knock over a bank or something, but let's not go chasing around now."

There was a long pause. The girl studied the guy. Hershy waited eagerly.

"All right," she said.

The guy sprang up and lifted the girl to her feet. He kissed her right on the mouth. Then, as they walked away, something dropped in Hershy. The lamplight, when they appeared under it, brought out their features, and, as they stepped into a parked automobile, he knew who they were. That was Joey Gans's car, and the girl with him was Rachel. The car started up and drove away. They were going to his house. They were going to do it in his house.

7.

"Where were you?" his father asked.

"In the park."

"Well, let's hurry."

Hershy realized, as they began walking, that they weren't going directly to Uncle Hymie's house across the park; his father was going home first.

"Ain't we going to Uncle Hymie's for the Seder, Pa?"

"Sure, but first we'll go home. I want to drop off my tallith and prayer book. It's only two blocks out of the way."

"I don't want to go home."

"We'll go home anyway. Look at you, how dirty you got. Mama'll get angry if she sees you so dirty. You'll shame her. Where were you to get so dirty?"

"In the park, I told you, and I ain't so dirty. Ma'll be madder if we come late to the Seder."

"We won't be late. Hymie's *schule* is farther away than ours. Irving and Ben have to come from their *schules* on the West Side. We won't be late. But hurry."

"But I'm hungry, Pa. I got a bellyache, I'm so hungry."

"All right, we'll go home and I'll give you something to eat. At Hymie's we won't eat for an age."

"But I don't want to go home."

His father ignored him and continued walking.

He had to keep him from going home. At the corner, he turned off toward the park, looking behind, watching if his father would follow or chase him, but his father walked directly ahead.

"Come on, Pa. Come on to Uncle Hymie's. Ma'll kill us if we're late."

His father disappeared after crossing the street. He couldn't go on alone. He ran back to his side, and glared at him, his fists clenched, his breath hard, his body trembling.

Help me, he prayed. Give me a stroke or something. Make me get runned over or something.

He ran out in the street and began kicking a stone slowly. An automobile appeared but he remained in the middle of the street, following the stone. The horn began blowing, but he paid no attention to it.

Run me over, he said inwardly. I dare you. I double dare you.

The automobile stopped and the man yelled at him and his father ran over and kicked the stone away and yanked him off the street.

"You crazy?"

He pulled away from him and kicked a can along the walk. His father rushed up to the can, and in the scuffle for control of it Hershy tripped. His father kicked the can into a passageway, then jerked him to his feet, and, as Hershy glared at him, slapped his face. The slap stunned him. He backed away, rubbing his cheek with his fingers.

"What's the matter with you anyway?" his father said.

"All right," he said. "All right."

All right, he said again in silence. Go ahead. You'll see. You'll see what's the matter.

"Come on now. No more nonsense."

"All right."

He stopped still when he saw Joey's car outside the house. Then he rushed past his father through the passageway that led to the back of the house and up the wooden stairs. The door was open. He ran through the kitchen. Nobody was in the dining room. Nobody was in the front room. Just as he opened the door of Rachel's bedroom, he heard the front door open.

"What is it, Hershel?" his father yelled. "What's the matter?"

He couldn't answer. Rachel, stark naked, had flung herself against the wall, pulling at the blankets desperately to cover

· 211

herself, her voice breaking from a gasp into a whimper. "No. Oh no. Oh no no no no no." Joey was sitting up, huge and matted, with a snarl on his face, and the muscular beauty that Hershy had once seen became a blur of flesh and hair and a tight ugly voice.

"Beat it, you guys. Beat it before I kill you."

Hershy backed up against his father, who was framed in the doorway. A firecracker seemed to have exploded in his father's face, and from the shocking pain his body tightened and reeled back, and then the life seemed to go out of him as the velvet bag that held his tallith, *t'fillin,* and prayer book slipped to the floor.

"Come on, Pa."

He took his father's hand and together they walked out of the house. Outside, at the foot of the stairs, his father sat down and buried his face in his trembling hands but didn't cry.

"We got to go, Pa."

The tears came at the opening of the Seder when Uncle Hymie's son, with a high silly voice, said: "Papa, why is this night different from all other nights?"

Hershy felt his heart break.

The others, thinking his father was moved emotionally by the service and the opulent table, stared at him a moment, then relaxed as his face gradually settled into a hard cast.

Later, his father approached Uncle Irving.

"I've decided, Irving. I'll buy the laundry with you."

Uncle Irving slapped his back joyously. He filled everyone's glass with wine.

"Next year, with luck," he said, "the Seder will be at my house."

BOOK THREE

THE MACHINE

CHAPTER TEN

1.

The incident came at a time of crucial change in Hershy's life, when the child was beginning to mingle with the adolescent that had taken root in him; it left him floundering, wishing to rush back over his early years into a corner of safety. But there was no escape, for the kids on the street were a part of his change.

Overnight, it seemed, the sight of a girl stirred something strange in them, as if they had seen a bud pop out on a tree or a worm crawl out of a cocoon or a butterfly flutter out of a caterpillar. Something seemed to reach inside them, shaking them violently, and suddenly a huge blob broke up into a hundred fragments and distinct forms began to take shape and they began to parade before the girls with a peculiar self-consciousness growing over them. Where before they were like shadow-boxers, involved wholly within themselves, now they felt that they were in a ring, surrounded by a whole new audience; now they found themselves reaching out, seeking a new kind of cheer and adulation; now, coming out of themselves, they found that they had to pause a moment to catch up with their new sensations of being, and they felt a need to talk about it. Society was taking its toll, especially at twilight, after a long day at school and at play. They'd sit or lie down on the slanting roof of a stable or garage, with the sky above and the alley below.

Hey, what makes the sky change all the time?

Look at all the colors, guys. Look at all the goddam colors.

The stars, guys. They're popping, guys.

How come the moon don't come up the same time every night?

All the things a guy don't know. All the things.

(A cat screeched, breaking their flight through the mysteries of interstellar space, flinging them hard against the one thing they tried to avoid but which was uppermost in their minds.)

I hear it hurts when a cat does it.

Yow, it must hurt.

How about when a man does it?

I don't know. Sometimes I hear funny noises from upstairs. Crazy laughing, screaming, moaning.

From next door I heard it. Holy mackerel, like a horse running.

You ever see it?

Once. A girl in the playground was riding on a swing. Yoppo, the wind picked up her dress. Yowie, the free show.

What'd it look like? What'd it look like?

You know.

Yah?

Holy mackerel.

Once I was in the yard. I looked up. Right on top of me, right on the second-floor porch, there was old lady Cohen. She didn't have no bloomers on.

Yah? Yah?

Holy Jesus, guys. Holy, holy, holy.

They sat or lay on the roofs with their hands folded behind their heads or around their knees, watching the night close in on them, listening to the cats and the rats and the dogs and themselves, feeling a strange bubble work through them. Wandering through the dark star-blistered night, they found themselves ganging closer together, forming a kind of protective society; but in reality they were preparing themselves for a day when one of them would spurt out and become a part of the world of women and then come swaggering back to the collective world of men to say: I know what it's all about now.

But Hershy, through all of this, felt as though split in two: one part of him involved; the other, violated and destroyed, cast out. He had a great need to purge himself of what he had seen and a still greater need to be told that it was nothing, it was normal, it was nature, it was a bad dream; but he had no one to talk to, not even his father, for, sensing the humiliation, shame, and heaviness his father felt about Rachel, he avoided mentioning her to the only one who shared his secret. He could hardly look at her without fantastic pictures rising in his mind. And, watching the growth of his mother, he began to look for Rachel's body to change and to shame him completely. Nothing, however, seemed to happen to her, except that she hardly ever talked. Even Joey, it seemed, had stopped seeing her, had stopped blowing his horn outside the window at night. Still, his sight and memory persisted, kept his lips sealed. But in his silence his ears were probed, his heart agitated, his hands and knees made to quiver. In his silence, locked with the grotesque images of his mind, a hard core of loneliness shut him out from everything. Spring released everyone but flung him into a dungeon of silence and fear: a kind of violence began to rage through him.

One Saturday, Cyclops began to tell a story. It seemed so much like what Hershy had seen in the park that he stiffened with fright.

"I seen it. A guy and a girl. I seen it happen."

"Who? Where? How? What'd they do? What'd they do?"

A fire in Hershey began to curl his hands and burn his eyes.

"I seen them. A guy and a girl. They was big, too."
"Yah? Yah?"
"They was on the grass. Laying on the grass."
"Holy. Yah? And then?"
"The guy kissed her."
"Yah? Yah? And then?"
"He kissed her."
"All right, all right, he kissed her. Then what?"
"He was on top of her, too?"
"Man, man. And then?"
"I couldn't see no more."
"Ah, you one-eyed punk. That all?"
"Then they got up and went away."

The fire in Hershy crackled and raged up beyond control. He lunged out and hit Cyclops, the wide arc of his blow crashing against Cyclops' ear. Cyclops fell down and looked up at him with his mouth open and his face white, rubbing his ear. A crazy desire came over him to kick Cyclops right in the mouth, but before he could do it he was tackled and pinned to the ground by the rest of the guys, and then the fire in him welled out of his eyes and scalded his face. When he was released, finally, he got up silently and walked away.

That evening, while eating the left-over chicken and soup from the night before, the sight of Rachel began to feed the smoldering fire that was still in him. There was a peculiar pull in his stomach and it brought thick nauseous saliva to his mouth. Glaring at Rachel, he spit at her and yelled: "I hope you die," then rushed to the bathroom, but got sick on the way, and then retched for a time. His father held his forehead and his mother trembled over him and Rachel kept saying: "What's the matter with him anyway?" But he thought he was going to die and somehow he didn't care; he just wanted to lie down and catch his breath and then die.

Afterward, his mother undressed him and helped him to his daybed, trying both to soothe him and to find out what the matter was, but, getting no answer, she went to the kichen to prepare some tea for him, while Rachel went out to buy a lemon. His father sat beside him and stroked his hair. Hershy finally took a shuddering deep breath.

"What's the matter, Hershele?"

"You know what's the matter?"

"Why did you spit on Rachel and then get sick?"

"You know why. It's what she did. She made you cry and broke your heart."

"But I'm not crying any more and my heart isn't broken any more."

"She made me scared and I hit a kid and almost killed him and now he'll be mad on me and all the guys'll be mad on me and I can't do nothing what all the guys are doing any more."

His father stared at him, his head wavering.

"See?"

"I see," his father said.

"So I hate her."

His father shook his head slowly.

"Don't you hate her?"

"No."

"But look what she did."

"I know. And I wish you could forget it. But you can't hate something you love. Sometimes you do horrible things to me and Mama, but do we ever hate you for it?"

"No," he admitted.

"You disturb us and irritate us and make us angry, yes; that's part of loving someone; but we never hate you. Anything you're responsible for you can't hate. I'm responsible for you. If you killed someone, the blame would be part mine, the fault would be part mine, but I'd never hate you for it, I'd cry for you, I'd cry for myself."

A lump formed in Hershy's throat; his father's voice seemed to quiver through him.

"I'm responsible for Rachel, too. If she did wrong, perhaps the fault is mine."

It ain't, Hershy wanted to say. It ain't, Pa.

"But if you love somebody enough, they can't do wrong. They may not always do the right thing, but they can't do wrong. Someday, perhaps, you will understand. But Rachel is your flesh and blood, and if she became weak it's up to us to protect her, to make her strong again, and you can't do that with hate. Anybody can respect the strong. But it takes a strong person to respect the weak. Let's be strong, Hershel, you and me, and be good to Rachel. Let's forget the muscles and bones and flesh, and let's live like giants in the heart and soul. Rachel needs us now more than ever. She is ashamed and has suffered. Let's not make her suffer any more."

"But what if she gets fat and makes a shame on all of us?"

"She won't get fat and she won't shame us."

"How do you know?"

"I know."

"Nobody'll find out?"

"Nobody."

"It's a secret then?"

"Between you and me."

"Not even Ma knows?"

"Nobody knows. Only you and me."

His mother and Rachel came in with a glass of tea. He looked away from Rachel, but when she leaned over and kissed the top of his head, a nerve in him quivered; he whirled about and flung his arms around her, and, through the trembling touch of her lips and her warm breasts he felt the throb of her blood flow through him; it was good to be good on everybody.

Nevertheless, he still couldn't trust Rachel fully; she might yet shame him and his family and cast them out completely from everybody's lives. He still felt shaken, and cringed before the images that kept flooding his head of Joey's huge hairy body and snarling face and Rachel's full naked body. He still became tight as a fist when anybody looked at Rachel, and he shrank before the eyes of every big guy that looked at him. He still ran every time he saw Joey; tired afterward, everything he had idolized in him felt mangled, left him rocky and unable to stand up. He still felt something hold him back from the guys, though he cried inwardly to become one with them. But he had lost his violent rage. He wanted to be good on everybody, but something held him in check. He strained for some kind of release through Cyclops.

"I didn't mean it, Cy." He put his arm around him but Cyclops shrugged it off. "Don't be mad, Cy."

He didn't know how to make Cyclops good on him. He didn't know what else to say. He fumbled through his pockets and found a wooden whistle his father had made and given him.

"Here, Cy. Take it, but don't be mad. Take it, huh?"

Cyclops looked away from him.

He didn't know what else to do. He scrambled through his mind for some stunt that might make him laugh, for something he owned which Cyclops really wanted. Feeling condemned, a sudden fear of losing Cyclops and all the guys came over him.

Out of sheer desperation he tackled him and began wrestling with him, and, as they rolled over and strained against each other, Cyclops got limp and stared upward as Hershy straddled him.

"You're not mad no more, Cy?"

"Ah, you're full of crap."

"But you're not mad no more?"

"Ah, let me alone, will you?"

"Sure, sure, but you're not mad no more?"

"No, for Christ sake."

"Here." He shoved the whistle in Cyclops' pocket, and, looking up for full acceptance at the guys crowded about, got off him. He helped Cyclops to his feet and put his arm around his shoulders. Then the guys began to yell and slap them on the back; the gang was still intact.

He was released to them almost completely the day Rachel came home so excited she could hardly talk or sit still. She had made good before a theatrical booking agent, whom Joey had introduced her to some time ago, and he had set up a long series of bookings for her. She was going all over the country. She was going to be gone a long time. She was going to dance on a stage all over the country. She was so happy she began to cry.

The day after she left Hershy skipped out on the springboard street ready to fall in love. He lay down with his pals on the slanting roofs, with the great sky above and the alley below, and let himself go.

Boy, if I only had a girl.

What if you did? What would you do?

Yah. What if I did? What would I do?

They would know everything, they felt, the very secret of life itself, if they only knew a girl.

2.

She suddenly appeared, like the word *mirage* which she was defining. The regular classroom work was finished, and whenever a few minutes remained until the bell rang, teacher played a game of giving value to words. Mirage was a fifteen-cent word.

"Mirage," she was saying, "is something which you think is there, way off in the distance, but it isn't. Like, a man is dying of thirst in the desert. All of a sudden, because he's been thinking of water so much, he sees a lake; but it isn't there, really. Mirage is an illusion."

"That's fine, Emily," teacher said. "You might call it an optical illusion."

Gee, Hershy thought. All the things one word can mean.

"Ah," said Cyclops, who turned about on the seat in front of Hershy. "I bet I can get it wholesale, for ten cents."

"Ah, you and your wholesale. Shut up. Don't bother me."

He wanted to look at Emily undisturbed.

There she had sat, without form, all that year. There she had sat: teacher's pet, a show-ee-off, an irritation. But now he thought: all the words she knew, dollar ones, too. Man, was she rich. Silver and gold, she had in her head.

There she had sat: a lump, blank, nothing. Now she had straw-colored hair that hung down in soft fluffy curls to the white collar of her middy blouse. There was a nice roundness to her features: nothing bumpy or broken or too long or too hooked: everything was in place, nice, with shiny dark eyes, like his bull's-eye knick, and a creamy kind of skin.

Emily Foster.

He wrote it on a piece of paper, but it didn't look right. He printed it. It looked just right. He let the sound of her name go through his mind. Some name, he thought. He wondered how somebody got a name like that. It sounded so right.

Hershel Melov.

He crossed out Hershel and printed Hershy.

Hershy Melov.

The printed name came to him forcefully, as something new, something to contend with. He balanced it against Emily Foster.

Hershy Melov.

· 223

He listened carefully to the sound of it.

"Hey," he whispered to Cyclops. "Say, Hershy Melov."

"You crazy or something?"

"Say it."

"All right. Hershy Melov."

He listened carefully.

"Say it again."

"Hershy Melov."

Yah, he decided, somewhat awed. That was a name. A good name. A peachy name. Boy, was he glad his father changed his name. Melovitz. Yach. Melov. Boy, that was some name.

He printed it beside Emily Foster. They looked very good to him. He printed: Tinkers to Evers to Chance. That was a good combination, too. Collins to Weaver to Schalk. That was okay, too. Foster to Melov. Wow!

He wondered where she lived and how he could get to know her. He wondered if he should ask to carry her books home. No, all the guys would see. Should he just follow her? No, all the guys would ask him where he was going. Besides, he might look like a dog. Besides, maybe she lived far. He had to be right home after school and take his father's supper to the laundry. His ma'd get mad if he didn't come right home. His pa'd get hungry and wouldn't be able to work. Suddenly, he got angry at her. Why didn't she live on his street, right next door? Why did she have to live so far away? But maybe she didn't live so far away and he could get to know her without being late. But what if it took a long time to get to know her?

The bell rang in the midst of his confusion. He was in back of the line and she was up forward as they marched out of the room. At the first landing he looked at the statue of an Indian, with his head thrown back and his humble arms stretched out, sitting on a horse. Help me, he pleaded. Oh,

224 •

Indian, with the sad face, help me. Then an idea came to him just as the class reached the last landing. He broke out of the building yelling as loud as he could, jumping and skipping and scattering everybody about him. He was going mad. He *was* mad.

Look out, he was an auto-racer. Look out, look out for that machine gun: tatatatatata. Make room, he was running the hurdles. Whango, the pole vault. Look out, the fly. Watch it, watch the ball. He can't see. The sun's in his eyes. He's blinded. Look out, look out, a beaner. Klunk. Run for home. You're making it. Slide, Hershy. Sliiiiiiiiiide . . .

He slid right in front of Emily, who flung her head to one side and stepped over him as he looked up eagerly for recognition, perhaps a sign of applause, and all the guys laughed. He jumped up and tore her books out of her hands and began running away from her, looking about to see that she followed, and the guys roared. She followed him, yelling and screaming and crying, as he trotted along. He teased her into thinking she could catch him until they were out of sight of their classmates, then he slowed down to a walk.

"Give me those books," she said.

He folded his arm tightly about the books.

"You give them to me or I'll report you."

He smiled at her.

"Are you going to hand those books over?"

His smile broadened.

"That was some trick, huh?" he said.

"You hand those books right over to me now."

"Boy, it came to me like lightning, that trick." He doubled over, hugging himself, and laughed out loud.

She stared at him. A sneer came over her face. "Look at him laugh," she said. "Horse. Horseteeth. Laughing hyena horseteeth."

· 225

The description shocked him, choking his laughter.

"Yah?" he said. He shut his mouth. His teeth suddenly began to feel huge, bulging his mouth way out. He turned his face away.

"Yah," she said, knowing she had hurt him, wanting to hurt him more. "You greenie, you."

"I ain't not a greenie. I'm an American. My father's a citizen and my uncle was killed in the war."

"Ho, ho. My great-great-grandfather was in the Civil War. He was a friend of Abraham Lincoln. And my great-great-great-great-great-grandfather was in the Revolution. He was a friend of George Washington. You call yourself an American?"

"Yah? What's so American about them? Didn't they come over on a boat from the old country? If you want to know, the only real Americans is the Indians."

"Yah, but you're still a horseteeth hyena. You're still a greenie. Don't you ever wash your teeth?"

"Sure," he lied. "Every day."

"Some washer, you are."

"Yah? If you're so great, is your father in business?"

"Certainly, he is. What do you think?"

"Well, so's my father. He's got a big business. That makes your father and my father the same."

"That's what you think. If my father was your father, he'd kill you."

"Yah?"

"Because you're a nasty . . ."

"Yah?"

"You're an obnoxious . . ."

The word stumped him. Still, he said: "Yah?"

"You're impossible." She stamped her foot on the ground.

"Why? Because I was doing a trick?"

"Some trick."

"I wanted to carry your books home, but I didn't know how, and I didn't want all the guys and girls to know so they should talk. See?"

"Oh?"

Suddenly she changed. Her eyes relaxed and she turned away from him and began walking. She held her head high and proud, and she seemed to bounce, like her curly hair, as she stepped along.

"All right," she said. "You may carry my books."

Hershy stepped beside her and walked along silently. Now that they had nothing to fight about, he didn't know what to say. He wished she'd start up again.

"What is your name?"

"Hershy Melov."

She began to titter.

"What's the matter?"

"It's a funny name."

"Yah? It's as good as yours. It's as good as Emily Foster any day."

"Is it?"

"Yah."

"Then why is it teacher sometimes calls you Herbert."

"Because she stinks."

"If you're going to carry my books you'll have to stop using that vile language."

"Why, what'd I say?"

"You're an uncouth young man."

"Ah, what are you talking?"

"I guess I'll have to teach you some manners."

"Ah, bushwa."

"See what I mean?"

He tried to see. She used too many big words, though. He looked at her instead. She looked like an expensive doll he had once seen in a store, with pink cheeks and soft curls. She

· 227

glanced at him and he turned away quickly, embarrassed, moving in awkward silence.

"You're the one who had a fight with Polack once and beat him up, aren't you?"

He nodded, thrilled by the recognition, feeling his muscles bulge.

"You must like me, huh?"

The question stunned him, made him retreat: it had never occurred to him.

"Do you like me?"

He couldn't answer.

"Then why do you want to carry my books?"

He shrugged his shoulders. He wished they had something to fight about; it was better.

"Cat got your tongue?"

He shook his head.

"Well, if you won't tell me, then give my books to me."

He stepped to one side as she reached for the books and he thrust them away from her.

"Then say nothing, tongue-tied."

She pouted and walked on silently. Then, flinging her head back, with her hair rushing along her middy collar, she said: "Do I look like Mary Pickford?"

He stared at her, said huskily: "Yah."

The haughtiness of her face broke down.

"Do I, Hershy? Do I, really?"

"Yah. I think so."

"Oh, you . . ."

"No. No kidding."

For a second there, she almost looked like Rachel. The similarity, and what he had really felt about Rachel before she turned bad and went away, astonished him.

"Well, here we are." She pointed to a yellow brick house.

The bay windows, bordered with stained glass and thick flowery drapes inside them, seemed to squirm in the sun. They hurt his eyes. He faced the park across the street and let only the sun pinch his eyes.

"I'm glad you stole my books, Robin Hood," she said.

"Yah."

"Will you do it again sometime?"

"Sometime."

She jumped up the broad white stone stairs. He called after her: "That was some trick, huh?"

She turned about, letting her chin rest coyly on her shoulder and shook her head, then she disappeared. Slowly, letting his arms dangle, looking at the glitter of the cement walk, he walked home wondering what had happened to him.

3.

His mother pounced on him and shattered the vague, oozy, spacious, dreamy feeling he had had.

All right, so he was late.

She'd give him an all right so he was late. Did he have no sense of duty, no responsibility? His father was working himself to the bone for him, but did he care?

Ah, he wasn't working himself to the bone for him. He was working himself to the bone for her. She was the one who had driven him into the business. She and Rachel.

She shook him. What was he talking about?

He knew what he was talking about.

What had Rachel to do with it?

He knew what Rachel had to do with it.

What?

He wasn't saying. He and his Pa knew but he wasn't saying.

She shook him again. What?

· 229

Nothing. Nothing. Nothing.

She could kill him, she said. He was turning out to be a fiend.

Exhausted, she released him. Her huge belly heaved for breath.

All right, he was turning out to be a fiend. What did she want, never leaving him alone?

She began to feel sorry for herself. She looked at her bulging figure. Give a child your blood, she said. Bring it into the world and let it almost kill you and what do you get? A demon.

All right, he was already at the laundry. So he was a few minutes late. It wouldn't kill his father.

She'd tear his tongue out if he ever used that expression kill again. Who was he talking about, some bum on the street?

Strange fears worked through his mother, but Hershy didn't know what they were, didn't know why she lashed out at him. With the business a reality at last, her aggressive forces suddenly became dammed up. Doubt and a sense of guilt crept through her. Fear also rose, as she watched a change come over Hershy's father and as the business began to drain him; and with the fear mingled a hope that he wouldn't be broken. The business had not only taken the seventy-five hundred dollar investment but also another fifteen hundred to get it going. That was something they hadn't counted on, but once in it there was nothing to do about it. Then, a few days after going into it, Hershy's father looked up from a newspaper and said: "The carpenters won the strike. A dollar an hour, a forty-four hour week." He looked bleak, denied a victory, with a sense of lonely defeat, as he said it. The business had to be a success. She could never ask: and if it failed . . . ? There could be no room for doubt; yet, in some tiny crevice, it crept in.

All Hershy knew was that since his father had gone into the business she yelled more and more at him, talked more and more about duty and responsibility, blamed him more and more for anything that went wrong, and that she grew more and more nervous. Was it because she was getting bigger, finding it harder to breathe and move and stand on her swelling legs? Was the thing in her an evil spirit, changing her, taking over her whole being? Or was she scared? Because once he heard her say to his father:

"I hope it comes easy."

His father tried to reassure her. "This time it will."

"I hope it doesn't tear me to pieces."

"Don't think about it."

"What else have I got to think about? Look, like something wild, it grows and grows. It's all of me."

"Try not to think about it."

"Hershel almost killed me."

Had he? Could he, a little baby, with no muscles, nothing, without knowing it, almost have killed her? How?

"He tried to come out feet first, the little devil. He tried to kick me into a grave. Oh, how he hurt. Then he turned around and came out right. Oh, how he hurt."

"That was in the old country. It couldn't happen here."

"You see what comes from love: pain, suffering, sometimes death."

"But here they have everything to make it easy."

"You can talk. You're safe, sound. You can enjoy your pleasure and go right to sleep. But for my moment of pleasure I'm doomed to agony. The devil must have a hand in this. In this, the devil must dominate God."

. . . Or was she like this because his father was hardly ever home now? He came home so late and so tired that he could hardly take off his clothes and lie down to sleep. He woke up so early that every nerve and bone in his body rebelled. It filled her with pity and complaint. He (Hershy) overheard her talking to the next-door neighbor, Mrs. Bromberg. It filled him with disgust.

"Business is no good for love."

"No?"

"It takes the life out of a man."

"So?"

"It tears the heart out of a woman. It makes you lonely."

"But you have plenty of company. Look at your belly."

"Yes, but without a man by your side the new company makes you feel lonelier. The bed sometimes gets so cold."

"It's a hard life."

"After all, what do we want out of life? Just a little warmth, that's all. Just a little warmth."

"True, true."

... It was all very bewildering. Love had the power to kill; without it, one could die. A baby, without a muscle in its body, could tear a mother to pieces; without it, there was no life. A baby was supposed to be a gift from God; but the devil, too, took his toll. His mother wanted his father to work like a beast, yet when he drove himself too hard she became frightened and lonely and cold. His father, meantime, tried to pacify her; it made him happier, it seemed, to see things in the abstract. For every feeling of joy, he said, there must be one of pain; otherwise one could never know what joy was. Things never came easy; they came with sweat and blood; only then could one realize the exaltation of a thing coming into being. You can't just want; you have to do something about it; and in the doing is the pleasure and the pain.

"Puff," his mother answered. "Puff up more clouds. A man philosophizes, a woman suffers: the man has it so easy."

But Hershy could testify that a man didn't have it easy. He knew. He had seen his father at work.

A terrifying world of heat, sound, and smell hit him the first time he came into the laundry off the cool shady street of a spring afternoon. The heat made him gasp and glued his nostrils together and burned his throat; for a moment he thought he was on the benches of a Russian steam room. Soon, dripping with sweat, he was a part of the consuming dampness: the steam, the sweating walls, the sloshing water, the wet clothes. Soon, within a building that had been an old stable, he began to vibrate as the whole plant shook with the working machinery. The gears clanked like the sound of freight cars moving on rails. The belts that whirled the washers screeched. The washers swish-sushed back and forth, with the soapy water gushing out of the pocket holes and splattering onto the cement floors and streaming into the foamy gutters. Off to one side two ringers began revolving with a hum, and then, as they hit a whirring speed, they went into a high whine. The sound was so great it was almost impossible to hear a voice. Separated from the plant itself was the boiler room; there, at the source of the plant's fierce energy and confusion, it seemed quiet and orderly, with only the hot fire sizzling in the furnace and the long flapping belt loping around two wheels and the well-oiled eccentric rods camming silently and the flyballs whirling on top of the engine.

Uncle Irving brought the bundles in with a horse and wagon. His father helped him unload, then both of them weighed and sorted them. Then his father dragged them to the washers, heaved them up, and dumped them into the pockets. His father mixed the soaps and bleach solutions and carried them in buckets and spilled them into the pockets. All the while he turned valves to get water into the washers and turned valves to drain them. Then he pulled the clothes out of the pockets and lugged them to the ringers to extract the water, then carried them to the bins where Uncle Irving was to pick them up for delivery.

His father wore big rubber boots, looked drowned in them as he sloshed up and down the wet pavement. He tended one machine after another, ending an operation and beginning it again. Up and down, over and over, carrying bundles and buckets, mixing solutions, turning valves and pulling levers, his wet hair plastered to his forehead, his damp face growing hollower, his lean body sometimes looking as wilted as the wrung-out clothes.

On Monday and Tuesday his father started the day at five in the morning and didn't come home until ten-eleven at night. Work slacked down on Wednesday, until there were only a few bundles to wash on Saturday. But then the machinery needed tending and fixing; the bins had to be rebuilt; business details had to be taken care of; there were a thousand things that had to be done to keep the whole plant going. Even on Sundays, he found it necessary to spend a few hours at the plant, to prepare it for the heavy Mondays and Tuesdays.

Hershy knew all this. So did his mother. What more testimony did she need of how hard his father worked than the way he came home at night? Even she, at times, seeing the way the flesh was tightening on his face and body, gasped and became overwhelmed with pity and warned him to slow down before he killed himself. To which his father answered: "The machine is a peculiar thing. It dominates a man. The tool—" he shook his head, remembering sadly, of something loved and forever lost "—is something a man dominates. But a machine—there is only one thing you can be to it: a slave."

Yes, Hershy could testify. A man did not have it easy. He knew. His mother knew, too. Maybe that's why she was so scared. But he really knew. He had seen his father at work. He knew another thing, too. He didn't like the laundry. He hated going there, but he wanted to help. Now, with something else on his mind, aside from the fact that it took him away from his friends and their games, he hated it more. But maybe, he thought, if his father was a success he'd make lots of money and he'd be able to get out of the inside of the laundry and become an office man like Uncle Hymie. Maybe Emily would like him better if his father had lots of money. All girls liked guys with money. He had to help out. It would be nice if he could show off a house nicer and bigger than Emily's. Ah, he'd say, my father's richer than your father. She wouldn't be able to argue back. A fact was a fact. He had to help out.

4.

Boarding a streetcar to go out of the neighborhood always brought a sense of adventure and fear to Hershy. His fear lay in the peculiar sensation of leaving home, that something unknown might happen which would keep him from ever returning; it lay in the hostile faces and bodies towering over him, in being a stranger among strangers, in feeling that nobody cared for him and that nobody would help him if he needed it; it lay in a sense that he might get lost suddenly, forever and hopelessly lost. To prevent this he began to memorize every detail on the way to his father's laundry, each one marked with a sign for his safe return. Leaving his own neighborhood with its familiar landmarks—Joey Gans's restaurant and poolroom, the two movie houses across the street from each other, the photo shop filled with familiar faces he could identify, the butter and egg store, the fish market, the butcher store, the barber shop and its revolving candy-stick pole, the baseball scores chalked on the sides of buildings, and the rusty corrugated tin fronts of buildings—a change didn't occur for a half mile.

Then a big car barn came into view with a hundred shiny tracks that curved into it. The stores began to fritter out. A quiet boulevard. A cigar-store Indian. The photo shop was the same but the faces of the people in the pictures had changed. The same chalk drawings and scoreboards on the sides of buildings, the same barber shops, the same flats on top of the street-level stores. The butcher shops changed, were filled with rabbits and pigs. No butter and egg stores. The same poolrooms, but the guys around them looking different: bigger, tougher. The people on the streets different: lighter hair, bluer eyes, blunter and broader faced, taller, heavier. Factories here and there with water tanks on top of them. A gas tank, a great big round gas tank. Empty lots, rubbled, the same. A drinking trough for horses and an iron post with a horse's head. The smell changed, heavier, like lard. The sky was more speckled, from smoke. A store with a head painted on the window, split apart with many colors, and gypsies sitting outside in a hundred dirty colors. Two big movie houses with vaudeville attractions. The YMCA. Three carlines crossing. One store like a triangle. Big stores. In the jungled depths of Polack-town. Next stop his.

Excitement also lurked everywhere: in the shiny rails that stretched endlessly; in the lurching motion of the streetcar, which sometimes transported him aboard a ship in a faraway ocean going to a faraway land; in the sense of rushing through space; in the signposts—like the cigar-store Indian and the water trough for horses which made the street open up to the vast expanse of the Wild West, like the gypsies outside their store who could make magic and read minds, like the vaudeville attractions in the big movie houses where he might one day see Rachel, like the YMCA where there were a million games to play; in the wonder, too, of what was going on all about him.

On this day, however, a new sensation worked through him on the way to his father's laundry. In passing the neighborhood movie house he saw a picture of Mary Pickford. Somehow, it began to blend into an image of Emily Foster and he felt a funny pull in his stomach; he wished he knew what had caused it. He looked up at the motorman, who had just spit a stream of tobacco juice over his head through the open window and was wiping a brown trickle off his chin, wondering whether he could tell him about Emily Foster.

Was it possible, he wondered, that this man with the beefy freckled hands and the bulky shoulders and thick belly, could have been a kid once with a girl like Emily Foster? Behind him stood a hunched-up man with vacant eyes and an open whistle-breathing mouth and deep creases in his cheeks. Ah, thought Hershy, he wouldn't know. Would anybody else know? He looked through the car: at the empty eyes, the distressed faces, the tense crouches, the uncomfortable slouches. Were all of them kids once with a feeling like he was having? Would they know what was happening to him? Well, maybe his father'd know. He didn't look like them. At least, he wasn't a stranger. But how could he talk about it with his father? The guys? Could he ask them? No, they'd kid him, they'd laugh at him. He wished he had a big brother. You could talk to a big brother; he'd know everything; he wouldn't kid.

The motorman began to dang-dang his bell. A horse and wagon rode the rails in front of the car. The motorman began to yell. The horse and wagon swerved off. Hershy stopped thinking about Emily. The man on the wagon, huddled up with his elbows resting on his knees and with the reins dangling in his hands, looked like Uncle Ben. In passing, he saw that it wasn't Uncle Ben, but his whole body froze: the motorman stuck his head out of the window and hurled a wad of brown spit at the peddler and yelled: "Hey, you kike bastard, next time I'll run you down." The peddler rode on indifferently. The motorman slammed his foot down on the bell a few more times, and, with the car away, looked down at Hershy.

"Boy, these kike bastards," he said, "clogging up the streets, making money money money, I could kill every one of them. Kid, when you grow up, be a man, don't let them walk on the same side of the street with you."

Hershy felt himself shrink from under the motorman's bloodshot eyes and reddish face.

"You going to be a man, kid? You going to do it?"

"Yah. Yah."

"Keep the country from going to the dogs. Me, I fought in the war. What did I get for it? A stool I never sit on, an iron fence behind me, a dirty window in front, a bell to dingle, a bunch of autos farting in my face, a Jew on a horse and wagon to slow me up and make me late and put me in dutch with the company, a bunch of fatheads who want me to roll out the carpets every time they get off. A guy goes away, gets himself shot at, and what does he come back to? A beefing wife, a couple of kids who don't know him from Adam, the same old varicose-vein job, and a bunch of Jews running free on the streets."

His throat dry, his knees quivering, Hershy backed away from the motorman, slunk behind him, and stepped to the door.

"Let me out, Mister. I got to get out here."

The motorman whirled his crank and slammed the door open. Hershy ran to the curb and swore defiantly at the motorman, but the door was already shut and the car had trundled past. Then, suddenly realizing that he was in a foreign neighborhood, he began to run. Maybe somebody on the street had heard him swear. He had got off the car three blocks before his stop and he ran hard over the distance. When he got to where he was to turn off to his father's laundry, he paused to catch his breath; he still had two dangerous blocks of foreign territory to pass before he'd be really safe.

He wedged the package of food under his armpit, pulled his

broken-peaked cap down to one side so that he might look tougher, took a deep breath, and then began to walk. The trees between the sidewalk and the curb were the same as on his block. The houses, some of them flush against the walk and some set back from it, were almost the same; they were only a little older and dirtier. A group of three kids were sitting on a porch. He tightened up and began to spit through the side of his mouth.

"Hey."

He looked straight ahead, his heart hammering and throbbing in his throat, his legs strained like a taut bowstring ready to whing him away.

"Next time we'll find out who the punk is."

Safe. He tried to relax but couldn't. A block and a half to go. A black iron fence began to flicker past. Set back from it was a church. In the garden was the statue of a saint in a long robe, with bowed head and a cross in his hand. A statue of Jesus Christ nailed to a cross, with a kind of diaper around his mid-section, loomed up. He stiffened and spit three times to keep his evil spirit away. (Once, a year ago, he had wandered out of his neighborhood and was attacked by five kids. Because he didn't know the catechism they knocked him down, pulled his pants off, and found out he was a Jew. Then they dragged him into a church yard to baptize him. They almost broke his arm, as they applied an upward pressure to it behind his back, to get him on his knees. Then, refusing to beg for mercy, feeling that if he did his own God would strike him dead, his mouth filled with blood as a knee rammed his chin. A clot of earth was forced into his mouth, and, when he saw a worm wriggle out in his sputtering, he vomited. He keeled to his side; then, pinned to the ground in the form of a cross, each one drew up a blob of phlegm, and, in the name of the Father, the Son, and the Holy Ghost, they spit on him and baptized him and ran away at the approach of a priest.

Only when the priest, in helping him clean up, assured him over and over that he had not been baptized and that he had not betrayed his father and his mother and his God and that the kids who had tortured him would be doomed to everlasting hell, did he begin to feel alive again.)

At the corner he saw four kids his size playing mumbly-peg. Then he couldn't help himself. He broke into a dead run and rushed into the laundry out of breath with his face white and his blood still racing madly onward. He had made it again. Once there, he calmed down quickly and the heat of the place helped bring back the blood to his face.

He walked over the wooden floor, parts of which were rotted and splintered from the dampness, through a wooden gate his father had made which led to the office. His father, who had watched the office girl sweat and squirm at work, had built a wooden partition separating the plant from the office. He had also built her two wooden desks. Uncle Irving had been opposed to it: what was he, still a carpenter? But his father said: "For a few dollars and a little labor let a person be a human being, let her be able to go home without having to wring her clothes out and without a broken back and splinters in her arms. God knows, we pay her little enough for her labor." To which Uncle Irving answered: "All right, break your back and spend our money, but don't come to me with complaints. Some businessman I've got for a partner."

Hershy tapped the office girl on the head. She looked up from her adding machine and smiled at him. Her wide face seemed to crunch together when she smiled.

"How's my little sweetheart today?" she asked.

"All right," he said, warmed by her welcome smile.

He liked her. She always had a big smile for him. Sometimes she let him brush against her, and, when she didn't move away, he got very excited. Once, when she was showing him how the adding machine worked, he leaned against her shoulder and accidentally put his arm around her and touched her breast. She looked up and shivered, then smiled and wagged her finger at him and said: "Naughty, naughty." Another time, after he had pecked his name on the typewriter, she pulled him to her. "Why, that's wonderful, wonderful." Then she released him and said: "My, my, but you're getting to be a big boy." He couldn't understand why, but when he was close to her he felt tense, dry-mouthed, heart-pounding. Was it that she held the secret that he and all the guys on the street were aching to learn?

He wondered if he could ask her about Emily: was it right that you should get a funny pull in your belly when a picture of a girl got in your head; and what did you talk about, without fighting, when you were with a girl; and how could you know if a girl was your girl? But the engineer stepped in, his white teeth flashing from his grimy face, his light hair coated with coal dust. The office girl looked away and slapped the engineer's hand down when he tickled her chin and said: "What's doing, cookie?"

Hershy wondered if she was the engineer's girl, if . . . but he was a married man; besides, in his overalls, he looked like a coal bag. Still, he liked the engineer, too. He had swum against the Duke Kahanamoku, the greatest swimmer in the world, and had pitched in the Three-Eye League, and had run the hundred yards in ten flat, and had been a crack fullback, and had done more things than it took the ordinary man a hundred years to do. Hershy, when he sat at his desk in the boiler room, didn't believe him, because he had a weak chest and his collarbones stuck out and his legs were bowed and his neck was scrawny and his gray eyes looked washed out; but he seemed to know so much about everybody and everything that it was nice listening to him. And when it came to machinery he knew everything.

"Someday," he warned him, "you're going to step in your

father's shoes, so you better learn what makes this place tick." Then he'd mystify Hershy completely as he compared the plant to the human body. "See that engine." There wasn't much to see, only the pumping rods and the flyballs. "That's the heart. Instead of blood it pumps power to all the machines in the plant; it makes all the belts flap and all the wheels go round. See the coal. That's food, that's meat and potatoes and bread. You feed it into that big ugly mouth, see. That's the fire box. See down below. I push and pull the shaker, the waste goes down the grate, and the system is cleaned out, just like when you go on the toilet. Now, that hot fire heats up the water in the boiler on top, and when water boils up what do you get? Steam. That's right, sonny. Now that steam is like your blood, see. It's what makes everything tick. It pops off against the engine; then, like the heart, the engine begins pumping, real hard, and it makes all the machinery move. See?"

Hershy'd say, yah, he saw, but he really saw nothing. Everything was hidden. He couldn't see the water in the boilers, nor the steam in the engine, nor the intricate connections between the engine and the machinery in the plant. All he knew was: it worked. His body worked, too; he didn't know why. He knew also that the engineer was important to his father and that he made more money than his father. That was another hard thing to understand: a boss making less money than a man who worked for him. His mother cursed the engineer for the salary he made, but his father stood in awe of him: without him, a man of science, the laundry was nothing; in fact, it gave him pleasure, he claimed, to watch a man go about his work with a sure skill and knowledge; the engineer was the master of the machine, just as he had been the master of the tool. As a result, with his father completely mystified by the machine and dependent upon the engineer's control of the machine's might, Hershy also stood in awe of him. He wondered, with all the engineer knew, whether he should ask him about girls. But then he might start talking about the heart and the blood and all the things inside that a guy can never see, and he'd get all mixed up, more than before. Maybe he'd ask him some other time.

"What do you say, champ?" The engineer pulled Hershy's cap down over his eyes. "Hit any Texas leaguers lately?"

Hershy pulled his cap up. "No," he said.

"Got to keep the balls hot, kid." The engineer winked at the office girl, who turned away red in the face. "Got to keep up that old batting average, champ. Remind me to tell you sometime what them Texas leaguers did to my batting average in the Three-Eye League."

No, thought Hershy, he couldn't talk about it with the engineer. He might say: Remind me to tell you about a little girl I had when I was four; by the time I was going on twelve, like you, I was an old old hand already.

He walked on to the wet floor of the plant. His father was walking down the aisle, pulling levers and twisting valves, amid the sliding belts and revolving wheels and washing machines. His boots were shiny and his bare arms were strained and his eyes looked buried between his forehead and cheekbones and his straight black hair was plastered to his scalp.

"How's it, Pa?"

"Oh, hello, Hershel. Look out, you'll get wet."

Hershy jumped back as a flooded washer, in its backward turn, gushed over. His father pulled a lever and let some of the soapy water splash into the gutter below.

"What's the good word, Pa?"

"Nothing. Nothing."

"Need some help?"

"No."

"Can't I do anything?"

"Later. Later."

His father stopped a machine and dragged the bundles to a ringer. He raised a lever. The high spin of the ringer began to slow down as his father walked away to the washing machines. The tight ball of clothes began to scatter, until, like a tightly woven rope had splintered to shreds, the clothes lay full and limp in the aluminum shell. Hershy wondered how, without hands, the clothes were wound up and wrung out and unraveled. His father came back, took out the water-extracted clothes, and dumped the wet wash into the ringer. Hershy pulled the lever down and started the spinning; he had helped out. His father patted his back.

"It's easy, Pa. Anybody can do it."

"That's right. Anybody."

"When you going to eat?"

"Later. Later."

"How come you don't go out to eat?"

"I don't have the time. Who'll tend the machines?"

"I will."

"When you get older. There'll be plenty of time for you to work when you get older."

"You mean you don't want me around?"

"No. You can go home and play. Play while you have a chance."

He lingered, feeling guilty; he really wanted to help. He also wanted to get back home, too. Maybe after supper he'd go over to the park and see Emily outside her house.

The engineer walked by. Hershy's father asked him if he'd watch the machines while he grabbed a bite to eat.

"Sure, sure," said the engineer.

Hershy followed his father with the package of food through the boiler room out into the alley. His father sat down on a wooden crate, and, closing his eyes for a moment, leaned heavily against the building. Hershy watched the sweat begin to dry on his skull-like face.

"You'll catch a cold, Pa."

His father shook himself and took a deep breath, as though coming out of a deep sleep. He opened the package and began to eat a salmon sandwich. He fumbled about the paper and brought up a pint bottle of milk. Opening it, he drained half the bottle before he set it down.

"Pa, we going to be rich someday?"

"I hope so."

"When?"

"Someday."

"Do all girls like rich guys?"

"I suppose so."

"Then we got to be rich."

"Why? Do you have a girl?"

"Who? Me?"

"Then don't worry about it."

"But we ain't rich now, are we?"

"No. We're poorer than we ever were."

"Why? Because the engineer makes all the money?"

"No."

"Because you used up all our money?"

"Yes."

"But when we get rich we'll have a big house, huh?"

"Yes."

"And a car and everything, huh?"

"Yes."

"When'll we be that rich? By the summer? By next year?"

"It takes time."

"Then maybe we'll move in a big house by the park on Sacramento Street, huh?"

"Maybe."

His father bit into another sandwich. Somehow, he wasn't interested in talking. He looked more like he wanted to sleep. Lately, he never seemed interested in talking. He didn't seem to care what was happening. He wiped his milky mouth with his hairy forearm.

"Pa, do I have a grandfather?"
"No. They're both dead."
"But I had a grandfather, didn't I?"
"Certainly."
"Did I have a great-grandfather, too?"
"Certainly. That was my grandfather."
"How about a great-great-great-great-grandfather?"
"You had them, too."
"Who was they?"
"I don't know."
"How come other people know who theirs was?"
"Why are you so interested suddenly?"
"Somebody said they had a great-great-great-great-grandfather in the American Revolution."
"Oh."
"What did mine do?"
"Yours? Your grandfather was the greatest of them all"
"Yah? Who was he?"
"Adam, the first man in the world."
"No kidding, Pa."
"It's true. All Jews are descended from Adam. Even the *goyishe* bible says so. So next time somebody boasts about their ancestors you tell them you're a descendant of Adam's. Hear?"
"Yah. How come you know so much, Pa?"
A weak smile appeared on his father's face.
"If I could only know so much as you, Pa."
"You will, Hershel. Much more. Much much more."
"I'd win every argument."

His father stood up and took a last deep breath of air and walked back into the laundry.

"You can go home now, Hershel."

"Okay. But any time you want some help let me know."

He still lingered on, feeling guilty in not helping. But his father paid no attention to him; the machines began to absorb him again. He wished his father was like he used to be, stronger-looking, and giving all his attention to him whenever he wanted it. Now he seemed to be inside himself all the time.

"Pa, do you wish you was a carpenter again?"

His father didn't answer him. A hundred spouts of dirty soapy water spilled out of the holes of a washer and splattered Hershy's shoes and stockings. Hershy decided, finally, to leave.

5.

Hershy began to train his hair with water and vaseline, and finally managed to get a clean unbroken part on the side. He brushed his teeth twice a day and no longer rebelled when his mother insisted upon his changing into clean clothes. He longed for long pants but was told he wouldn't get them until he got into high school. He studied the big guys, especially when they were with girls: the way they walked and talked and looked, wondering what they talked about and what was happening to them as they walked or sat or stood still. The image of Rachel and Joey began to blur: as something without meaning which he could no longer relate to himself; as something, almost, that had not happened, though sometimes it disturbed him in his sleep. In fact, with her gone, he began to miss her, as his mother and father did, for it felt strange and lonely about the house without her.

From time to time, when she sent a picture postcard from some different part of the country, he could almost see her getting dolled up and eating supper with him, and he could almost hear her singing voice and smell her nice powdery skin. And he could almost hear himself say to her, after a breathless trip through all the wonders she had seen and done: Rachel, what's a girl really like, what do they want, how do they like a guy to be, what do you talk about with them, how are you supposed to feel? Maybe she'd tell him. He wished she was home again, as much as his mother and father did.

He also wished, as he observed himself in the mirror and began to estimate himself, that he had dark curly hair and that his ears didn't stick out and that his teeth wouldn't make his mouth bulge and that his nose wasn't so bony and that his eyes were wide and dark insead of light and sunken. He wished he was six feet tall, with broad shoulders and a big chest and narrow hips and strong legs, with muscles busting out all over. For, when he looked at his bony knees and the thin fuzz on his shapeless legs, at his tight white skin with only his ribs and two nipples designating his chest, at his flat waist and bony pelvic region, and at his narrow arms and shoulders, he saw himself as something not yet formed. He became helpless at the sight of himself; he'd never become a man. Time, to him, became a stationary thing; it never moved. It seemed to him that he had lasted a century and that nothing had changed about him. Growing up was endless.

His mother, noticing his change (though he thought she was too absorbed with worry about the business and his father and the growth within her), clasped her hands and screamed with delight: my, how he was growing.

Yah-yah, he sing-songed.

She concluded that he had a girl.

He wouldn't admit that he had a girl, not even to himself.

Soon he'd be coming to her, she knew, to say he wanted her to meet his sweetheart.

He didn't have a girl, he growled.

Who was she? What was she like?

She was like nothing. He didn't have nothing.

Then why was he so impatient about long pants and growing tall? Why did he glare at the clock and the calendar and curse them? Why did he brush his teeth and wash himself and comb his hair without being told?

Because. That's why.

Pisher, sissy, monkey-face, she ridiculed him. So young and he had girls on his mind already. How time flew. Yesterday he was in diapers. Yesterday he had stood up and had taken a step and had fallen on his face. Yesterday he was a sick baby on a ship crossing the Atlantic Ocean. Now look at him. Look at him bristle. Look at him worry. Look at him die with impatience. Look at him. Look at him. How time flew.

She crunched his face in her hands and kissed him on the lips. He broke away from her, bewildered by her emotion. Then she got sad. Her face blurred in the shadows of Time. Yussel was gone: forever. Rachel was gone. Soon Hershy would be going away. Oh, she knew. A girl came and the boy went. A girl came and a child suddenly became his own boss. Soon everybody would be gone. Soon, though she was going to give birth to a new baby, she'd be left alone with only his father. Soon, soon. Yesterday's dream, today's past. How time flew. . . .

Time.

For his mother it flew. For his father there was no time; there wasn't a second of the day that didn't consume him; time was a hungry mouth; it ate him up alive. For Hershy, time stood still. It was a funny world.

Time left him in a state of suspense, too. Was Emily going to be in school the next day? What was she going to look like? What was she going to wear? Would she turn around and glance at him? Would she talk to him? Would he walk her home? Could he think up a stunt to get him away from the guys so that he could walk her home? Then what would they talk about? What would they do? Couldn't he think up any games both of them could play? . . . Time left him with a sense of entering unknown vistas of experience; it left his cluttered heart and mind on the brink of bottomless chasms. He wanted to give but didn't know how. He wanted to take but didn't know what. Time brought him to a dictionary; it solved a problem.

"Hey, you're so smart, tell me what this means. Quagga."

"What, smarty?"

"It's a horse, see; like a zebra, see; with stripes, see."

"Where'd you learn that, from a dictionary?"

"No," he lied. "Think I read the dictionary like you? I seen a quagga in the zoo."

"You mean, you *saw* a quagga."

"All right. *Saw*."

"And I don't read the dictionary, smarty."

"You do too."

"How do you know? Have you ever seen me?"

"*Saw*, not *seen*. See?"

"*Seen* is right, the way I used it."

"*Saw-seen*, what's the diff? I know you read the dictionary."

"You're a dirty, nasty, supercilious, unconscious, for saying that."

"Yah? Then how do you get them dollar words, from your own head?"

"Yes, see? At night, when I'm asleep, they come right into my mind. Sometimes I make up a whole poem from my own mind when I'm sleeping and it has the most beautiful words in the world. See?"

"Ah, baloney."

"If you talk to me like that, I won't let you talk to me any more."

"Okay, don't talk to me then. Who can understand you anyway?"

Silence.

"Then don't talk to me."

Silence.

"Ah, for Cry Yike."

Silence. Then:

"You going to use that word, quagga, tomorrow?"

"No."

But when teacher began weighing the value of words, Emily gave the class the word he had presented to her, and his heart turned over.

Once he gave her a real present, at a priceless cost.

Many times, after delivering his father's supper and trying to help out at the laundry and after eating his own supper, he sneaked out of the neighborhood through the alley, so that he could avoid meeting his pals, and went to where Emily lived. On the park side of the street, opposite her yellow house with the squirming bay windows, there was a large clearing of soft earth and grass, which, as the sun sank, became shadowed and cooled by the tall trees surrounding it. There, he'd do handstands and cartwheels and somersaults, hoping she'd see him through the windows. Sometimes she came out and passed by with a girl friend and, watching him begin to perform twice as hard, she said: "Who is that strange little boy over there? What queer things he does!" Sometimes, though, she came over alone. "You get away from in front of my house, you conceit, you show-off, you braggart, you acrobat." But he knew that she liked his stunts, because after a little fight she'd sit down on the grass and she'd scream with

· *251*

delight as he wore himself out with more stunts; then tired, he'd sit down beside her and feel himself drawn very close to her, beyond their desperate awkwardness and agonizing silences.

But one evening she didn't appear at all, neither in her window nor outside. He wore himself out, performing and watching for her, wondering what had happened to her; but when the lights went on in her house and came out on the street, he knew that she was home and had ignored him and that she wasn't going to come out. He dived into the grass on his hands and stretched out exhausted. Presently, through the swelling sound of the crickets and the soughing of the trees overhead, he felt the whole earth move against him, lifting him high high, until it became a huge ball with himself dangling over a curved edge of endless space. Then, looped in the incessant swirl of the cricket's sound, he rolled up to his knees, rolled up to his feet, and, feeling as small as the cricket, began to walk home.

On his way, he heard the sound of a mandolin. It seemed to reach out to him and, as though grasping him by the hand, it led him to Old Man Parker's basement flat. Mr. Parker was the only real American that lived on the street. Nobody knew what he did and how he lived, but Hershy's mother once said: "What does he have to do? He's a genuine American. Isn't that enough?" Outside of his mandolin playing he was always reading books and sometimes he recited poems. When he talked his words sounded more foreign than anybody Hershy knew.

Hershy looked through the window and saw the old man sitting in candlelight, plunking his mandolin, his shadow huge on the wall and his gray beard and hair and clothes yellowed by the light. Mr. Parker saw him suddenly and stopped playing. He rose slowly and seemed to creak himself as he opened the creaking door.

"Come in, son. O enter, son."

Hershy walked in timidly. The place was dusty, as unkempt as Mr. Parker, and smelled of old age, loneliness, and mothballs.

"Sit down. O please sit down."

Hershy sat down stiffly on a soiled wooden chair and leaned against an old coat that was draped around it. A cloud of dust rose and the springs began to screech as Mr. Parker eased himself into a rocking chair. His eyes seemed to run and his tongue was a fiery red in his yellow-gray beard when he spoke.

"Anything wrong, son? What makes you so pensive and silent?"

Hershy felt that an ant was crawling down his back. He glanced at a spider web across a shelf of books and wriggled his shoulders. He said: "Nothing."

"Have you lost your best friend? Your dearest sweetheart?"

The phrase frightened him, in the way it was said. He felt himself wanting to leap up and run, in the way Mr. Parker's head wobbled as he leaned forward.

"Do not worry, son. I am an old man dried by a century. I am a lonely old man with an ancient past. Do not see sadness in my weak eyes. If there are tears, see gratitude in them."

Hershy gulped and tried to relax. Mr. Parker always talked funny, like he was remembering something and reciting it, his voice dry and froggy, the words matted by the shaggy hair that covered his whole face. Hershy could almost feel Mr. Parker's voice boom in his belly. He could almost feel the heavy-veined, wrinkled, shaggy hands upon him, as they quivered. He felt himself recoil. But the old man was a real American. Maybe he'd know Emily better if he could know a real American.

"Why don't you play some more, Mr. Parker?"

"Do not be frightened, son. I am an old man in a dusty

basement. But you are youth. O youth. The lovers, the creators, the vital ones. I will write you a song."

Mr. Parker rose and went to a cluttered roll-top desk. He fumbled about for some paper, opened a book, and with a trembling hand began to write. Hershy watched, both frightened and fascinated, rooted to his chair. Mr. Parker folded the paper, then got up and put it in Hershy's shirt pocket. And then Hershy almost leaped with terror as he felt the trembling old hand on his head and heard a new note, almost of frenzy, come into Mr. Parker's voice:

"*O camerado close! O you and me at last, and us two only.
O a word to clear one's path ahead endlessly!
O something ecstatic and undemonstrable! O music wild!
O now I triumph—and you shall also;*
(Mr. Parker fumbled for Hershy's hand)
*O hand in hand—O wholesome pleasure—O one more desirer and lover!
O to haste firm holding—to haste, haste on with me.*"

Hershy flung Mr. Parker's hand off his head and rushed out of the door. He ran wildly down the block and finally stopped. He didn't know what had happened, except that he had had a feeling of being engulfed, that he couldn't breathe, like suddenly he was drowning in a sea of wriggling veins and yellow-gray moss. It was when he began to scratch his head, puzzled and wondering why he had got so scared, that he missed his skull cap. He walked back stealthily to the basement flat. Mr. Parker was hunched over his desk, his head on his arms, his back shuddering, and great sobs tore out of his throat. The terror Hershy had felt had run out in his flight; in its stead a deep sense of pity welled up. He tiptoed in through the open door and took his cap off the floor and stepped out without making a sound.

The following day he couldn't help but dramatize the evening before to himself. And when he presented Emily with the poem that was written for him he thought he had risked his very life for it.

"Here," he said. "A poem I wrote for you. I almost died to do it."

She pecked his cheek and ran away and left him standing in a bewildered straitjacket of joy. But the next day, without warning, she stepped up to him in the park, just as he was getting to his feet from a somersault, and slapped his face.

"You're a dirty, nasty, filthy-minded person, you, and you ought to get your mouth washed with soap and water until the day you die, you you you filthy."

"Why, what'd I do?"

"My mother told me what you wrote. You're a foul, evil-minded, dirty little boy, she said, and I must never see you again."

She handed back the poem; it was what Mr. Parker had recited to him the night before, and below it was written—*by Walt Whitman, who was also so misunderstood.*

"Besides, my mother said I have no business playing with a dirty little Jew. See?"

The words shocked him: he had never considered whether she was Jewish or not.

"Yah?" he said, his breath coming hard.

"Yes. I'm never to see you again. Now beat it, you dirty little Jew."

His fists tightened and he glared at her and for a moment he couldn't move; but when she turned her back on him and walked away and he saw her curls bounce haughtily on her shoulders, something inside him seemed to tear loose. He ran over and kicked her with all his might. He looked down at her as she screamed and cried on the ground, then his heart seemed to drop out of his hands as they uncurled, and

· 255

he walked home with a great emptiness. He met some of his pals sitting on the curbstone under the light of the lamppost outside his house. Listening to them talk and yearn, he declared solemnly: "Ah, they all stink out loud."

CHAPTER ELEVEN

1.

Every other year, as the school term drew to a close, Hershy felt like a wild bridled horse, bucking and straining against rein and saddle and bit. And, when released finally—the rein loosened, the bit snapped, the saddle flung off—he burst out in a frenzy of joy: school was over: he had passed: it was summer summer summer ... A time for liberation and belonging: all outdoors was his.

But this year, after the initial outburst of joy, he learned for the first time in his life that summer was also a time for oppression; in its vivid and luxuriant growth, corrupt bodies entered with seeds of despair and decay. For it was evident by then that the laundry, as well as his father, was slowly disintegrating.

"The devil," his mother said, mopping her wet face and groaning with the burden of her added weight, "has come to spend his holiday with us."

Hershy noticed that she long ago had stopped welcoming his father eagerly each time he came home.

"How was business today?"

"So-so."

"Was it good?"

"So-so."

"How many bundles did you wash today?"

"A hundred."

"But Irving said you can handle two hundred a day."

"What one says, what one dreams about, and what is really true, are three different things."

"Still, a hundred bundles isn't bad. At a dollar a bundle, it's a hundred dollars. You made a hundred dollars today."

"If only it were so simple."

"If you washed them you made it."

"All right, then I made it."

"So where is it?"

"In a piece of coal, a barrel of soap, in a fixed machine, in the landlord's pocket, on the engineer's table; in a thousand things a business consumes. So tell me, where is it?"

"Don't worry. You just started. Wait, business will get better. You'll expand. You'll hire more workers. You'll have it easy then. You'll just sit in the office. You'll see."

"I hope so, I hope so, I hope so."

But when he began staring at her as she talked, falling asleep at the table while waiting for his supper, becoming more and more silent, her eagerness died away. In its stead rose a sense of guilt. A dim hope, vague and aching, mingled with fear, took over. She became concerned more with survival than with success.

2.

Hershy was at the laundry the day a city inspector came to look the plant over. He showed his badge and Hershy noticed his father become nervous as the man walked about and noted things down in a black notebook.

"What is it?" his father asked. "What's the matter?"

The man didn't answer. He observed and made notes in his book; he mopped his thick red face and the leather band of his straw hat. Finally, having obtained the fear and respect he wanted, he cleared his throat and said:

"Mr. Melov, you're in a jam."

"How? Why?"

"You're not operating according to regulations."

"How is that? What do you mean?"

"I could close you down tomorrow, like that." The inspector snapped his fingers.

Hershy watched his father's body twinge, as though he had been cracked with a whip.

"Yep." The inspector snapped his fingers again. "Like that. Tomorrow."

"But this place has been in business for years. Why suddenly, now, is it operating against the law?"

"Well, for years we didn't know about this place, see? But people have started to complain about the smoke from your stack. It's too low, not according to regulations. If they hadn't complained, nobody'd have known the difference. But now that they have and I've come to look things over, I see you not only need a higher stack but you also need a brick wall instead of wood to separate the boiler room from the plant. That's a safety regulation."

"But who has to worry about safety? I'm the only one in the plant. I don't have any workers here. If anybody is unsafe, it's me, the owner, the boss, nobody else."

"It makes no difference, Mr. Melov. You got to operate according to regulations. That's the law."

"Who complained?"

"Why? You think you can do anything about it?" He looked his father over, with a slight chuckle and a sneer, his bulky body towering over him. "The neighbors around here are big fighting Polacks."

His father shook his head weakly and wiped the sweat from his eyes.

"Well, what are you going to do about it?" said the man.

"I don't know."

"Do I put in an order to close you up?"

"No. No."

"What are your plans then?"

"Where will I get the money?"

"That's your worry."

"Can't you help me? You see, I just started the business. Give me a chance to get on my feet. I'll do everything right. God knows, I want to do everything right. Just give me a little time, I beg you."

The man stuck his thick lips out, thinking.

"Well," he said, "I don't have to turn in my report right away."

"No. Please give me a little time."

"I don't like to see a guy trying to get along put in a jam."

His father's eyes began to look grateful.

"I figure," the man said, "it'll cost you a good five hundred for the job, maybe closer to seven-fifty before you're through, what with labor costs and all that going up. I'll tell you what I'll do. Would it be worth two hundred bucks to you if I don't turn in my report?"

His father's eyes seemed to spin, then grow wide and rigid.

"For two hundred bucks," the man said, "I'll tear up this report and I'll turn in another one saying the plant is in perfect order, operating according to the law. How's that, Mr. Melov?"

His father's mouth began to quiver and the man, mistaking it for heartfelt gratitude, said:

"After all, I know what it is to get started. I know what it is to get a good break out of life. And after all, what's a couple hundred iron men compared to five hundred or seven-fifty. . . ."

"Get out." His father's extended arm and pointing finger shook. "Get out of here."

"Okay. That's your business. I'll give you till the end of the day to change your mind. If you do, call me at the city inspector's office. Ask for Mr. Mahoney."

"You grafter," his father called after him. "You swine. You nogood bloodsucker. Two hundred dollars today: how much next week? A simple, honest man tries to get along; he kills himself. Day by day the life is sapped from his body. For what: to fill your pockets with two hundred dollars every Monday and Thursday?"

He sat down on a bundle, choking and trembling. Then he clutched the bundle and, in looking about the plant for something steady and secure to brace himself, it seemed that he was becoming engulfed in the steaming heat and the grating gears and the swirling belts and the sloshing washers and the whirring ringers, and a look of terror came into his eyes. He closed them quickly, reached for Hershy, and clutched him to his chest. Hershy gradually felt him calm down. When he was released, his father sat, almost helpless. Then with great effort, he rose and began to tend the machines.

3.

Uncle Irving, hearing of this when he came off his route later with a load of bundles, was rocked to his toes. He flared up beyond the sound of the machinery and followed Hershy's father down the wet aisle between the washers.

"Fool. Lamebrain. Idiot. A man tries to do you a favor and you spit in his face. Idiot, idiot, you. Have you forgotten the heavy thousands we have invested here? Have you forgotten that our lives are sunk in here? Have you forgotten our whole future? And for two hundred dollars you want to throw all of it away. What happened to you? What?"

"I don't know."

"What kind of an answer is that? What are you, a baby? Couldn't you think?"

"I don't know. Suddenly I felt trapped. One thing after another. One thing after another."

"Trapped? The man tries to let you squirm out, he tries to do you a favor: you call that trapped?"

"Suddenly he looked so corrupt I could see the maggots crawling out of him."

"So you saw the maggots crawl out of him. For that, you want to throw away fifteen thousand dollars? For that, you want to spend another seven hundred and fifty dollars to fix the plant? Where can we possibly get so much money, you fool, you?"

Hershy's father didn't answer. A washer overflowed and got Hershy and Uncle Irving wet. Sweat streamed down their faces and their clothes stuck to their bodies. Uncle Irving jammed a lever down and stopped the revolving motion of the flooded washer.

"We can afford two hundred," he said, "but not seven-fifty. The man takes pity on you. He sees we're just starting in business. He takes one look at you, he sees you're worn out, his heart turns over. He thinks: all right, he'll do us a favor and let us go until a time comes when we can do things right. And you, with your false sense of honesty, your fear of corruption, throw him out. Oh, why did I ever go into business with you? Why?"

"I can ask the same question. Why?"

"You came begging me to go in with you."

"I? Begging? Who had the money?"

"What's the difference? Without me you couldn't get along."

"No? What did I need you for? What did you put into the business: fifteen hundred dollars? But me, I put in thirteen thousand five hundred dollars, and then I put in another fifteen hundred for one thing after another. I don't have a penny left in the bank. If the business fails I'm ruined. And you stand there and tell me that without you I couldn't get along?"

"Wait a minute, don't talk so fast. We're partners. Half the money in the business is mine."

"Sure, half of it is yours. But out of whose pocket did you get it? Mine, mine. Outside of your fifteen hundred dollars, not a penny in the business is yours."

"What, are you crazy? I put in seventy-five hundred dollars, half the investment. Don't forget I borrowed six thousand dollars."

"And who's paying on the loan?"

"The business."

"Certainly, the business. But out of whose pocket is that money coming from? From mine. I'm paying your debt, don't forget. That's the kind of partnership we have. Do you pay the loan out of the wages you draw? Tell me. Tell me."

"But I have to live. My children and my wife can't go without a piece of bread, can they?"

"What about me? Because of the loan I have to draw less wages. Week after week I draw less money because the business has to pay the loan. So who's paying, if not me?"

"All right. You don't want to pay, don't pay."

"Smart one, you. All we have to do is miss a payment, then what have we got: the street, a job to beg for? Is it any wonder I feel so trapped, so helpless. Oh, why did I ever meet you? Why did I ever listen to you?"

"Don't be so upset. I'll call the man and we'll pay him his two hundred dollars and he'll let us alone. Just attend to your work and we'll be all right."

"I'm attending to my work. It's you who's not attending to it. Two hundred bundles a day, you said. Profits we'll make, swollen profits. We'll expand, you said, move to another building, hire more inside workers and drivers. If Hymie can do it, why can't we? Dreams. Idle dreams. And you tell me to attend to my work. I'll attend to all the work you can bring. I know what I do with my time. But you, outside, on the street, what do you do with your time while I slave: play cards, chase after women?"

"Never mind what I do. Look after yourself. Do you get the bundles out on time? And why do you let clothes get torn and lost, and make me the victim of complaints? Because you don't pay attention to your work. Every time I see you, you have a hammer or a saw or a chisel in your hand. What are you, a baby, still playing with pieces of wood?"

"I build things because the plant needs them."

"They don't have to be so fancy."

"When I build something it has to be good. You're not talking to an ordinary laborer. You're talking to a man who was once a skilled carpenter."

"And you don't have to waste your time building desks and fixing things for the help."

"What do you want me to do: buy desks, hire a carpenter to make things we need?"

"Ah, shut up already. I'll call the man up and tell him to tear up his report and come in for his two hundred dollars. But shut up already."

"Don't tell me to shut up."

Uncle Irving poked his finger in Hershy's father's chest.

"I'll tell you to shut up and you'll like it," he said.

Hershy cringed under their blazing eyes and tense bodies. Suddenly, his father slapped Uncle Irving's face.

"Nobody can tell me to shut up."

Uncle Irving stumbled backward and then struck back at Hershy's father. It was the strangest fight Hershy had ever seen. They stood toe to toe, slapping each other's faces with the front and back of their open hands. Saliva ran out of their mouths and tears out of their eyes. Then they began to grapple. They slipped on the wet walk and rolled over and over each other on the soapy floor. Spouts of dirty water from the pocket-holes of an open washer gushed over them as they tore at each other's mouths and eyes and hair. Hershy rushed in and locked his arm around Uncle Irving's throat. He held on with all his might. Then all his air was sucked out of him as Uncle Irving smashed his elbow into his stomach, and, flung off, he blacked out just as his head struck a protruding pipe.

They were on their knees, breathing heavily over him, their faces scratched and bloody and running with sweat, when he opened his eyes.

"See, he's all right," said Uncle Irving. "He's all right, he's all right. I told you he's all right."

"Are you all right?" his father asked.

Hershy swallowed hard and nodded.

"Thank God."

He cried out in pain as his father touched the swollen part of his head that had hit the pipe. He touched it himself and winced; the wetness, thinking it was blood, sickened him; but when he looked at his fingers he saw that there wasn't any blood, only the moisture of his own body.

". . . I didn't mean it, Hershele," Uncle Irving was saying; he began to cry. "It should have happened to me."

He felt peculiar at the sight of Uncle Irving crying. Then he wondered if he could get up. He sat up and blinked his eyes. His strength was coming back.

"Here," said Uncle Irving, fumbling for his hand. "Here's a quarter. Spend it. Be a king. Buy candy. Buy anything. Here."

Hershy closed his fist around the quarter.

"Can you walk now?" his father asked.

Hershy nodded. He got up. His head throbbed as he walked. But he wanted to get out. He wanted to get away.

"I'm going home," he said.

"Good, good," said Uncle Irving. "Go home. Go in a candy store. Spend the quarter. Have a good time."

"Don't tell Mama we fought," his father said.

"No, Pa."

"He's a good boy," said Uncle Irving. "A Samson."

"I'll tell Ma, if she sees the bump, I fell down."

His father patted his back and kissed his forehead, then Hershy left. Outside, shimmery waves of heat rose from the street, but he felt cool coming out of the laundry. A rock seemed to swell in his heart as he walked to the streetcar. It felt like it was going to burst through his chest—right up to the time his father came home; then, for a while, he felt it begin to crumble and patter down through his insides.

His father told his mother about the fight and that they had decided to pay the inspector. He was talking, he said, so that he might try to recognize himself once again; for a change, he felt, had come over him. It seemed that a new force had come to dominate his life. He had never known himself to become so violent before. Twice in one day, everything in him had suddenly turned black, as though a terrible disease had ravaged him, and all at once he was shaken with a crazy desire to kill. Not only did he want to kill but he also felt that he wanted himself destroyed at the same time. What was happening to him? . . . He looked up and shook his head in bewilderment. And then, as Hershy's mother moved toward him, he buried his head above her swollen stomach and let himself, like a child, be patted and soothed.

The rock in Hershy formed hard again. He gritted his teeth and prayed: Kill the laundry, God. Make my pa like he used to be. Make my pa strong again. Make us all like we used to be, and make us all happy and good on each other all the time. Kill the laundry, O God.

4.

Summer . . .

A time of quick growth and quicker decay; of hot winds blowing off the prairies and shaking the ragweed and sunflowers; of heat blasts melting the asphalt and choking the air out of a room; of prayer for rain and a cool off-shore breeze and an apartment on the lake front; of damp faces and sticky flesh and fly-pocked stores and limp bodies and asthmatic breathing and sharp garbage smells; of bedding down on the back porch at night and waking up in the cool fly-buzzing dawn and dragging your sleep-heavy body back into the house.

A time for ball games and swimming, crickets and birds, hotdog and popcorn stands. A time for diving into new-cut grass and climbing trees, for slingshots and bows and arrows, for boatrides in the park and gulping fishes making rain circles in the lagoon, for riding bronze buffaloes and firepumps and swings, for banging down the chute-the-chutes and hurtling through space on the Cyclone, for lightning and thunder and ever-changing skies, for exploration and discovery, for shadows in the night and mysteries, for talk and talk and horseplay.

O kid, whirling on the high-flyer, wandering on a path, chasing a ball in flight, hooking a worm, studying the agitated lips and squirming bodies in lover's lane, thrashing in water, lying in a leafy shade—what's it like, what's it like?

I don't know, he says. It ain't like it used to be.

. . . A time to hear from Rachel. A picture of her lying on a beach in a bathing suit. Look at me, I'm laughing, she writes.

We die of the heat, says Hershy's mother, and she laughs. It's her America.

Another picture. One of a stranger, puzzling everybody. Isn't he cute, she writes.

Rachel must be going crazy, says Hershy's mother.

It was a picture of a clown, with a duncecap on his head, a face dipped in flour, balls of paint on his cheeks and the tip of his nose, little sad eyes, and the widest mouth anybody had ever seen.

Another picture. The same clown and Rachel in her spangled dancing costume. Look at us, we're hysterical, she writes.

What could possibly be happening to her, the wild Indian? says Hershy's mother.

And another picture. Another stranger, with a soft face, a straight nose, a nice mouth, curly hair, but the same sad eyes. Meet my hubby, she writes.

The news comes with a shock. Hershy's mother cries. His father's shoulders sag, he looks helpless, he feels guilty. Rachel is really gone.

. . . A time for pity and worry and responsibility.

A different kind of summer.

Hershy worried about his mother. The heat wore her out, making her groan and catch her breath; with her energy sapped, the house began to look dirtier and less orderly, and she seldom washed the floors to cool the house, and she dreaded her duties over the stove. She could never get comfortable and all of her seemed to stick together. The heat, it seemed, contracted her face and at the same time puffed up her whole body. The sight of her, and a sense that she was very far away from him, gripped Hershy's heart. Sometimes he looked up at the sky and said: "God, don't let nothing happen to my ma." That was when he felt that the baby had taken her over completely and a fear rose in him that it might transform her into something else that he couldn't name or wouldn't be able to recognize.

His father, struggling against his inevitable fate, not daring to admit failure, for in it was a kind of death, was crushed between the simple life he had always wanted and the complicated life that was demanded of him. Sunk in everyday worries, wallowing in dampness, eroded by the biting salt of his sweat, exhausted by the daily demands of the business, his body began to rebel but his mind held it in check and would not let it defeat him. The rebellion took form in a cold that lasted all summer; with it came a hacking cough, splintering him to pieces. He had never been sick a day in his life and, not understanding illness, refused to submit to it. But sometimes he felt his mind would snap. When this feeling came over him he did the only thing that gave him a sense of order and accomplishment and pleasure; he would begin to make something out of wood, whether it was necessary or not. The surface of the wood and the sight of the grain and the feel of a tool over which he had full control was like water to his dehydrated body. It revived him and gave him a sense of being.

Hershy, however, heard only the cough. He saw only the eyes blurred with fatigue, the sagging shoulders, the skin drawn thinner over bone and muscle. Sometimes, when his father had his teeth out, his face looked so shrunken that Hershy thought he was staring at a skull. Once, on a Sunday, he saw him asleep in the rocking chair. The gentle face he had known was sunk in the hollow of his cheeks and seemed to spew out in the trickle of saliva on his chin; suddenly he looked very old and wasted away, and for a moment he thought he detected an odor of death rising from him. A lump came to his throat, but the shocking thought made him wake up his father. He watched his father stare at him without recognition and then go back to sleep again.

"I hope," he prayed, "the laundry burns. I hope the boiler explodes and the machines break. I hope."

Yet once there, after bringing his father's lunch or supper, he tried to help and he tried to pull his father back to himself.

"Today I swam twenty strokes, Pa."

"That's good."

"Yesterday we beat the Wyandottes, a great team, a real great team. Eight to seven, Pa. Some game, Pa."

His father dragged a bundle of clothes across the wet walk and dumped it into the ringer. Hershy helped him fill up the machine with other bundles.

"You know who's the new world's champion, Pa?"

He wasn't interested.

"Jack Dempsey, Pa. He beat Jess Willard. What a fighter. What a socker. The Manassa Mauler, that's who he is."

The ringer was full. Hershy started it up. It began to hum, then whine, higher higher.

"Maybe someday I'll be a fighter, Pa. I ought to start taking boxing lessons. They make lots of money. Lots and lots."

His father didn't protest. He hated the thought of fighting but he didn't say a word against it.

"Or maybe a ballplayer, Pa. They make lots of money, too. And it's healthy. All day long they're outside in the fresh air."

"All right, be a ballplayer. Be a fighter. Be anything."

Something was wrong. His father didn't care; he didn't care what happened to him.

"What's the matter, Pa?"

"Nothing. Don't talk so much."

"Who's talking? I'm only saying things."

"Go home and say them to your friends."

"But I want to help."

"Then help, but keep quiet."

All right, he thought. But he couldn't help himself; his need for his father to forget himself and reach out for him was too great.

"Hey, Pa, the Sox are in first place in the American League. Boy, what a ball team. They're going to win the pennant and then the World Series will be here in Chicago. Boy, will that be something to see."

His father looked beyond him.

"Hey, Pa." He drew his father's eyes to himself, then wondered what to say. Finally: "When's Ma going to the hospital?"

"Soon, soon."

"But when?"

"When the time comes."

"Then will she get skinny again and be like before?"

"Yes, yes." His father was irritated.

"What's the matter? Can't I even ask a question no more?"

"Go home. You helped me enough. Now go home."

"Okay."

He went home angry, promising himself that he'd never come back. But when he saw his father come home with his wet hair and damp clothes and blood-drained face, when he heard him cough at night, and then groan as he stiffly got up in the morning, the lump would rise in his throat again and he would go back the next day.

Sometimes, while out in left field waiting for the play to come to him, he'd suddenly think of his father or mother and miss a ball when it sailed out to him. They were even making a lousy ballplayer out of him.

It was the loneliest summer of his life.

5.

A huge hole developed in the structure of the business over which neither Hershy's father nor Uncle Irving had any control. During the summer, all of the larger laundries installed mangling and ironing machinery in order to give their customers complete service, from washing to finished work. It left their laundry with only one service to offer; gradually, even the customers they had began to drop away. To plug up this hole, another driver was hired and prices were cut to get more business. But a representative of the Laundry Owners' Association threatened to put them out of business completely unless prices were maintained. With more expenses added, and less and less money drawn weekly to bring home, and the monthly payments on Uncle Irving's loan draining their resources, hope for a miracle was slowly squeezed out of them. The only thing that could save them was more money for additional machinery, larger space to house it, and more workers for the new operations. Where could they get it?

The thought of salvaging what they had by selling out occurred to Hershy's father and Uncle Irving, but neither of them would come to grips with it. Though it was what Hershy's father wanted, he found himself fighting against it, unable to admit complete failure; once committed to the standards of business, he became their victim without realizing it.

Uncle Hymie, their last resort, simply didn't have the money. He advised them to sell out or get another partner. Would he be interested in coming in as a partner? they asked. No, he wasn't interested at all; he had enough troubles of his own. And, while they tried to interest a man with money to come in with them, a payment was missed on Uncle Irving's loan. It was then that Hershy's father realized fully that he was driven to his knees; the laundry, with his whole investment in it, could be taken away. Uncle Irving was unable to borrow the money anywhere and finally, after he agreed to sell the business, Hershy's father borrowed the money from Uncle Hymie. But as people came to the plant, not to buy the business, but to estimate the value of the machinery, it slowly dawned upon Hershy's father that they couldn't even sell the laundry. He felt trapped completely. He had nothing. He couldn't even escape, for the plant wasn't a job which could be left at will; it still demanded a moral and financial responsibility. It left him utterly helpless, yet he continued to drive himself, hoping beyond hope that perhaps the next day might bring a new turn in events.

6.

With the close of summer, a terrible heat wave moved over the city. Hot winds swept in from the prairies, prematurely withering the leaves and grass, and the cold Hershy's father had grew worse. He refused to see a doctor: it was nothing, he insisted, a slight cold.

One night, Hershy woke up in a sweat. He heard his father coughing and gagging. He heard him get out of bed and go to the bathroom and turn on the faucet and drink and then climb back into bed.

"Are you going to go to a doctor?" his mother said.

"No."

"Why are you such a stubborn fool? First I have to drive you with a whip, God forgive me, to go into business; then with a horse, when I see you killing yourself, I can't drag you out. Why are you so stubborn?"

"What will a doctor tell me? I have a cold, he'll tell me. That I know."

"Maybe he'll give you a medicine to stop the cough."

"It'll go away."

"All summer you've been saying that."

"As soon as it gets cooler it'll go away. Summer colds are hard to throw off."

"But maybe it's more than a cold. When I touch you it feels like you're burning up."

"It's the heat."

"Maybe, on purpose, you want to stay sick."

"Don't talk such nonsense."

"Who knows? Maybe you want to punish me. Maybe you want to ruin yourself forever. Maybe you want to ruin all of us."

"Sonya! Stop talking like a fool."

"What have you got against me, David? Why don't you go to a doctor and prove you have nothing against me?"

"I haven't the time. Go to sleep."

"Time. You'll have a million years to remain buried, but how much time is there in a life? How much time is there altogether if you try to kill yourself sooner? David, listen to me."

"Go back to sleep. I'm tired."

"If something should happen to you what will happen to us?"

"Will you go back to sleep?"

"Remember, you're not made of iron. You're only a man."

His father kept silent. Hershy thought he could detect his mother crying:

"I thought: money comes to money. A little money will bring more money. All one needed to do was go in business and one became a success. Don't blame me, David. If anything should happen to you, I'd die. Oh, David, what will I do with you?"

There was no answer from his father.

"Oh," his mother said. "How he's burning up!"

There was a kind of rattle coming from his father's throat as he fell into deeper sleep. A wet kind of breathing came from his mother's sobbing nose and throat, and then she fell asleep. Hershy felt himself carried away and then flung, in his sleep, into a violent storm at sea. A huge wave crashed against the side of the ship he was on and turned it over.

Suddenly, he saw his father and mother drowning. He swam over to them and held them up. Slowly, being tossed madly up and down by the waves, his arms got limp and he felt himself begin to sink with his mother and father. Then, just as a wave came up to engulf them, a whale rose from it and ate them alive. They rode in the whale's belly for days. His mother and father sat helplessly about; it was he who knew just what to do and who kept them alive. He explored all over and found a knife one day, some flints, and driftwood. He cut the meat from the whale's ribs and built a fire and saved them from starvation. He did not know how long they lived in the great dark belly, but one day when the whale came up for air he heard the roar of surf. He knew they were near shore. He began to tickle the whale with his knife. The whale began to laugh. It opened its mouth so wide when it laughed that they could see the light and the land. He told his mother and father to make a run for it and swim to shore while he tickled the whale. When he saw them dive out he tickled the whale so hard that it heaved him right onto the shore.

He woke up from the impact of hitting the shore and found himself laughing. He wondered if the dream meant anything. In it, he had felt so strong. He knew everything and he was able to do anything. And he had saved his mother and father, even himself. Now, in the dark, he felt small and helpless. He tightened up wishing he could do something. But he knew that he could do nothing. He lay back limp, heavy with helplessness.

CHAPTER TWELVE

1.

The following morning the landlord's wife called Hershy's mother to the phone and when she came back she said: "Papa wants you at the laundry right away."

"Why so early?"

"The engineer didn't come to work today. Papa needs some help."

"But I got a ball game this morning. We're playing the Eagles."

"The Eagles can wait but Papa can't."

"Ah, I never can do what I want no more."

She prepared a lunch for him and his father and he left for the laundry. Outside, his pals were beginning to practice for their game with the Eagles.

"Hey, Hersh. Where you going?"

"I got to go help my father."

"You mean you ain't going to play?"

"No."

"Aw, show up later."

"I can't."

"Ah, you're never any fun no more. Ever since your old lady got fat and your old man went in business you're never any fun no more. Always got to do this, always got to do that."

"Ah, shut up already."

He left the street slowly, wishing he could play. Niggy hit a high fly. Lala ran under it and caught it against his chest, then whipped it down to Moishy, who whirled about and whipped it back to Niggy.

"Attaboy, Lala."

"Right in the old socker, Moishy."

Niggy batted another one. Lala caught it on the bounce and hurled it back to Niggy. Jesus, said Hershy, and turned the corner wistfully. He boarded a streetcar and, in passing Joey Gans's restaurant and poolroom, felt like throwing a brick through the window. If it hadn't been for Joey that day, maybe his father never would have gone into business. Someday, when he grew up, he was going to kill Joey. He felt, in the drag of the wheels against the rails, that he himself was being dragged to the laundry by Joey and Rachel and his mother and Uncle Irving, and that pieces of himself, which he might never be able to find again, were being ripped away. He wished, when he got there, that he'd find the laundry burned down. Then he could rush back and play against the Eagles. Then everything might be like it used to be. Then maybe his father would stop looking like he was going to die.

When he got there his father was in the boiler room shoveling coal into the fire box. His clothes were wet, his breathing heavy, his eyes bloodshot; the flame of the fire highlighted the hollows of his grimy face. Hershy's self-pity was snuffed out by the sight of his father and he became eager to help.

"Here I am," he announced.

His father glanced at him and motioned him away.

"What do you want me to do, Pa?"

"Wait a minute."

Hershy watched the strain of his father's body as he dug into the coal pile, turned about with the full shovel, and dumped it into the hot fire. The veins stood out on his arms, one vein on his forehead wriggled like a worm, and the top of his head seemed to be yanked downward by the cords of his neck each time he heaved the shovel. He could hardly straighten his back when he finished. Then he doubled up suddenly, wracked by a coughing spell, and began to vomit.

"What's the matter, Pa?"

"Nothing."

"You sick?"

"No."

"Ma said you was sick. I heard her last night."

"Shut up and come with me."

"Ma said you should see a doctor."

"Don't you nag me, too. I asked you to come and help me, not talk."

"You don't have to holler, Pa."

His father stared at him silently. His pupils were glazed and it seemed as though a blood vessel had burst in the white part of his eyes. A nameless ache rose in Hershy's throat as he followed him to the washing machines.

"I want you to watch these three washers, Hershel. Can you do it?"

"Sure."

"Before when you helped me it was fun. Now it's serious. I need your help. I need it bad."

"Don't worry, Pa. I can do it. Watch. I pull this (he touched a lever) and the machine stops. I push it the other way, it goes. I turn this (he pointed to a valve) and whoosh, water comes in. I turn it back, the water stops. I turn this (he pointed to another valve) and I make the steam. See, I know everything."

"Good. Every ten minutes empty the machines. Then let in clean water and open the steam valve and then throw in the bucket of soap and the bleach. Call me when you need me."

"Okay, Pa."

His father left him, came back and worked beside him, left him again. It felt good to be trusted. He felt important. After each operation he called his father to check on him and to show him that we was doing things right. His father patted his head. He felt very close to him. He almost wished he could work with him all the time. Teamwork. You and me, Pa.

It was exciting, too. He turned a valve. The belly-button of the machine opened up and the dirty water drained out. He turned another valve and he could hear the water rush in from the overhead pipes. Another valve: steam cracked through another pipe, popped into the washer, and wet clouds rose. He pulled the lever, slish-slosh, like a big round barrel the washer rolled back and forth, back and forth, the belts swishing and sliding on the shiny wheels, the soapy water spilling out of the pocket holes. Boy, was he strong. Man-mountain Steinmetz, that's who he was. With a touch. One little touch and he made the water boil, the steam crack, the clouds come out, the machine turn, the gears clank, the belts slap and swish. One little kid, with an iron muscle. Powerhouse Melov, that's who he was.

"Am I doing good, Pa?"

"Good, Hershel. Good."

You and me, Pa, he thought. O you and me.

But turning valves and working the levers wasn't all that he had to do. There were buckets of soap and bleach to carry to the washers. After each wash, which took four operations lasting ten minutes each, he had to empty the pockets and carry the clothes to the ringers and then pick up more bundles to dump into the washers.

Soon the sweat began to pour out of his body and his soggy clothes began to stick to him. His armpits, then his face, then his whole body began to itch. His eyes got bleary and stung

· 279

from the sweat that streamed off his forehead; even his lips had a salty taste. He couldn't get enough water to quench his thirst. He drank and drank, and it poured right out of him. The life in his arms and legs seemed to go dead. He could hardly bend over, he could hardly lift a bundle, he could hardly straighten up. He had to grit his teeth and summon all his energy to dump a bucket of soap into a washer.

"Don't drink so much," his father warned. "You'll catch cold."

"I can't help it, Pa."

"It'll drain your energy."

"Yah, but I'm thirsty. My throat hurts."

"You'll get used to it."

When? he wondered.

"Maybe you better have something to eat now. Go to the grocery store on the corner and get two bottles of milk."

"Okay."

He ran to the store and ran back. Even running was easier. He sat in the alley outside the engine room, ate a sandwich and gulped some chocolate cookies down with a pint of milk. Some small kids came by rummaging through the garbage, hoping to find something of value.

The lucky punks, he thought.

From the distance he could hear a horseshoe striking an iron post. A ringer, he thought. Through a passageway across the alley he saw a gang of guys pass by swinging bathing suits. He shuddered as he felt a blast of heat from the laundry strike his drying skin.

I got to go back, he thought. But he couldn't get himself to move. He sat on an empty orange crate and began to watch an ant drag a dead fly along the ground. He wondered, as he told himself to go back inside, where an ant got all its strength. Soon he was looking at it without seeing it.

"Hershel." His father had come into the engine room to fire the boilers. "What's taking you so long?"

"Nothing, Pa. I just got through eating."

He stood up stiffly. There was an ache in his muscles. His skin felt very tight.

"Go back in and don't drink so much."

"Okay, Pa."

Sweat began to pour from him again. His skin loosened up quickly, making him feel soggy and itchy all over, and then his throat began to feel as though there was a raw sore in it. He tried to stay away from the fountain, but when he tried to wet his parched lips he tasted the salt of his sweat and got thirstier. He ran to the fountain and, feeling his belly swell, he became frightened as an image of a bloated dead horse formed in his mind. He came back to the machines, finding it harder to reach for the levers and valves. At times the clock he had to watch, with its face and hands blurred by the steam, never seemed to move. Suddenly, the engineer's grimy face, with his white teeth flashing and his mouth wide in laughter, appeared through the clock. Hershy waved his fist: "You sonofabitch. You dirty dirty sonofabitch."

"What's the matter, Hershel?"

"The engineer. Why'd he have to get sick?"

"A man gets sick, that's all."

"You're sick, too, but you're working."

"I'm different. I'm a boss."

"Yah?"

His father moved away from him, went into the delivery room, and came back with more bundles. The sight of them made him feel weaker. The sweat on his body seemed to turn into jagged teeth biting deeper and deeper into him.

"How long do I have to keep on, Pa?"

"Wait, you just got here."

"Yah? I been here all morning."

"I've been here since five o'clock."

"I missed the ball game against the Eagles."

"You'll play tomorrow."

"But the game was today, not tomorrow."

"Save your strength and talk later."

"And we was going to go swimming in the afternoon. To-day's boys' day in the park pool."

"You'll swim tomorrow."

"Tomorrow's girls' day."

"Don't you want to help me?"

He looked up at his father, at the eyes burning in his sweat-blackened face, at the wet coal dust on his black hair, at his sloping shoulders.

"Yah," he said.

"All right then."

A sense of pity welled up in him as he watched his father slosh down the aisle in his boots. He glared at the clock, where he thought he had seen the engineer's face laugh at him. He swore at the engineer anyway; it made him feel stronger. The clock, however, seemed to mock him. He thought the day would never end. Time stood still in a steaming maze of soap suds, rusty pipes, revolving machinery, screaming belts, whining-swishing-sloshing-clanking sounds, and wet clothes. He moved away from it to the delivery room. His father was sorting the soiled clothes. Then he couldn't believe his eyes. There were only a dozen bundles left.

"Hey, look, Pa. We're almost finished."

"Almost."

"Boy, I thought we'd never get through."

"Feel better now?"

"Yah."

The bundles became light. It was still daylight, it was still early. Maybe he could get back to the neighborhood on time and go to the pool and take a swim. He'd swim and swim. He could almost feel the shock of the water upon first jumping in. It revived him. He couldn't get the bundles to the machines fast enough. He dumped them into the pockets with a vigor he could hardly believe. One more operation, he thought. Four times. Forty minutes. Throw the wash in the ringers. Through. Finished. Forever. He could hardly contain himself. He saw the minute hand on the clock jerk. Move, clock. O move and let me go. It even seemed, as he worked the valves and levers, that he sparked the machinery with an added strength. Move. Faster. Faster. O hurry hurry hurry. . . .

In the midst of what he thought was the last batch of bundles Uncle Irving arrived with a new load. Everything in him caved as he saw his father and Uncle Irving drag the new bundles into the sorting room, heap upon heap. I quit, he said to himself. I quit, see. He looked up at the clock, but couldn't see the time, for mingled with the steam and the stinging sweat in his eyes were tears. He tried to wipe them away with the back of his wet hands. The added moisture of his hands bit deeper into his eyes.

". . . A regular man," Uncle Irving was saying.

He looked up and saw Uncle Irving, with his hooked nose and high forehead and smiling lips, in a reddish blur.

"Yah?" he said.

"You're a good boy, Hershele."

"Yah? Why don't your kids come and help?"

"They're at the beach."

Uncle Irving seemed to waver over him in a hazier blur and he felt a sharp thump in his chest.

"Yah?"

"Keep it up, Hershele, and maybe I'll give you a job."

"You and who else?"

"What are you so angry about?"

"Keep your job. Stick it, see. I'm helping Pa. I ain't working for you. I'll never work for you. I'm only helping Pa, see."

· 283

"All right, so you're helping."

"I don't want to help, see. I don't care if the whole laundry blows up, see. I'm quitting, see."

"Listen, snotnose. Don't do me any favors and don't help and go home right now for all I care. You're not helping me, you're helping your papa. I don't need any help, so my boys are at the beach. Tell your papa your troubles, not me."

The sharp thump in Hershy's chest began working like a piston. He clenched his fists, thrust his head forward, and began shouting: "Go fuck yourself. Go fuck yourself."

Uncle Irving reeled backward. He brought up his hand to strike him.

"Hit me. Hit me. I'd like to see you hit me."

Uncle Irving turned about and walked to the sorting room.

"Go fuck yourself, fuck yourself, fuck yourself," he yelled after him. "You yellow bastard."

He sprang to the valve of a washer and made it overflow as he let the water gush in. He ran to another valve and made another washer overflow. His father rushed over, grabbed his shoulders, and began shaking him. Then his father released him, turned the water off, and came back to him with his jaws quivering in anger.

"What's the matter with you? Have you gone mad?"

"No."

"What did you say to Uncle Irving?"

"Nothing."

"Next time you talk like that to anybody I'll kill you. With my own hands I'll kill you."

"He was teasing me."

"He was proud of you, your good work. He was grateful to you."

"He made me mad."

"And what were you trying to do with the machines?"

"Nothing."

"You wanted to destroy them."

"No, Pa."

"You did."

"No, Pa. He made me so mad I didn't know what I was doing. He didn't have to tell me his kids are at the beach. He didn't have to tease me."

"Will you attend to your work now?"

"Yah."

His father stared at him, shook his head, and began to walk away. His body doubled up suddenly; he reached for a pipe to support himself, and became shaken violently by a coughing spell. Then, straining to straighten himself, he disappeared into the boiler room. Hershy wished with all his might that he had been able to destroy the machines. He watched them spinning back and forth, relentlessly. Nothing, it seemed, could stop them. Nothing could hurt them. A man started them, but once under way, nobody could stop them until the last bundle was done. They were killing his father, yet he made them go; he couldn't stop them. Now they were killing *him*.

He had wanted to kill them, but he was stopped. They still went on and he fed them soap and water and clothes. More. More. Slopping over with soapy water, draining them, filling their bellies again, swishing, gurgling, sucking, spouting. More. More. . . . The new driver came in with another load. His father called him. More bundles dragged to the machines. More bundles, wet and heavier, sopping to the slippery floor, lugged to the ringers. More bundles to the delivery room. Uncle Irving picks them up, takes a nice ride on his horse and wagon in the fresh cool air, stops for a glass of soda water or lemonade, stops to play a fast game of cards, stops to talk to a lady and maybe does funny business with her, his kids at the beach splashing around. More. More. . . .

"My back hurts, Pa."

"Soon, soon you'll go home. Tomorrow, after a good night's sleep, you'll never remember this day."

"My throat hurts, too. I can't swallow, it hurts so much."

"Take a drink of water."

"But you said I shouldn't."

"If you need it, take it."

He went to the fountain. He drank and drank. The water seemed to gush right out of him. He could hardly get back to the washers. His father looked at him sadly and then left. He was always going away and coming back, going away and coming back; but he never seemed to be paying attention to the washers any more. He was making him do all the work. He was beat, a weakling, letting him, a kid, do all the work. No wonder he was failing, no wonder he was losing everything. He was finished. Why couldn't he admit it? Why did he keep on killing himself? All he had to do was say: I quit, see. That's all. I quit, see. Three little words. And he'd be like he used to be. Why wasn't he strong enough to say it? Why wasn't he strong, just plain strong, like Uncle Hymie? He'd be at the beach now. He'd be in the water now, the cool cool cool water. He wouldn't even try to swim. He'd just let the waves roll him around. So cool. Or he should be out in left field now, running way way back, the ball sailing high in the sky, a spinning dot in the blue blue sky coming down down down. . . .

Let me go, Pa.

A sharp pain began cutting into his side as he bent over to take the wash out of a machine. He could barely drag it to the ringer. He began looking for his father, but could hardly see in the wet haze. The pain began moving up his chest.

O let me go, Pa.

His father didn't come back. Maybe he wasn't coming back. Maybe he had left the laundry, left him alone.

O no, Pa.

He left the washers to look for him. He wasn't in the office. He wasn't in the delivery room. He wasn't in the boiler room. He wasn't in the stable.

"Pa," he began to yell. "Pa. Pa. Pa."

He started running from one place to another and then stopped; his father was shoveling ashes out of the ash pit.

"Where was you, Pa?"

"Here."

"I mean before, where was you?"

"Maybe I was in the alley."

"Yah?"

"Why, what's the matter?"

"Plenty. You're making me do all the work. You go out in the fresh air and make me do all the work."

His father dug the shovel into the ashes and dumped them into a basket.

"Let me go home, Pa."

"As soon as we finish."

"When'll that be?"

"When we finish."

"But I'm tired, Pa. I hurt all over."

"You do a little work and you're tired. What would happen if you really had to work?"

"I'd quit, see."

"Not if you were a man. A man never quits."

"No?"

"No."

"How about you?"

"What about me?"

"You're making me do all the work. I'm a little kid and you're making me do all the work."

He felt trapped in the glare of his father's eyes.

"You never worked so hard like me," he said. "Never in your whole life did you work so hard like me."

"Stop your crying and go back to the washers."

"If you don't let me go—" He hesitated.

"Then what? Then what?"

He reached for it in the far recesses of his mind, grasped it fully and pulled it forward, then let it fumble at his throat.

"Then what?"

His whole body strained for balance, and then he let it go.

"I'll tell everybody about Rachel and Joey Gans. Everybody, everybody, everybody."

He saw it come, the swift movement, the curled lips baring the thick false teeth, together with the sweat running out of the grimy face and the blood swirling in the eyes, but couldn't ward off the blow. He seemed to leap up to it and, as the hand struck his head, he fell to the ground, cringing and yelling: "No, Pa. Don't, Pa."

"I'll kill you the next time you say that."

"No, Pa. I didn't mean it. I won't say it. I won't."

A wild pain rushed through his body with the impact of his father's kick against his thighs.

"I'll kill you the next time you even think about it."

In a boiling mist he saw his father reach for him. He tried to scramble away; he had never seen his father like that before; but he was lifted off his feet and shaken until he thought his insides were going to tumble out. He clutched at his wrists and tried to kick. Then his shirt ripped and he fell to the ground.

"Now get back to the washers."

He crawled away slowly, not daring to look away from his father's tight quivering body. Then he rose to his feet and started back to the washing machines.

"I'll get even," he said. "I'll grow up, I'll get bigger, I'll get even."

He turned about to see if his father had heard and saw him sag to the coal heap and begin to beat the pile helplessly with loose fists as his body became shaken with a great sob.

But he was going to get even, Hershy vowed. As he resumed work he began to plot his revenge. The clanking sound of the gears, reminding him of freight trains clattering over tracks, gave him the perfect idea. Slowly the sound bore down on him, and presently it lifted him out of the laundry and he felt himself land on top of a boxcar. A breeze hit him and he jumped with joy. Air. Wind. He cupped it in his hands and washed his face in it. Man, O man. He felt the shaking of the car and heard the rapid clacking and the roaring engine. Faster, faster, faster. Louder, louder, louder. Farther, farther, farther. Until he was alone, whipped by the wind, free of everything, roaring through vast space, lost from his father forever.

But maybe his father wouldn't look for him. Maybe he wouldn't risk his life searching for him. Maybe he'd just let him go, as he had let Rachel go. He had to get another idea. Something that would make his father suffer for the rest of his life. Something terrible. Something *now* that would get him out of the laundry. Something to get him away from the blinding sweat and aching body and itching skin and sore throat. Something to hurt his father. Something. . . . Maybe hurt himself. Maybe kill himself. Then his father would see. It'd be his fault. His father'd cry after he was hurt or dead; he'd tear himself to pieces for making him do it. His mother'd kill him. Nobody'd ever talk to him. He'd be alone. Everybody'd spit at him.

He'd do it now. He'd show him. He'd get even. Now.

He saw the leather belt as it slid around the wheel. If he got his arm caught in it, where it crossed in the figure eight, it might lift him to the wheel on top. His father'd see him on top there, unable to get loose, the belt whirling him around and cutting him up, and maybe his father'd get killed trying to rescue him. Or if he got his arm caught in the gears. No. Nobody'd see him. But way up on top. He tried to brace himself.

Make me move. You're going to be sorry, Pa. O Jesus, make me move. Ma'll kill you, Pa. God'll kill you. Make me do it. Make me not be so tired. Make guts in my belly. The whole word'll kill you, Pa. O make me make me make me.

A hand kept him from moving. He was all set to do it and he was stopped. The hand on his shoulder was his father's.

"You tired, Hershele?"

He didn't answer.

"I know it's hard. But what else am I to do? I don't know where to turn. I came to the only person in the world I could turn to. Forgive me, sweet son. Forgive me."

He stepped away from his father's hand.

"I have something easy for you to do now. You'll take a rest, sit in a chair. All your hard work is finished. It'll be easy, you'll see. Come with me."

Reluctantly, he followed him to the boiler room.

"I'm pumping water into the boiler. All you have to do is sit there (his father pointed to a chair) and watch that gage. When the needle points here (his father drew a black line over a number on the gage), call me and I'll turn the water off. All right?"

He sat down sulkily and looked up at the gage.

"Remember to call me when it's time or something terrible might happen. All right?"

"All right."

"Remember, something terrible might happen if you don't call me on time. So watch carefully and rest. Tomorrow you'll feel proud of the help you gave me. You'll see."

His father moved away.

I'll never see, he told himself. He looked up at the gage. A strange mist seemed to cover it. He could almost see it, but not quite.

Pa!

Something: a hand, claws, clutched his throat.

I can't see, Pa.

Sure, you can see, he could hear his father saying. It's only in your mind.

I'm telling you I can't see. The sweat, I'm blinded.

Sure you can see. You're only making believe you can't.

I'm telling you, Pa. I'm telling you. You don't believe me?

You can see, all right.

All right then, don't believe me.

Don't lie. I know you. You want to go home. You want to get away.

Honest, Pa. Honest.

A stinging sensation twitched his face, as though he had been slapped; red whirled out of his eyes.

Now can you see? Can you, can you, can you?

He wasn't going to answer. His father didn't have to believe him. Nobody had to believe him. But something terrible was going to happen. Something so terrible there wouldn't even be a laundry any more. What? What could happen? Something terrible, his father said. What? How terrible?

This was the heart of the plant. That's what the engineer said. There, the boiler, like a face. The doors on top like cheeks. Below, the hungry red mouth, a dragon's tongue with fire on it. The jaws seemed to move. Stopped. The throat tightened. Gulp. A hot coal fell into the heap of ashes in the pit below. It startled him and his eyes leaped upward. The gage!

Pa! It's going up!

Still time. Still time.

Up! It's going up!

· *291*

Don't bother me. I'm busy. How will I ever get anything done if you keep calling me?

But something terrible . . .

Still time. Still time.

Pa! It's going up!

Nobody was listening. Nobody came. All right, he didn't care. But something terrible . . .

Behind the face, the long black body filling with water, the fire making it thirsty, more water, thirstier, the water boiling, parching the body, the more you drink the more you want, thirstier, filling with water. Something terrible . . . What? Steam. The fire made the water steam. The steam went to the engine. Big wheels. An arm moved the wheels, made the belts slish and slosh. Ssssss. Swish-swush.

It was hot. He felt his face on fire, his throat burn, his eyes heavy, his body slipping, slipping, slipping.

Slide! Slide! Slide!

Safe!

He woke up with a shock.

Pa!

He struggled against the claws on his throat.

It's going up!

He fought hard against the tight grip.

Something terrible . . .

Safe at home!

He rose out of a swirl of dust, was lifted by a thousand eager arms, thrown high in the air, landed softly in the net of arms, thrown high high again, carried away by a puff of wind, like a pennant flying, up up up . . . Over!

Pa! It's over!

The black line his father drew like a wire pulling at his eyes.

It's over! Something terrible! Pa! Pa! Pa!

His voice jolted back into the pit of his stomach, stunning him, leaving him gasping for air.

A strange ringing sound in his ears. His voice, screaming, coming back to him in a gurgle.

Like a gasp from his own body, he heard a sucking sound: the engine, laboring through the overflow of water in the boiler, began to suck water instead of steam into the cylinder, and, with the piston unable to compress it, the engine began to rebel. Hershy heard a hollow gurgle, like a fantastic underwater laugh, followed by a pop, like a cork being pulled out of a bottle. Then came a shrill whistle as the piston blew and a deafening crash as it smashed through the wall. For a moment, as the whole plant screeched to a violent stop and in the awful hush that followed, Hershy felt that the whole universe had altered, with everything dead, even himself, with only the wild pounding of his heart alive. Then his heart lifted him to a fearful frenzy and a wave of black terror engulfed him as a pipe broke and the hiss of live steam began to fill the room.

He dived into the coal shed and scrambled into a corner. Through a chink in the wood he saw his father rush into the room. He backed deeper into the corner, trying to stifle his breath, as he saw the wild bulge of his father's eyes, the terrible twist of his face, and the tight cords of his neck pull his voice out high above the hissing steam: "Hershel! Hershel!" Then he saw him duck under the shooting cone of steam. It seemed, for a second, that it had blown his body away. Then he saw a hand rise up from the swirls of steam, turning a valve, another valve, another. Suddenly the hissing stopped. In the awful cloudy silence that followed, it was as though the steam had choked everything, even his father. He waited for a sound of his father. Nothing. Only the steam crawling up the coal heap, coming at him with a deadly silence. Then his voice came back to him: "Pa! Pa!" It shattered the rising cloud and he scrambled through it over the coals and came out in the blinding mist not knowing what to do. He called and called, turned and turned, not knowing which way to go. Then his voice and his agonized body broke suddenly as he saw an opening through the steam: at the open door that led out to the alley his father lay crumpled up, with a trickle of blood running over his chin, his mouth sucked in between his sunken cheeks, his eyes staring.

Hershy fell to his knees and ran his hands over his father's face and chest, beside himself with terror; then he clutched his shirt, begging for a response, and tried to pull him to himself. But his father's dead weight was too much for him and he slowly slipped from his grasp. He stared at him a long while, a slow numbness creeping down his body, then something in him turned over as he saw the bone in his father's throat slide up under his chin. He fell on him and smothered his face with kisses. Then his father turned his face slowly toward him. Weakly, very faintly, and as though amazed at the fact, his father said:

"Hershel, I can't get up."

A note of fear rose in his voice.

"I can't get up."

CHAPTER THIRTEEN
1.

"Help me," said Uncle Irving. He had driven his horse and wagon to the doorway of the boiler room.

Hershy sat on his heels beside his father, staring down at his glazed feverish eyes, and couldn't move. Uncle Irving yanked him to his feet and shook him.

"Help me."

He didn't know what to do. He watched Uncle Irving prop his father against the back of the wagon.

"Now hold him while I get up."

He held his father, feeling his helpless weight. Uncle Irving jumped up on the wagon and grabbed his father under the armpits, then lifted him up and dragged him onto a bed of bundles.

"Come on up and sit with me."

Hershy climbed to the seat of the wagon. The horse strained in the harness and made the wagon creak as it moved off.

"What happened?" said Uncle Irving.

"I don't know."

"You were there. Why don't you know?"

"It wasn't my fault."

"Who's saying it was? But what happened?"

"I don't know."

He saw Uncle Irving's lips move, asking more questions, but he didn't hear him. He didn't hear the clomp of the hooves on the street nor the clattering of the wheels, nor did he feel the rocking of the wagon. All the way home he sat rigid, packed with the image of the statue that stood on the first landing of his school building: of the Indian sitting on his horse with his head tilted back and his arms stretched out to the sky. A scream crumbled the statue to bits when his father was carried into the house, and he saw his mother's face rip open. Her whole body shuddered and she reeled backward, as though the hands that crushed her breasts had a knife in them; but she hung on and recovered her balance and led the way to the bedroom and ordered Uncle Irving to call a doctor.

Again he was asked to help. But in his quivering eagerness he couldn't even unlace his father's shoes. She shoved him away and told him to get out of the bedroom; she'd undress his father herself. As he stepped backward he felt that he had been lifted high in the air, flung out of the room, and dashed to bits against the floor.

2.

The doctor, after his examination, came into the kitchen and sat down at the table. Hershy stood stiffly by, watching the doctor search gravely behind the mysteries of his wrinkled forehead.

"Well?" said his mother. "Well?"

"Fortunately, the burns he suffered are only minor."

"Yes," said his mother eagerly, waiting.

"But he's a sick man, a very sick man."

"How sick?"

"Pneumonia."

"No!"

"Why wasn't he in bed days ago?"

"He wouldn't stay in bed. He said he only had a little cold."

"Didn't you know he was sick? Couldn't you make him stay home?"

"He wouldn't listen to me. David, I said, stay home. You're burning up with fever, I said. But he wouldn't listen to me. I only have a little cold, he said."

"Yes, that's what they all say, all you people fighting against nature." He took out a pad and began writing. "Let's hope he passes out of the crisis and no complications develop."

"Doctor, what does that mean?"

"If he passes out of the crisis, he'll live."

"But can't you do anything?"

"I'll do my best. He's in his crisis now . . ." The doctor continued talking. Hershy caught a word here and there. "Delirium . . . Fever . . . Every four hours . . . Careful, Mrs. Melov . . . Oh, in a week? . . . Careful . . . The baby . . . Hope . . . Fight . . . Constitution . . . Hope . . ." For inwardly, his eyes dry, drained of tears, he cried: Don't let him. God God God, O don't let him. Make him strong, make him jump on his feet, make him fight, make him mad, make him fight like crazy, make him make him make him.

"Hershel," his mother called. "Go to the drugstore with this prescription. Tell the druggist to make it in a hurry. Wait for it and bring it right back."

The streets terrified him. Everybody was after him. Everything was trying to get him. The whole world was after him. Fence posts reared up, rushed at him, and clattered behind as he ran, dodged, and ducked by. A high screech bore down on him and the giant eyes of an automobile caught him in its glare. He lunged aside from the gaping mouth of the radiator and the big shoulder of the fender. The telegraph wires overhead became long, streaming, crackling hair, attached to the stony, yellow faces of lamplight which raced after him. A streetcar, like a one-eyed monster, bore down on him, gonging and roaring and snarling in its wild stampede. People were trying to grab him, stop him, their hands shooting out of the dark, their faces broken with yells. He escaped them all, banging the door of the drugstore shut behind him, and gave the prescription to the druggist. The man led him to a chair and told him to sit down. But even in sitting he felt himself running hard. Finally:

"Here you are, son."

He grabbed the medicine.

"Wait a minute, kid. That'll be a dollar."

He dug into his pockets. He didn't have any money.

"Hey, you! Come back here, you . . ."

He was out of the door, across the shiny tracks, past a rackety horn, over the sparks on the cement, rushing from yellow light to dark shadow, behind him heavy breathing and the hard driving sound of running and a million voices yelling: Get him get him get him.

Safe!

In the house: quiet. He watched his mother give his father the medicine. He followed her out into the front room. Suddenly everything became as still as a winter day in the park, with a heavy snow on the trees and the ground. Everything seemed far far away.

From a great distance he saw his mother swaying back and forth on the rocker, her arms around her swollen belly and her back humped. He saw himself reach out to her. She seemed to back away slowly. His whole being reached for her, but she retreated from him slowly.

"Wait," he thought he heard her say. "Not yet. We'll see. Wait."

Waiting, hanging in the balance of space and time, he saw himself alone on a great flat land with no horizons. He dropped to his knees and stretched his arms out; with his head raised upward he saw the blue sky turn hard and cold, and the sun began to move away as he asked for somebody to come to him. Then, in reality, he saw his mother move. He prayed for her to place her hand on his head. Even a glance would satisfy him. But she moved past him, her face tense with listening. His father was talking in the bedroom. He talked and talked, but Hershy couldn't make out what he was saying. He was about to step into the bedroom, but his father's voice froze him: he saw himself once again diving into the coal shed and scrambling into a corner and looking through the chink of wood.

"Hershel! Where are you, Hershel! Look out, you'll get burned! Look out! Hershel, Hershel, Hershel . . ."

His father's voice dwindled, muttered out. A gasp from his mother accented his father's quick rasping breath. Then his mother came out slowly with her face drawn, saying: "Can it be? But it's not time yet."

"What's the matter, Ma?"

"Nothing." She sat down in the rocker and felt her belly. "Nothing." She folded her arms across her belly and rocked back and forth.

"What's the matter, Ma?"

"He's delirious."

"What's that, Ma?"

"He's out of his mind."

No, he wanted to say. He's not. He *was* looking for me. I was afraid. I was afraid he'd kill me. I made the machines break. I made the explosion. But it wasn't my fault. I was tired. I couldn't see. It wasn't my fault. But he's not crazy. He *was* looking for me. He was he was he was . . .

"He's burning up with fever."

He wished he could say something.

"How long will the night last?"

Mama Mama Mama, what'd I do?

"I wish Rachel was here."

"Why?"

"I just wish."

"Why?"

His mother didn't answer. Instead her face twitched. Her arms tightened around her belly and she held her breath. Then she took a deep breath and sighed.

"I wish she was here," she said.

"Why?" He had heard that whenever somebody died the whole family got together. Whenever somebody was dying you wanted the whole family around you. Mama, what'd I do?

"Better go to sleep, Hershele."

"No."

She had no strength to argue. She began to stare and mumble, as when she prayed over the Friday-night candles. "*Gottenyu, Gottenyu, Gottenyu.* Dearest, dearest God." More mumbling. She stopped abruptly. His father was laughing. At first it sounded like crying, then it turned into laughter: wild, uncontrolled, gasping, a laugh he had never heard before: it ended in a violent fit of coughing, with his mother rushing into the bedroom. Then it became quiet again. He heard his father suffer through his breaths, a sign from his mother. Then the clock started ticking, faster faster, louder louder; it seemed to rock the whole house. He covered his ears but couldn't escape the sound. When he took his hands off them his father was talking again: this time, it seemed, to his mother.

"Listen. Who you calling a failure?"

"Nobody," his mother said softly. "Nobody."

"Who is it calls me a failure?"

"Nobody, David."

"My wife? Have I not always been a good husband, have I not always loved her? . . . My son? Wouldn't I die for him? . . . My friends? Don't they trust me, don't they have respect for me? . . . Who is it calls me a failure?"

"Quiet, David. Rest. Shhhhh."

"Oh, the world. All right, let the world call me a failure. What do I care about the world? Let the world go to hell."

It dawned upon Hershy that his father wasn't talking to his mother but to himself, perhaps to an accuser hovering over him. Who? Who could it be? God? Don't Pa. Don't make Him mad on you. Don't.

"I don't care for a world that measures a man by the money he has in his pocket. To hell with a world that kills a man like my brother. To hell with a world that makes whores out of people."

"Shhhhh, David, shhhhh."

"I don't believe it. Measure a man by the work he does, the love he has for his family, his not hurting people, his respect for people, his being content with what he has, not by his ambitions, his cruelty, the rock in his heart. Can't a man be a success without gaining an empire? What more is expected of a human being than just being a human being? What more?"

"Nothing, nothing, nothing."

There was a long pause: exhaustion. Then, the voice breaking:

"Don't blame me, Sonya. I tried. God knows I tried. O how I tried . . . Yussel, Yussel, Yussel, what did you do to me? I was happy before. I had everything. I had respect, love, contentment, everything. Why did you tempt me? Why was I driven? Why did you shatter my world? Why did I hold on for dear life to a thing I didn't believe in, a thing I was afraid of? Why? Why? Why?"

"Shhhhh, it's over now, David. Get well, rest, it's over. Shhhhh."

"Rachel, come back. Nobody will ever know. My sister, my dead sister, your mother, will never forgive me. Come back. Come back . . ." The voice grew tender, trembling. "I know you're tired, Hershele. You don't know how my heart is breaking. But I'm a sick man. I can hardly move. We should go away, take a boat ride in the park, sit in the sun, you and me. But I can't tear myself away. A monster is holding me.

Help me, Hershele. Help me . . ." The voice rose in terror. "Look out! You'll get burned! Hershel! Hershel! . . ." The voice broke, faded in exhaustion. "No. O Sonya, Sonya, Sonya . . ."

His mother came into the front room finally, her face bathed in sweat. She sat down in the rocker and swayed slowly back and forth. Another twinge on her face, baring her teeth, stopping her breath, and she held herself in studied readiness, waiting. Hershy moved to the couch and watched her. The slow rocking and her stare began to blur his eyes. They grew heavy, so heavy. But he was afraid to fall asleep. He began to fight against it. He tried to listen hard only to his father's raspy gasps, but the deep swell of his mother's breathing and the ceaseless motion of her rocking began to overwhelm him.

I don't want to. Ma, don't make me. What if Pa should . . .? But he can't. He can't. Ma, don't make me. Wake up, Ma. Don't make me to. I don't want to. He can't, if I didn't mean it, if it wasn't my fault. He can't. I don't want to. Let me stay. Let me up. Up. Up.

He struggled to get up, but a pair of strong hands were pinning him down. He couldn't move. He was trying. Everybody could see he was trying. See, he was trying. Look, everybody could see he was trying. Look. He looked up himself, in his sleep, and cried out. The hands that held him down were claws, and directly above the thick, shaggy arms were a nameless jumble of heads. A scream peeled out, bursting him into wakefulness; and in the terrifying silence that followed it was as though his open eyes had nailed the sound deep into the ground.

3.

It was morning. He was not on the front-room couch; he was in his underwear in his own bed. He heard a noise in the kitchen, bringing him back to life, to the memory of the day before. He crawled into his pants and ran into the kitchen. His mother wasn't there. Aunt Mascha, (Uncle Irving's wife) was there. He saw her and the clock at the same time. It was past noon.

"Where's my ma?"

"In the hospital."

The news stunned him.

"Reva took her there. She's having the baby. It's a week beforetime, but the shock of your father coming home the way he did brought the baby to life sooner. What does a baby know of time and tragedy?"

"But Pa?"

"And you—" Aunt Mascha paid no attention to him—"like a dead one you slept. Wild horses couldn't even get you up. I had to carry you to bed and undress you. A ton you weighed. What were you yelling about in your sleep?"

"Nothing."

"Oh, but you're a devil."

"Is my pa still here?"

"Yes."

"How is he?"

She shrugged her shoulders. He ran to the bedroom. His father was asleep, still breathing fast and hard. There was a stubble of beard on his face, making it look hollower. He looked worse. Hershy was afraid to wake him. He was afraid to look at him. He walked back to the kitchen feeling numb.

"Aunt Mascha, will he get better?"

"Sure, he'll get better."

He wondered if she meant it. She didn't look like she meant it. She looked like she hoped it.

"Will Ma get better?"

"Certainly."

She meant that.

· *303*

"When?"
"As soon as she has the baby."
"When'll that be?"
"Wait. It takes time."
"Can I go there?"
"Tomorrow, maybe."
"Why can't I go now?"
"They won't let you in. Even Reva can't go in. She has to wait there. Tomorrow, maybe, you'll go see her."

A sudden sense of loneliness engulfed him, bigger than he had ever felt. He didn't know what to do with himself.

"Here, I'll make you some breakfast."
"I don't want none."
"You have to eat."
"I don't want to."

He sat down at the table and began to wait. He drank a glass of milk Aunt Mascha placed before him without knowing it. His father began mumbling, then he yelled: "No! Get out! Get out, you you you . . ."

Aunt Mascha walked into the bedroom and then came out sighing with her face crunched.

"A human being," she said. She looked up at the ceiling. "*Gottenyu, Gottenyu, Gottenyu.*"

She started cleaning the house. He watched her, waiting, going deeper and deeper into his loneliness. Then he walked out of the back door with his aunt calling after him. He walked through the alley. He didn't want to meet anybody. He walked into the park, over the walks and the heat-withered grass. Some kids stopped him. They started talking at him, but he didn't hear. They started pushing him around, but he paid no attention. Finding no resistance, no fear, they swore at him and left after pushing him to the ground. He lay there a long while, then got up and started walking again. When the night came and the lights went on he wandered out of the park and stopped to look into the dark windows of a sporting goods store. Exhausted, he slumped down in a corner of the entrance about six feet in from the sidewalk. When he looked up a cop was tapping his shoe with a club.

"Get up, kid."

He crawled against the corner of the entrance. The cop lifted him to his feet.

"I didn't do nothing."

"Who's saying you did?"

"I didn't do nothing."

"What's the matter, kid?"

"It wasn't my fault."

"Who's fault was it?"

"I was tired."

"What'd you do?"

"Nothing. I didn't do nothing."

"You're making sense, kid. Where do you live?"

"There."

"Where, there?"

"There."

"What's the matter? Your old man beat you up?"

"No!"

"Your ma?"

"No."

"Then what's the matter?"

"I don't know." He was finding it hard to remember.

"Come on. I'll take you home."

"No."

"You know what time it is? After midnight."

The time meant nothing. He was waiting. He didn't want to be there when it happened. What? What was going to happen?

"All right, I'll take you to the station. You want to be locked up in jail?"

"No."
"Then go home."
"Okay."
"You sure you're going home?"
"Yah."

The cop let him go. Down the block, Hershy looked back. The cop was following him slowly, swinging his club. He broke into a run. When he turned the corner of the next block the cop was gone. He slowed down to a trot, then to a walk. He didn't know where to go. He knew he didn't want to go into the house. He was afraid. It might happen while he was there. What? What might happen while he was there? Something terrible. What? He was less afraid of the dark.

4.

Mr. Pryztalski found him asleep the next morning in the front hallway on his way out to work. Hershy was lifted high in the air and he looked down at Mr. Pryztalski's small eyes and big mustache.

"You little sonofabitch. You tiny little sonofabitch. Your aunt almost went crazy: I almost went crazy looking for you. You crazy little sonofabitch."

Mr. Pryztalski lowered him to his feet. Gradually, Hershy's senses came to him: with it full memory tightened his throat.

"Running off, with your mama in bed with a boy and your papa past the crisis. Oh, you little bastard."

Mr. Pryztalski lifted him off his feet and carried him into the house.

"Don't hit him," he said to Aunt Mascha. "He was crazy. Besides, he's a man. Never hit a man."

Hershy found himself alone with Aunt Mascha.

"Yah?" he said. "Is it true?"

"It's true, thank God."

"O Jesus Jesus Jesus."

"The fever went down. The doctor said Pa's still very sick, but he'll get well. Your pa, he said, has a will like iron. He wouldn't let himself go. He'll get better."

"And Ma, too?"

"And Ma, too."

He rushed into his father's room. He felt his legs cave at the sight of his wasted, bristly face. But his father was better. He didn't know what to do with himself. His father was better. He was strong like iron. And his mother was better. The whole world was better. He was better, too.

"Well, Hershele?" His father's voice was weak.

"You all right, Pa?"

"Better. Don't come too close. I don't want you to catch my germs."

"Ma's better, too."

"I know."

"Pa." He flung his arms around him. "It wasn't my fault. I didn't mean it."

"No, baby." His father soothed him. "It was my fault. I should have known. But a devil was in me. It wouldn't even let me lay down when I was so sick. Now that nothing has happened to you, thank God, I'm glad the engine broke. I don't have to worry about it any more. To hell with it: it's only a piece of machinery." He pushed him away gently. "Not too close, Hershel. You'll catch my germs."

"You're not a failure, Pa."

"No, dearest. How could I possibly be called a failure?"

"I don't know."

"Because a piece of machinery broke, because I have no money? With my family and my hands we'll live again. That's important. To live again."

5.

The following day, at the hospital, he saw it for a minute beside his mother. Its eyes were crushed shut, its face raw and red and puckered and old, its hand clenched. It was like a monkey, something primeval, defying all age.

His mother looked exhausted but calm. She was transformed, too. She no longer bulged under the blankets. She looked nice. She looked tender. It was like the baby had given her life back to her, and she could come back to him again.

He felt, looking at her, that he himself had died somewhere and had just been born, with a whole lifetime ahead of him.

THE END